Somewhere Else

Alex J. Milan

Original cover image courtesy of Getty Images/ iStock.com/fcscafeine

Formatting by Polgarus Studio

The following quotation 'The Edifício Panorâmico de Monsanto is abandoned and in a run-down state. Some people believe that the building is haunted by bad luck that doesn't allow any project to move forward.' is reproduced by kind permission of the discoverwalks website.

ISBN (print) 978-84-09-41825-1
ISBN (ebook) 978-84-09-41826-8

It has been a privilege to work with the same team who helped me to produce my previous novels, The Last Carriage and The Ghosts of Summer. I would once again like to thank Jessica Espejo Hernández for her work in producing the cover and Polgarus Studio for preparing the text for publication. My thanks also go to all the people who have given me encouragement and support.

Then hate me when thou wilt; if ever, now
William Shakespeare,
Sonnet 90

Ten Years Ago
Woolacombe Sands, Devon, England

I flailed around, gasping for breath as the freezing water engulfed me. I knew the theory – turn on your back and float, and theory was fine when you were splashing about in the local pool under the watchful eye of a lifeguard. It didn't translate so well when the danger was real, the cold was biting into you, and the force of the water was threatening to pull you under again at any moment.

Another wave broke over me, leaving me lashing out more helplessly than before. I could feel my strength draining away as I thrashed about. The water rushed into my nose and mouth and burned as it hit my throat. I choked on it and tried to force my head above water as I began to cough violently, desperate for air. I looked up, hoping to see land or something, anything, beyond my nightmare, something to help me to orient myself, but there was no up anymore; I was being spun around, and the world turned over and over. I felt myself beginning to fade away, and then some momentum from outside my body started to propel me.

I remembered nothing from then on until I realised I was lying on the beach and saw anxious faces looking down at me. The red kite I had seen a boy flying earlier floated high above me, dazzling against a sky now bleached of colour. Dazed, I drifted with it, and then the full force of what had happened hit me. 'Finn. Where's Finn?' I gasped, and the world went dark again.

One Month Ago
Seville, Spain

It was the middle of May; the month of beauty run riot. The jacaranda trees were in full bloom although some of the flowers had fallen already and were starting to carpet the streets with crushed velvet. Meanwhile, the swifts had reclaimed the skies. It was warm, but the relentless heat of summer was still a few weeks away. It was perhaps the most enchanting month in Seville, the city deep in the south of Spain which had been my home for almost a year. The anniversary was fast approaching, but it felt different; worse in a way I could not define, which, in turn, made it more unnerving. Clouds were gathering on a brilliant horizon. I could sense the trouble closing in, threatening to suffocate me. Just like before.

Finn was always in the background, but I rarely dreamed of her. She was with me every day but not in conscious acts of remembering; I could only describe her memory as an intrinsic part of me, a scar perhaps, something I was aware of and carried with me all the time. The previous night, though, she had finally tiptoed into my dreams, not quite centre stage but not hiding in the wings either. One faltering step after another, I could feel her moving closer, the harbinger of something I was yet to understand.

Part 1

Present Day
Seville, Spain

Chapter 1

As I forced my eyes open, I sensed how painfully dry they were, parched by the temperatures which never completely relented even in the depths of night. My sleeping pattern, erratic at the best of times, was becoming more and more disrupted. I stretched my hand out across the sheets, relishing the momentary coolness where my body hadn't touched them, but the heat soon tracked my hand down and the sheet grew warm.

The room came into focus, and I squinted into the glare caused by the sun reflecting off the tiled floor. At some point during the night, the fan had switched itself off. It needed to be fixed or replaced. The internal wooden shutters were doubled back against the walls, and I remembered I hadn't bothered to wind the outside roller blind down the night before either. It sagged on one side and every time I tried to move it, it jammed, and I had to wrestle it into submission. I thought I should ask the landlord to get it repaired. Like the fan. I never seemed to get round to asking him to get them fixed; a symptom of my lack of attachment to the place.

It took me a moment to register that it was the twenty-third of June, and then to realise the significance of that date. Having looked forward to the start of the summer holidays for so long, I felt the familiar sensations I always had when the date finally arrived: a measure of relief at having made it through the school year and the luxury of freedom from deadlines but also weariness and a sense of redundancy.

Pulling on a T-shirt and shorts, I ducked under the blind and went out onto the tiny balcony, just big enough for one chair. It was still early enough for the world beyond my window to be quiet. I loved the peace and the soft golden light at that time of day; it compensated for the lie-in I hadn't managed to have. Early-morning Seville in summer always felt like a city with a hangover, slowly realising that another day had rolled around and had to be faced, ready or not.

The first signs of life appeared at the bar in the square below. *Square* was perhaps a generous description; it was more of a widening in the narrow maze of streets in the old town of Seville. Streets so narrow in places that if you were to stand in the middle of one of them with arms outstretched, you would be able to brush your fingertips against the walls of the buildings on both sides. The ubiquitous orange trees of Seville were dotted around the opening in the labyrinth and would provide welcome shade as the sun climbed ever higher.

I watched the owner of the bar going about his work, setting out metal chairs and tables, polishing them until they gleamed, preparing for another long, hot day. His body language suggested that great effort was involved in the task. From my observations of him, I knew by now he wasn't good with early starts, but once he had got going, he would work until late at night, catching the final revellers just when they thought the supply of bars still open had been exhausted. I had no idea about the rules on closing times, but if they existed, he obviously paid no attention to them. I knew him only in passing, in the same way as I chose to know most people, but I felt an affinity with his struggle with early mornings.

I would never have been able to afford to rent a flat in such a beautiful location if I hadn't shared it with four other teachers. I wasn't keen on sharing, and there were tensions between them I could have lived without, but I'd had to find somewhere at short notice after my previous living arrangements had changed so unexpectedly a few months previously. It was surprising what you could tolerate when you had no choice because the other choices were not even worth serious contemplation.

After a brief trip to the kitchen, I returned to the bedroom with a cup of coffee. I heard my phone buzzing and in the fleeting moments which passed as I reached for it, I wondered if it might be someone at the school asking me to cover some summer classes. That was something I wasn't keen to do, and I picked up the phone, thinking about what I would say. Instead, I was presented with an entirely different proposition.

Hi Isabel. It's me, Vanessa. I really don't know where to start, but I was wrong about everything. I realise that now. I'm so sorry. I feel terrible about what happened. I wish we could meet and talk everything through.

Vanessa. To say I was surprised would have been an understatement. We had parted on bad terms. It would have been hard to imagine worse terms, in fact. Yet there she was apologising and wanting to repair our friendship or at least resolve our differences.

I went back out onto the balcony and settled in the chair, the sun not yet intense enough to burn. At that time of day, it was fresher outside than inside. I would gladly have slept on the balcony if it had been just a little bigger. I allowed the coffee to work its way through my system while I reflected on the last time I had seen Vanessa and whether I wanted to risk a repeat of that experience. Opening up old wounds didn't appeal, but equally I hated the way we had left things. The events of the Easter holidays, just over two months ago, had played on my mind since and so often I had wished things had turned out differently; that the one person who had been my friend was still my friend. For the last few months, I had wanted to make peace with her as much as I had wanted to make peace with myself. Both had seemed unobtainable.

Still cautious about speaking to her despite her conciliatory tone, I decided to follow her lead by sending a message rather than calling her. I started typing, trying to keep it as neutral as possible. I looked at my message, my finger hovering over the send button, deleted it and started again.

Hi. Yes, I'd be happy to meet you. Where are you?
Lisbon.

I paused, looking at the single word staring at me. For some reason, I had expected somewhere closer although I had no idea where she had gone after her abrupt departure. I realised she could have been anywhere. Vanessa had started typing again. I waited.

I know it's a long way but how would you feel about coming over here? I can't get away at the moment.

The summer stretched ahead, disconcertingly empty after the routine I was so accustomed to even while I so often simultaneously railed against it. I thought of the stifling heat of high summer in Seville when the city would grind to a halt as locals fled the city if they could or retreat inside as often as possible if they could not. I thought of the sun which would turn even the narrowest, darkest corners of the old town into a furnace. I thought about my need to get away, and I thought about making peace with Vanessa.

I tapped the phone against my palm, contemplating the idea. Over the last few weeks, I had been thinking about going away and a trip to Portugal appealed, whatever awaited me in Lisbon with Vanessa. I needed time to think about whether I would stay on in Seville for another year. If I decided to move on, I would need to apply for jobs, but I would still have time to do that. I looked at the screen again and the new message which had appeared.

What do you think? Vanessa asked.

Yes. I could get there. The holidays have just started.

Yes, I knew the term was ending around now. That's why I thought this could be a good opportunity to get together.

Shall I phone you now so we can arrange it?

Better not, I'm at work. Shouldn't even really be sending messages! When could you get here?

I thought about practical arrangements. *I'll need a couple of days.*

OK. Well, let me know when you're on your way so I can be ready for you.

You must be close to finishing for summer yourself. For some reason I was keen to keep the conversation going.

Yes, not long to go now at all. Oh – boss is here. Better go before he spots me on the phone! Loads to do. Bye. With that, Vanessa disappeared.

I reviewed the messages. I wasn't sure what to make of them, and after my initial impulsive agreement to go, I wondered if I had done the right thing.

The sun was starting to burn so I retreated from the growing heat. I fiddled with the fan and after hitting it a few times, it reluctantly juddered into action. I lay down on the bed and drifted off to sleep despite the best efforts of the coffee. The sound of two of my flatmates arguing woke me up. As I heard a door slamming, I was sure agreeing to go had been the right decision. Looking back later, it would seem strange that I would simply get up and drive all the way to Lisbon on the basis of a few messages from someone I had fallen out with so dramatically and hadn't spoken to since. Yet somehow it was inevitable that I would go. I wanted to put things right, and I had other reasons for wanting to escape Seville. Not all of them were to do with the thermometer as it continued its journey north.

* * *

Javier had agreed to meet me by the Fountain of the Lions in the María Luisa Park. As I walked through the city, the sun, now higher in the sky and gaining in intensity, stung my skin. I had forgotten my sunglasses and as I narrowed my eyes to avoid the glare, the world became a red filter beyond my eyelashes.

As I entered the park, the relative calm and welcome pools of shade enveloped me. The haven which was the María Luisa Park never ceased to delight me and fill me with something close to tranquillity. Checking my watch and seeing that I was early for our meeting, I slowed my pace and found a place to sit, just across the path from the vast semi-circular building of the Plaza de España. The building's red bricks glowed in the sunshine. The fountain in the centre of the square was in full flow, and the dazzling light playing on the water was hypnotic. Fountains I could appreciate; it was rivers, lakes and, above all, the sea, I couldn't cope with.

A row of bird of paradise plants with their vibrant orange blooms flourished in the flower bed between my vantage point and the square. The sounds of Paco de Lucia's Entre Dos Aguas drifted on the balmy air, but the busker was nowhere to be seen; wisely, he had found a spot in the shade and was tucked away under the arches of the building.

As the music faded away, I checked the time again and reluctantly got up. Walking further into the park, the hum of traffic receded to be replaced by bird song, the rasp of cicadas and the calls and laughter of children as they chased each other along the parched pathways.

I passed grandmothers fanning themselves on benches

while watching over their grandchildren and groups of elderly men, setting the world to rights. The horse-drawn carriages waited for passengers, the men who relied on their trade sitting on a nearby bench while their restless horses kicked at the ground.

For many years after the accident, I had refused to get close to anyone. Meeting Vanessa, and inadvertently becoming friends with her, had restored a fragile amount of belief that having friends might be possible and welcome after all, and Javier had been my first tentative dip into the world of dating since university. Our relationship had been slow to get started due to my reticence, which he had not understood and, to be fair to him, I had not explained. Equally, though, I hadn't found it easy to explain anything to Javier; he was an impatient person, not given to taking the time to listen to others. I had started to realise he and I were not a match made in heaven. We were not any kind of match at all.

He had been all for going from zero to one hundred in the first week, but I had kept applying the brakes, unsure of myself, of him, of us. Nevertheless, he had insisted that I should meet his family, an experience I had endured a number of times, each one worse than the last. There would have been other such occasions had it not been for my repertoire of creative and credible excuses. The last get together had been the previous weekend, and we had not spoken since.

I spotted him by the Fountain of the Lions, gazing into the water. It occurred to me that if there had been something to fight for, I would have felt something, or at least felt something according to my own scale of emotions, which I had a suspicion was not quite the same as those of other people. I would have felt some pull towards him, a ripple of affection, but there was nothing. For the first time, I realised there never really had been, and I wondered how we had got to this point where we were dating and yet not.

'Thanks for agreeing to meet me,' I ventured.

A shrug was all I got in return.

'Do you mind if we go to the café? It's pretty hot. I could do with a drink.'

'Sure.'

We walked in a silence which became increasingly uncomfortable, and I was grateful when we arrived at the café and the waiter appeared and asked us what we wanted. When it became clear Javier had nothing to say even after we had ordered, I made a start. 'Are we going to talk about last weekend?'

'What is there to say?' Javier asked.

'I don't know really. I just thought we should clear the air.' I wondered if my meeting with Vanessa would prove to be equally as awkward.

'You embarrassed me in front of my family.'

I burned at the injustice of the statement. 'Your mother embarrassed me in front of everyone.'

'Don't insult my family.'

'I'm not insulting your family.' I heard the way I spat out the final two words and took a deep breath. 'If you recall, it all started when your sister kept insisting that I should go to the beach with her. She couldn't just let it be.' I was tempted to add that she could never let anything be, but I restrained myself.

'Rocío,' Javier began, referring to his sister, 'was just trying to be friendly.'

'And I appreciated that, but I didn't want to go to the beach. I don't like the beach.'

Javier threw his hands in the air and dropped them back in his lap in exasperation. 'Everyone likes the beach.'

'I don't,' I replied, annoyed with myself for sounding like a petulant child. 'Besides, you shouldn't try to force people to do things they don't want to do.' I had reason to know that better than anyone.

'She wanted to make you feel like part of the family, and you threw it back in her face.'

I felt anger rising inside me. 'I did not "throw it back in her face". I said I'd prefer to go to the park, the cinema, anywhere but – '

'The beach?'

'Yes. And then your mother started going on about my Spanish. She made fun of my accent and all my mistakes when I speak Spanish, and then they all started laughing and making comments. Most of which I understood, by the way. How do you think that made me feel?'

'It was a joke.'

'Yes, it's always a joke, isn't it? Even when it's hurtful and embarrassing.'

Javier gave me a look. 'My mother was right.'

'What a surprise,' I muttered. 'Right about what?'

'She said I shouldn't have got involved with a foreign girl.'

'Oh really?'

'Yes, after she first met you she said you were nice, but you didn't understand our culture and you would never fit in.'

His words stopped me in my tracks. I felt my throat tighten. 'She said that?'

'Yes.'

'Is it really because I'm not Spanish?' I paused long enough to make sure I could control my voice. 'Or is it me?'

Javier moved his glass around the table, creating a puddle of condensation, which he proceeded to examine. He couldn't look at me. 'It's not just about language or even culture. It's about the way we are … and the way you are.'

I had no desire to find out what he meant by that, and I could feel the rejection coming so I was determined to act first; to rip the plaster off. 'I'm going away for a while. I think it's good timing.'

'Where?'

'Does it really matter?'

'I suppose not.'

'So this is goodbye then.' It didn't matter how many goodbyes I had had to say; I had never truly got used to them. Every single one, even those which had been necessary or self-inflicted, chipped another part of my heart away. It was one of the reasons why I usually avoided getting close to anyone and one of the reasons why I never stayed anywhere too long. And I had just learned my lesson again.

Javier nodded, and I watched as he got up. He bent to kiss me on the cheek and as he did, I wished he hadn't. The moment of tenderness without any true feeling attached to it hurt more than a smack across the face.

'Goodbye, Isabel.'

'Goodbye, Javier.'

I watched as he walked away without a glance back; another ending. The timing coming straight after the messages from Vanessa left me feeling as though I were on shifting ground. Everything seemed uncertain when only a few hours before, I had been contemplating a relaxing if empty summer with only two intertwined decisions to make; whether I would stay in Seville for another year and whether Javier and I had any sort of future. Even though I had known for a while that my relationship with Javier had not been going well, I had hoped it might somehow work out. Now, though, that much at least had been decided and staying in Seville hung in the balance. I felt the familiar urge to run, to be somewhere else and to recreate myself yet again; a blank page with no mistakes; no judgements against me or about me. I bit back the feeling of loss, got up and headed back to my room.

* * *

The next morning, I felt more exhausted than when I had gone to bed. The heat and the jagged shards of the past as the anniversary grew ever closer had punctuated the moments when I had started to doze, until sleep had finally deserted me.

When I slipped out of the flat, it was around half past five in the morning and still dark. While most of the world was asleep, I immersed myself in the life of pre-dawn Seville; a culture of its own populated by people who had jobs which demanded unearthly hours and who frequented the cafés which kept similar hours to accommodate them. The cafés were pools of light, of refuge and, for some, of companionship, in a still darkened world.

As I passed one of them, I smelled the sharp tang of coffee and heard the clatter of cups and glasses being slammed down on counters and teaspoons rattling against saucers. I went in and ordered a coffee. It arrived in a glass, which meant I had to wait for it to cool down. I had never mastered the art of grasping a piping hot glass of coffee.

While I was waiting, I spent some time people watching. All of the people around me knew at least one other person in the bar. The realisation I was an outsider looking in and the sensations of isolation and rootlessness had never been stronger. I knew I had no reason to complain; I was the one who had chosen that life, but sometimes an aching sense of loneliness within me crept through the gaps in my defences. It was a question of waiting it out; daylight would banish it, even if only temporarily.

One of the men – and it was almost always men who populated those cafés – was proclaiming about something to anyone who would listen. The words tumbled out of him so fast that I could not keep up. Those around nodded and continued to sip their coffee until he jumped up, thumping a fist into the palm of his other hand. He continued his rant and received more murmurs of agreement until he seemed to feel sufficiently placated and sat down again.

There was no such thing as silence in a bar or café in Seville, but some level of peace, at least, had been restored. Without any further diversions, I contemplated the trip to Lisbon and wondered what Vanessa and I would find to say to each other. I was curious as to why she had suddenly decided she had been wrong about everything, when back in the spring she had been so furious with me and adamant I was the one who was to blame.

I pulled my phone out, half inclined to phone her and then realised that it was an hour earlier in Lisbon and a horribly unsociable hour to call anyone. Instead, I started scrolling through hotels in Lisbon and made a reservation for a week, starting in two nights' time. Having done that, I gingerly picked up the glass of coffee. It was cool enough to hold and bitter to the taste but welcome. I drained the glass, paid and walked out to see a deceptive, milky sky, which betrayed no hint of the heat to come.

I walked through the city, dodging people washing pavements and buckets of water being tipped into gutters, the smell of bleach strong in the air. After a long wait for the car hire agencies to open, several unsuccessful attempts and a lot more walking, I found a company which would allow me to drive a car into Portugal without charging me a fortune. I settled on renting a car for three weeks, thinking I might take a road trip between my visit to Lisbon and heading back to Seville. I sent Vanessa a message.

Hi Vanessa, I've hired a car. Leaving tomorrow.

She started typing immediately.

Great. What type of car did you get?

Her reply surprised me. She had never shown much of an interest in cars before. *A Fiat 500. Why?*

That's good. You don't want to be driving a big car in Lisbon. Have you got parking at your hotel? Can be hard to park here.

Yes. I'm staying at place called the Hibiscus near the Edward the Seventh Park. Got a good deal including parking.

Tell you what, give me the registration number. I'll see if I can get a permit for you to park near me. You never know – might be handy at some point.

I consulted the paperwork from the hire car company and sent her the details.

OK. No promises but I'll see what I can do. What time are you leaving?

About 11.30 but expect me the day after tomorrow. Going to break the journey and stay somewhere on the Algarve overnight. Not sure where yet. Faro maybe? It's about halfway, I think.

OK. Keep me posted. Looking forward to seeing you.

I walked back to the flat through the Murillo Gardens, taking a break on a ceramic-tiled bench to sip the drink I had picked up earlier. I recognised it as a delaying tactic as much as anything else. I was starting to hate my room; it was not home but merely the place I went to when I had nowhere else to be or in order to sleep, which was becoming harder. Absent-mindedly, I traced the lines of the yellow and blue design of the tiles until I realised there was no exit route, and I had ended up where I had started. Somehow that seemed fitting.

Chapter 2

After another fitful night's sleep, I left a note on the table in the kitchen, explaining I was going away, threw some clothes in a bag, sent a message to Vanessa to tell her I was leaving and set off.

I estimated it would take me an hour and a half to reach the border with Portugal. The GPS guided me through Seville and over two bridges which were short enough not to allow my fear of water sufficient time to rear its head. An urban landscape gradually changed into an uninspiring and scrappy view of low-rise workshops and warehouses, punctuated by hoardings advertising supermarkets and fast-food outlets. It was vaguely depressing, but then it all melted away and the GPS fell silent. It was just me and a burning stretch of tarmac in softly undulating countryside dotted with stone pines and slender cypress trees but otherwise mainly featureless, allowing other thoughts free rein.

I had tried to block out the fact that it was the anniversary of Finn's death, but it was pointless. The memories shimmered in the heat haze in front of me, and I was moving towards them yet never quite reaching them. Salvation was always just out of range. I might have been driving along a motorway in Spain, but my mind was back in England ten years earlier.

Devon: a spontaneous trip to celebrate the end of our studies at university had been prompted by a spell of unexpected good weather. Finn was due at her parents' house in Norfolk the following weekend. I had met her parents on a previous occasion but, having found myself concurring with Finn's view that they were an acquired taste, I had bowed out of the option to meet them again. After her visit to see them, Finn and I planned to go travelling for a month and then head to Hungary to take a course to qualify us to teach English abroad.

Devon was a relatively short drive from Bristol, where we had spent our university years, but what had been meant as a couple of days away to let off steam after the pressure of the last term at university had changed everything.

But that was later; still in the future; a future which, on that weekend, seemed to contain so much promise. On the day we had arrived, Woolacombe Sands had fulfilled all of our hopes; a glorious beach which stretched for miles, backed by sand dunes and cradled between the twin headlands of Morte Point and Baggy Point.

We had arrived on the Friday afternoon and had planned to return to Bristol on the following Tuesday, when the weather was due to break, with storms forecast. When Tuesday rolled around and produced another day of brilliant sunshine, we had decided to postpone our departure until the following day and headed down to the beach, enjoying the warmth, the sand beneath our feet and the sea air. The scene was utterly peaceful; the waves broke gently on the beach and Lundy Island floated far out to sea on a hazy horizon. At the top of the dunes, a boy was flying a bright red kite, his laughter and excited chatter drifting towards us before being caught on the breeze and blown away. I was utterly content and felt we were so lucky to have an extra day there.

So often since that day I had thought that if only the weather had changed earlier, if only it hadn't been so good in the first place, if only we had stuck to our original plan and returned to Bristol that morning, if only there hadn't been any spare rooms at the hotel, if only we had gone somewhere else … and always the biggest if only, the one which dogged my every moment. I shook my head, trying to dislodge it, but that other *if only* was still there. It was always there; it was the one which I could never accept or escape. I tried to stop thinking, but my memories had other ideas and took me down another road just weeks after our trip to Devon.

Norfolk: unrelenting flat fields under an unforgiving, heavy grey sky. It was as if summer had forgotten that corner of the world. The bleakness of the day was surpassed only by that permeating every part of my body. I thought the fact I had not received an invitation to the funeral had been an oversight or perhaps a sort of kindness to spare me from reliving the day of the accident. I had been given the details by a mutual friend who was travelling down from Lincoln while I was driving up from Southampton.

The weather had been fine when I had left, but as I had passed London the sky had grown darker, and I had been delayed by an accident on the motorway, slick with recently fallen rain. Lane closures had compounded the delay, and progress on the country lanes which followed had also been slow, leaving me furious with myself. I could not even manage to make it on time for Finn's funeral. I had slipped quietly into the back of the cold Norman church, unseen by the mourners in front of me whose attention was focused on the vicar and the coffin, caught in a shaft of light.

The coffin; I stared at it. I knew on an intellectual level that Finn had gone, but still it was not real. I hadn't cried even when I had been told they had found her body. I had wanted to; there was a dam of grief building inside me, and I feared what would happen if the pressure could not be released and, equally, if it could. I wished it had been me who had died, not only so that Finn would still be alive but, selfishly, so that I would not have to endure the pain of her loss.

The service drew to a close, and the mourners began to file out. I saw Finn's parents, Jennifer and Robert, etched in partial silhouette, move towards the coffin. Robert had his arm around Jennifer's shoulders and she, in turn, had her arm resting on the shoulder of Finn's youngest sister, Suzanna. Beyond them, I saw a shadowy figure with her back to me, closer to the coffin. It had to be Finn's other sister, Caitlin. I had only met her sisters in passing the year before. Suzanna had been three then and had not made much of an impression on me. Caitlin, at thirteen, had been a blur of Gothic moodiness with black lipstick, black eyeliner and spiky purple hair.

I wanted so much to go up to them and say something, but I couldn't find the words. I shuffled out of the oak pew and into the aisle and then stopped. What could I possibly say that would be appropriate? I was still rooted to the spot when her parents turned to leave and then froze when they saw me. Time slowed. We all waited for someone to make the first move; to speak first. My heart was pounding so hard it hurt, and I felt slightly dizzy.

I heard my voice start to say something and then Jennifer cut across me. 'What are you doing here?'

I shook my head, trying to free myself from the lack of comprehension I felt. 'Finn is –'

'Fiona,' said Jennifer, her voice tight. 'Her name is Fiona.'

I noticed the use of the present tense and how I had slipped on it myself. 'Fiona is – Fiona was – my friend. My closest friend.'

'Some friend. There is no way she would have gone into the sea if you hadn't encouraged her. If it weren't for you, she would still be with us.'

If she had tried to find the words which would hurt me, she could not have done better.

'No, no, it wasn't like that,' I stammered, trying to convince myself more than her. I looked from Jennifer to her husband, who was staring at me with an impassive look which was equally disturbing. Then my eyes moved to the figure behind them, kneeling down now, her arm over the coffin as if trying to embrace her sister. I looked down at four-year-old Suzanna, who was chewing on her fingers with a confused, slightly reproachful look on her face. I looked back at Caitlin; her hair, no longer the purple of the previous summer, but dyed jet black, a stark contrast to the pale wood of her sister's coffin. She seemed oblivious to the exchange.

'It wasn't like that,' I repeated, not believing myself.

'You should leave now, Isabel,' said Robert. His voice was calm, but there was an undercurrent to his tone which suggested the veneer might shatter at any moment.

'I just wanted to say goodbye.' I could feel the dam coming close to collapsing, the fractures widening, but it wasn't quite at breaking point, and I couldn't let it happen in front of her family.

'You're not welcome.' Jennifer said. Her voice was brittle and sharp. 'Please leave.'

'No, please, let me just …'

Jennifer turned away, stifling a sob, and I heard her impossibly high heels catch on the rough stone floor and echo around the church. Robert moved swiftly down the aisle, grabbed my arm hard enough for it to hurt and escorted me out of the church.

A brisk wind had picked up, and it cut through me. Robert turned me to face him and let go of my arm. 'After destroying our family, I don't know how you had the effrontery to come here. I'm holding it together for Jennifer and the girls, but I won't be responsible for what I do if you don't leave now.'

I didn't understand at the time; I was too young. But I would learn that about people; they couldn't deal with grief and guilt whether it was theirs or yours. And grief and guilt were always the close companions of death.

I looked up at him and around at the church and the graveyard. I knew then the truth of what he had said; there was nothing there for me and no way I would ever be able to make things right. It was my fault, I did not belong, and I had to go. Without a word, I turned and walked down the gravel path, the stones grinding beneath my feet and the wind whipping my hair across my face. I pulled my coat tightly around me, but the wind found its way through it and bit me to the bone.

I continued out of the gate and down to where I had parked my car. I noticed Josh, who had told me about the funeral. He raised his hand to acknowledge me, but I pretended not to see him. I got into the car and pulled away as quietly as the gravel beneath the tyres would allow. I didn't look back once, but I had looked back every day since.

With all that had been lost to me, that day and every moment, every gesture, every word was indelibly stamped upon me. My final doubts about my guilt had been extinguished. I had driven as far as London when fatigue, which I knew did not come just from the driving, overtook me. I found a turn off and checked into a dismal hotel for the night. There, surrounded by fraying carpets and damp, peeling wallpaper, I cried for the first time and thought I would never stop.

I ran a hand through my hair, forced myself back to the

present and concentrated on the motorway; no longer transported to England, but back in Spain. My thoughts drifted from my friendship with Finn to my one with Vanessa, and I wondered again how everything had gone so terribly wrong and how we had ended up having such a huge showdown instead of talking things through. It seemed as though everything had been fine, and then a switch had been flipped.

I focused on the road again, trying to ignore the thoughts which gnawed at me. I suddenly realised I had passed all the points at which I could have turned off, turned round, abandoned the whole business and driven back to Seville. But now it was too late; there were no more places at which I could turn back. In the distance, I could see the tops of the pylons of the Guadiana International Bridge which would take me into Portugal, where it was an hour earlier, and I would get to live the last hour of my life again. I recalled the other times I wished I could have done that. And done it so much better.

I saw a flash of the Guadiana River ahead and tried to ignore it. It was true that my panic was only fully realised if I had to come into physical contact with a body of water, but I wasn't great with bridges and this one was considerably longer than the ones I had had to cross to leave Seville. I tried not to think about it. I noticed the oleander at the side of the road, its pink flowers glowing in the sunshine. A memory of a student telling me it was a deceptive plant, beautiful but deadly, flashed through my mind. I pinched the bridge of my nose and rubbed at my eyes with the heel of my hand as if the actions would enable me to break loose of both my memories of Finn and my fears. And then I was on the bridge, trying to ignore the drop; the water below me.

The fan-like pattern of the stays splaying from the pylons to the deck of the bridge wrapped around me, making me feel claustrophobic. The sense of not being able to turn back, of having no choice, intensified and sweat crawled down my back. I felt my hands becoming slippery on the steering wheel and tried to keep it steady. I passed under the first pylon and focused on my breathing. Somewhere high above the water, I crossed the border and then the second pylon was behind me and the shadows of the cable stays peeled back, releasing me into a new country.

Part 2

Portugal

Chapter 3

As I drove off the bridge, I realised how much it had cost me to get across it. My heart was beating unnaturally fast and my skin felt clammy. I continued to concentrate on my breathing, reminding myself I would be turning off the motorway in a matter of minutes anyway. The slip road diverting me to the Algarve Welcome Point appeared; I took it and pulled over with a sense of relief.

Ahead of me were the complexities of the toll booths, but just to my right was a small tourist office. I got out, locked the car and went in. It was as good an excuse as any to stop and get myself together. I came out clutching a handful of leaflets extolling the delights of the Algarve and a map of the region. I hadn't asked for them, but the woman in the office had been so keen to tell me how lovely the Algarve was that I hadn't had the heart to tell her I was only passing through.

The stop had given me time to calm down, and my breathing and heart rate had returned to normal. I hovered under the sparse shade provided by a tree and looked idly at the information. Something made me glance up, and I saw a car parked further down by the police station. My interest in cars was no greater than Vanessa's, but I noticed that one. It was a muscular SUV in a dark olive green matte paint with tinted windows. It vaguely resembled a small tank and gave the impression that the surrounding light had been sucked inside and could not be released. It was a strange and unsettling illusion, and I wondered who would have chosen to buy a car like that.

I walked back to the hire car, got in, reread the information I had found about paying the tolls and inched towards the end of the queue. As I passed the SUV, I turned to try to see the driver, but the car was not divulging its secrets.

The toll system proved less painful than I had expected and before long, I was on my way again. I continued along the motorway with the GPS set for Faro, where I planned to make a stop. When I finally turned off the motorway, the GPS seemed keen to lead me in long, looping spirals until I ignored it and simply followed the first sign I saw for the centre, where I found a car park shaded by jacaranda trees, stripped of their flowers but with the foliage still lush and green.

A walk around the old town with its whitewashed houses and cobbled streets, followed by lunch at a small restaurant tucked away in a side street, refreshed me. I returned to the car, debating what to do. I could push on to Lisbon and be there before nightfall, but I wanted to take a break and my booking at the hotel in Lisbon was for the following night anyway. I had told Vanessa not to expect me until the next day so it was not as though I would be late.

In the car, I consulted the map I had been given, looking at the towns along the route. I noticed the movement of a car behind me and glanced in the rear-view mirror. A green SUV. Matte paint. It was parked up some way behind me, and it seemed to be waiting for something or someone. I tried to quell the strange flame of anxiety the sight of it lit inside me and continued flicking through the leaflets I had been given, looking for a place to spend the night.

Faro made sense as I was already there, but Olhão caught my eye or rather the description did – a little off the beaten track even in summer, peaceful, quaint. It sounded like a good place to break the journey. It meant going in the wrong direction, but it was only a fifteen-minute drive from Faro. It wouldn't involve backtracking a long way.

I pulled out my phone and sent Vanessa a message. *Decided to stop off in Olhão for the night.* I started the car again, one eye on the car in my rear-view mirror. I reversed out, and it edged forward into the space I had occupied. It made no move to follow me. 'Paranoid,' I muttered to myself.

The road to Olhão was busy, and rather than drive around the town and risk getting lost in a maze of streets, I pulled up at the first hotel I found on the main road, which had parking and a *Rooms Vacant* sign.

'Just one night?'

'Yes.'

'You should stay longer. Take a boat trip through the Ria Formosa Natural Park. It's like another world over there.'

I could think of few things I was less likely to do. 'I'm on my way to Lisbon. Maybe another time.'

'Very well. So, here's your key – you have room twelve at the end on the left. Breakfast is from eight to ten-thirty. Card or cash?'

I paid and made my way to the room, which was cool and more luxuriously furnished than my own room back in Seville, not that that was saying much given my austere existence. The old saying that a rolling stone gathered no moss was certainly true in my case. It was not that I didn't appreciate the pictures on the wall, the scatter cushions on the bed or the vase of flowers, but I liked the fact that they were not mine to care for. I could pick up and be gone from anywhere in less than an hour.

In the early evening, I took a walk through the streets of Olhão, which was as charming as the leaflets had proclaimed although it also had a strangely drowsy, dreamlike atmosphere. As always, I was happy to be in a place where nobody knew me. I felt free. I had no way to know it then, but it was to be the last moment of anything akin to peace I would experience for some time.

As I slowly walked back to the hotel after dinner, I was in my own world, mulling over what might happen in Lisbon. I pressed dial on Vanessa's number before I had even had time to consider what I wanted to say. I imagined the other end – the phone ringing, echoing around her flat in Lisbon. I waited, hoping she would answer so we could talk and hoping she wouldn't in case we ended up arguing. There was no answer. I hung up and sent her a message instead.

Hi. Managed to find a place in Olhão for the night, but I'll be in Lisbon tomorrow as planned. See you then?

I waited, hoping for a reply, but there was no response. It occurred to me that if the volume of Vanessa's paperwork at the end of the school year was anything like mine, she was unlikely to reply until the following day. The last few days of term were always filled with long days and nights of marking and report writing.

As the night wore on, I lay in the dark remembering; my thoughts tripping over themselves as they drifted from my parents to Finn to Vanessa to Javier and back again.

The only – and I suspected accidental – child of a marriage between a French mother and English father, my childhood up to the age of twelve had been spent moving between France and England as my parents tried to find a place to settle. It had occurred to me as a teenager, and many times since, they were always looking for something they could not define and so could not find. My life had turned out much the same. Whether I had inherited their restless nature or not, it had become apparent and grown in me since what had happened to Finn.

At the age of twelve, I had been sent to boarding school in England, while my parents drifted from country to country on their endless and fruitless search for a place to call home. It was a disjointed childhood, one which had required me to be self-sufficient and never to bother too much with friends as I learned quickly how painful the goodbyes could be. I also learned that those who were supposedly the closest to you could be the ones who hurt you the most, whether intentionally or, worse, through casual indifference. It was simply better not to get too close to people in the first place.

School holidays were spent either in Southampton with Sylvia, the elderly friend of my father who had taken me in, or in the latest random corner of the world in which my parents had found themselves. Among the more memorable if not necessarily enjoyable trips, there had been the Christmas spent on the beach in Goa, where my parents had gone in search of the long-lost hippie trail, leaving me feeling deeply embarrassed as they obliged me to follow them around while they hunted for their elusive dream.

There had also been an Easter break spent travelling around Sicily by a combination of hitchhiking and public transport, an endeavour which had left all of us bad-tempered and relieved to part ways for a while. Our final meeting had been in Peru, where my mother had ended up in hospital for a day with altitude sickness. When she had recovered and they waved me off at the airport for my flight back to England, I vowed to avoid the next trip they suggested, however tempting the destination sounded. I didn't know then that I wouldn't see them again. Perhaps I would have made more of an effort at a heartfelt goodbye if I had.

When the news of the death of my parents reached me, I was strangely detached, which only served to make me feel guilty. The fact that we had not been a conventional family, and my parents had cut me adrift years before, did little to allay the feeling. I was still just young enough to be spared the need to organise their repatriation and all the subsequent arrangements. The boarding school did all they could to support me for the last two terms, but then I was ejected out into the world.

Helped on my way by a modest inheritance, I was able to go to university. Amongst the many dubious things my upbringing had bestowed on me, the inheritance and dual nationality were the two for which I was, and would remain, immensely grateful.

Having decided early on not to let people in, I was content in my own way, and then I had met Finn. Finn. I turned over in bed, reached for my watch and checked the time. Eleven-thirty. Only half an hour to go until the anniversary was over. I tried to tell myself that once it had passed, I would feel better. I got up, had a glass of water and then tried to settle down again. I closed my eyes and willed sleep to arrive, but the memories were too strong.

Finn and I had met at university, and we had clicked in that indefinable way that instantly makes you realise the person you have just met is going to be an important part of your life. We were yin and yang. She was the extrovert to my introvert, the sunlight to my shade and would rush in where I feared to tread. She was sympathetic about the death of my parents without being mawkish or making me feel I had to apologise for their loss as so often happened.

She was the one who would propel me towards dates, which usually turned out to be disastrous. And then she would make me laugh about them. When I brooded, she would pull me out of it. For all of those reasons and so many more, she became the sister I had never had, and I adored her. Remarkably, for me, she seemed equally fond of me although I never quite understood why. I never asked her for fear of looking foolish or prompting her to question it.

After the accident, I had shut down completely. I had never managed to recall the immediate aftermath, but I was aware there were a few people who had tried to reach me and pull me out my despair, but they had gradually given up and slipped away. I couldn't blame them; their phone calls and texts had gone unanswered; their visits had been evaded, or cut short when evasion had not worked. The blame I heaped upon myself became an ever more intolerable burden. In those days, people were supposed to get on with life rather than admit they needed help, but I didn't know how to move on. I knew only a few incontrovertible truths: Finn was gone, it was my fault, I hated myself, I wanted to punish myself, and I wanted to run away from everything, including my life. I had experienced an overwhelming urge to run as far and as fast as I could, and I had never really stopped.

The incident at Finn's funeral had only made it worse and emphasised my culpability and since that day, I had gone through the motions of life but with everything strangely blunted and slightly out of focus. I had emotions, but it was as though I experienced them through a filter.

I had taken a voluntary job in Nepal, thinking that if I could only do something good, I could make up for what had happened, but I found I couldn't. Combined with my new, ever-present companion of ceaseless restlessness, I had been on the move again when my time there came up for renewal.

After Nepal, I had become a teacher of English as a foreign language, just as Finn and I had wanted to do, and in the years which immediately followed her death, my job had taken me to Thailand, Vietnam and Turkey, but always with one eye on the next destination; the next fresh start, which would miraculously make everything right. The hectic pace of life in Bangkok and Hanoi had not helped me to move on although the retreat I had gone to during one of the school holidays in Thailand had enabled me learn how to deal with my panic attacks. Istanbul's chaotic beauty had not cured me either.

The only times I had returned to England had been to see Sylvia. The last time had been for her funeral, and with her passing, I had felt even more of a stranger there than ever before. I had left again as soon as possible and headed for France, wondering if I would feel more of a sense of connection with my mother's country of birth. I hadn't. After two years, one in my mother's home town of Rennes and one in Toulouse, I was on the move again, having accepted a job in Gdansk on Poland's Baltic coast.

Part of my inability to stay in one place was a yearning for something else although what that something else was remained tantalisingly unidentifiable. A clean slate, I sometimes thought. The other part of it was that moving on so frequently made it easy to avoid any close attachments. Friendships, if they could be called that, were fleeting and superficial. I had lived my life like that for so long that I had ceased to question it; that was just the way things were.

Frustrated by how elusive sleep had become, I switched on the TV. I flicked through the channels, hoping to find something to distract me. There was nothing. I turned it off and the darkness closed in around me again.

My thoughts turned to Vanessa. I had met her in the September of the year before last. She had arrived at the school in Gdansk at the start of my second year at the school which, by definition, meant my last year, as two years was my self-imposed limit anywhere. I had almost left after the first year, but a job offer in Morocco had fallen through.

In my first year, I had been sharing with another teacher in a flat belonging to the school. It was small and cramped and offered little privacy; I had absolutely hated it. When I realised I would be staying in Gdansk for another year, I knew I would have to find a place of my own and moved into a small studio a few minutes' walk from the market square. Vanessa took my place in the flat belonging to the school and so I suppose I immediately felt sorry for her. My ex-flatmate, who had now become her flatmate, was not the easiest of people to get on with, certainly not at such close quarters.

Vanessa confided in me about her problems with her flatmate, along with the fact that she had only been teaching for a year and was concerned about making a good impression. I found myself taking her under my wing. She was keen, bright and personable so it wasn't a hardship and, despite my self-imposed rules, we slowly started to become friends.

Over time, the occasional tipsy nights led to shared confidences although that was not quite the two-way street it appeared to be – I knew she was twenty-nine, that she had on older brother, loved teaching and liked Gdansk but disliked the flat and her flatmate in almost equal measure.

All the little – and sometimes not so little – trivia we pick up as we get to know someone. And what had she learned about me? Certainly not a lot I was sure for I preferred not give too much away; to retain some distance between me and the rest of the world. Anything I did say was carefully considered first. However much I might have appeared to be an open book or occasionally have one drink too many, I never lost control.

One thing Vanessa did know was that I hated swimming. I hadn't been able to avoid telling her as she had once suggested a trip to the local pool. However, my perfectly plausible story about being pulled underwater during a swimming class at school had served me well. I had rehearsed it, and I had had to pull it out a few times over the years. I had even almost started to become convinced by it. Except in the quiet moments I could not avoid. That was when I remembered the inky water, the shock of the cold, the burning in my throat and the conviction that my final moments had come.

On one particularly freezing cold evening out in Gdansk, we had agreed that the beauty of the city could no longer compensate for the grinding cold and, as the hours passed and the drinks flowed, we searched the Internet for lists of the warmest cities in Europe and came up with a shortlist of three: Athens, Valencia and Seville. For reasons lost in the fog of a late night, we decided Seville was the place to head for. Unlike in most cases, it still seemed like a good idea in the light of day when the hangovers had gone. In fact, as the days passed and the cold seeped deeper inside of us, it gained traction. As I shuffled around my flat swathed in blankets, scraping frost off of my windows, the thought of moving somewhere warm again grew more and more appealing.

Vanessa and I were the fortunate ones at our school; with her Irish passport and my French one, we were able to consider moving on to other countries in Europe, while our British colleagues were still reassessing their futures. Before long, job applications were sent, interviews were conducted online and job offers were received and accepted.

Before the move, Vanessa had gone home for a couple of weeks, leaving me kicking my heels in Gdansk. I had nowhere to go and nothing to return to. She had not invited me to accompany her, nor had I expected or hoped that she would. The thought of staying in a stranger's house for days on end would not have been something I would have enjoyed, and I thought perhaps she had understood that.

When she had returned she had seemed changed in some indefinable way at first, but then the old Vanessa had returned and my overriding memories of the previous summer were happy ones; travelling through Europe by train, arriving in Seville, finding a place to live and getting to know our new surroundings.

We wandered through streets scented with jasmine and honeysuckle, savouring the new food and drinks, having swapped stews, dumplings and ice cider for tapas and wine. The sound of flamenco lured us into intimate bars, where we were captivated by the passion and beauty of the music.

Everything was wonderful at first. We were both in the honeymoon stage of being in a new place; enchanted by everything, including those things which would eventually become sources of frustration. Even the intense heat of August in Seville could not dampen our enthusiasm. When the honeymoon was over, though, it seemed to be harder for Vanessa than for me. After all, I had had to do it so many times before that the constant adaptation and reinvention were not even conscious actions anymore. Vanessa envied my easy transition to acceptance, but she didn't understand the downside, the why. I didn't struggle and protest against something new because I had no core of fixed ideas and expectations. I had lost myself long before.

At some point in my recollections, I must have drifted off, but it was not to be for long. I woke up, surprised by my unfamiliar surroundings and had to remind myself where I was. I tried to go back to sleep again but ended up pacing the room. Something was eating away at me, a sense of unease I could not define and all the worse for that. The feeling I had had in May was back and that night in particular, it was stronger than ever.

I went back to bed and stared at the ceiling. I turned off the light and moved from my back to my left side and then to my right, increasingly restless as proper sleep eluded me, and I managed no more than five minutes here and ten minutes there before another look at my watch. At some point, I was fully woken by the sound of a knock on the door. I groped around and switched on the bedside light. Two-fifteen.

Still trying to wake up fully, I heard a key being inserted into the lock and although it was not followed by the sound of the lock releasing, the handle turned. I was rooted to the spot, unable to look away as the handle moved up and down.

I wanted to call out, to sound assertive and tell the person to go away, but when I opened my mouth, no words came out. After two or three further attempts it went quiet, and I waited as my watch ticked a minute off. The door handle rattled again. There was another pause, and then I heard footsteps receding down the hallway.

I turned the light off again but any remaining chance I had had of getting a good night's sleep seemed to have vanished. I checked my phone and saw three o'clock and then four o'clock roll round. I got up and had another glass of water. Whoever had been at the door was long gone and unlikely to return, I reasoned. There was no need to worry.

I went to the window and nudged the curtain back. In the sallow glow of the sodium street lights, the colours of the cars in the car park below were dull and less distinct than they would be in daylight, but in the far corner, I saw it. Unlike the other cars, no light reflected off it. Matte paint. It was the car I had seen behind me earlier at the Algarve Welcome Point and also in Faro. Despite the lighting conditions, there could be no mistaking it; I was struck again by its similarity to a small tank and its strangely intimidating presence.

I hurriedly pulled the curtain across again and scuttled under the covers like a child frightened of monsters. It would be a long time before I managed to sleep, and when I did, I was on an unending road, burning under a bright sun with the occasional glimpse of something I could not identify in the rear-view mirror.

* * *

I awoke to someone knocking on my door again. Remembering the incident in the early hours of the morning, I felt my heart start to pound and called out. 'Who is it?'

'Housekeeping.'

I found my watch. Midday.

The knocking resumed. 'Hello?'

I forced myself out of bed and cracked the door open. The woman peered at me. 'You are checking out today?'

'Yes, yes, I am.'

'Check out is now.'

'I'm so sorry. I didn't sleep well. Can you give me fifteen minutes?'

The woman sighed. 'I suppose so. I have to clean next door. I will come back after that.'

I thanked her, closed the door, showered quickly and threw the few items I had unpacked back in my bag. Apologising to her again as I left, I hurried to reception. Nobody was there, and I cautiously looked out into the car park. The green SUV was nowhere to be seen. I dashed to my car and drove away before anyone from the hotel had the chance to tackle me about the fact I had overstayed and request payment for an extra night.

* * *

The need for something to eat prompted me to stop before too long. At a small café on the main road between Olhão and Faro, over a breakfast of fresh bread, cheese and milky coffee, I studied the two routes I could take into Lisbon. Both would take me along the same stretch of motorway.

Then there would be a choice between the direct route and the more circuitous one which would add time to my journey. On paper it was an easy choice, but the direct route would mean conquering another bridge, a long one; the 25th of April Bridge. I looked it up; at over two kilometres long and seventy metres high, it was far longer and higher than the Guadiana Bridge, which had induced such panic in me the day before. I looked at the alternative route which would make the journey longer. Then back to the bridge. Even given its length, it would take only minutes to drive over it.

I twisted the silver bangle on my wrist, the bangle which I rarely took off. It had been the present I had planned to give to Finn at our graduation ceremony, the ceremony which had never come for her and I had failed to attend.

I thought about how much the drive over the Guadiana Bridge had drained me the day before. Then, defying all logic, I told myself I could manage the drive over the 25th of April Bridge. Despite the uncertainties in store at the end of the journey, I felt better as I returned to my car.

In the bright light of day, it was easy to convince myself that the events of the day and night before were nothing to be concerned about. The person who had been trying my door had just gone to the wrong room before realising their mistake; no doubt someone who had had a drink or two more than was wise. I was annoyed at how agitated I had allowed myself to become.

My reaction to the SUV also seemed absurd. I had seen it a couple of times, it was true, but I had only noticed it because it was so striking. The Algarve Welcome Point to Faro was hardly an unusual route and as for seeing it at the hotel in Olhão, well, that was just one of those things. Of course, it was.

Traffic was sparse as I continued to retrace my route back to Faro, thinking about seeing Vanessa again. I negotiated the outskirts of Faro and settled myself in for the rest of the drive up to Lisbon. I passed a petrol station and became aware of a car pulling out and falling in behind me. A matte green SUV. My heart started to beat faster, all thoughts of meeting Vanessa and tackling bridges forgotten.

I thought about looking for a route which would take me back to Faro, where I could stop somewhere with people around, but somehow I knew the car would simply melt away if I did that. On the other hand, it would be a safe option. But Faro was behind me now; I had no idea how to get back there without pulling over and finding a route back to the city, and I had no desire to do that. I looked at the petrol gauge even though I had filled the tank the day before, needing confirmation that I was, at least, unlikely to find myself stranded.

Torn as to what to do for the best, I took the path of least resistance and continued driving, trying to focus on the road ahead. Some people might have looked for a place to stop and confronted the situation head on. I was not one of those people. I considered that stopping in the middle of nowhere to confront what I perceived as a threat would have been downright reckless rather than brave. At best, the car would drive straight on. At worst — a hundred lurid newspaper headlines flashed through my mind.

The one reckless moment in my life had ended with Finn losing her life and me losing mine as well, albeit in a very different sort of way. So recklessness was not even an option when I knew only too well how that could end.

I thought about who I could call, just to hear a friendly voice to give me some reassurance and realised there was nobody. Once upon a time, it would have been Finn. What she would have said to me I couldn't imagine, but it would have been something simultaneously comforting and funny. She would have made me feel better that was for sure. I tried to recall the sound of her voice, but it was lost to me and the more I tried to capture it, the more elusive it became.

Later on, it might have been Vanessa I would have turned to, but we had not yet reconciled. I still had no idea if we would. I could hardly call her. No, the truth of the matter was that I had deliberately chosen a solitary path so I could not complain about the consequences of that choice.

The minutes crept by, five turning into fifteen; thirty; forty-five. I wasn't sure I could stand the drive to Lisbon with the car following me or whether I even wanted to. I had no desire for the driver to know where I was going and perhaps even follow me to my hotel there.

On the overhead gantry, I saw that the road was about to split. I could carry on to Lisbon or turn off and head for Castro Verde. I knew nothing about the place, though, and I had no idea if I would be able to shake the car off there or find help if it became necessary. I saw the SUV starting to steer towards the right so I stayed on the motorway, willing it to turn off.

As it did, I gradually felt the anxiety start to drain away. Surely, I told myself, the driver could quite innocently have been following a similar route to me. After all, the SUV hadn't followed me from Olhão and the driver would have had no idea I was planning to drive from there to Lisbon. 'You don't own this road, Isabel,' I said to myself. 'Don't be so ridiculous.' But in some shadowy corner of my mind there existed a doubt that refused to be fully quieted.

* * *

The rest of the drive towards Lisbon was uneventful. I kept glancing in the rear-view mirror, but the car which had caused me so much concern made no reappearance. Finally, the distinctive orange-red towers of the 25th of April Bridge appeared in the distance. I passed through the tolls and the bridge loomed in front of me; just as the day before, there was no way back from that point. I felt the tension in my body and my hands growing clammy again. I wondered what had possessed me to think that saving some time was worth the ordeal which now lay ahead. I drove onto the bridge. Why had I ever thought it would be a good idea?

I saw a flash of deep blue far below me and willed myself to look straight ahead. Don't think, I ordered myself. Just keep driving. Keep taking deep breaths. But still I felt my body tremble, and I gripped the steering wheel harder. The Guadiana Bridge had been nothing compared to this one.

After what seemed like an eternity suspended over the Tagus River, I chanced a look up from the stretch of road directly in front of the car. I had seen photos, of course, but nothing quite prepared me for that first view of Lisbon, nestled on hills, basking in the warm amber glow of a perfect afternoon. For a moment it took my mind off of the bridge until my eyes wandered to the Tagus far below. A bead of sweat rolled down my forehead and dropped into my eye. I rubbed it away and forced myself to concentrate on the little patch of road in front of the car again.

Finally off the bridge, my breathing started to return to normal. The GPS directed me to my hotel, and as I approached it, I glanced behind me. There was no green SUV in sight. I turned off the road and drove into the underground car park with a sense of relief. I retrieved my bag, checked in and flopped on the bed.

The room was much the same as any hotel room; a double bed, bedside tables, a luggage rack and a small table with two chairs. I was cheered by the sight of a kettle and a supply of coffee. At the far end of the rectangular room was the bathroom. It was all simple but clean and far more pleasant than my room in Seville. Not that that was saying a lot, I realised. I phoned Vanessa, but there was no answer so I sent her a message.

'Hi. I've just arrived in Lisbon. We can meet tomorrow if you're free.'

I kept checking my phone, but there was no reply.

Part 3

Lisbon, Portugal

Chapter 4

The tree-lined Avenida da Liberdade sweeps through Lisbon taking multiple lanes of traffic with it, majestic yet intimate in parts. The avenue deposits the visitor in Restauradores Square, taking in everything on the way from expensive hotels and luxury shops to kiosk cafés set amongst the gardens which dot the avenue.

I looked up from the guide book I had been reading and surveyed the scene. When I saw the city on that clear summer morning, standing at the far end of the Edward the Seventh Park with the Tagus River providing a distant backdrop, I could understand why Vanessa had chosen to flee there. The sloping lawns and manicured geometrical hedges of the park led the eye to the statue of the Marquês de Pombal in the middle of a busy roundabout and beyond that, a smudge of greenery, which indicated the path of the Avenida da Liberdade. The light was extraordinary in its clarity and the air was warm, but it was not as stifling as in Seville, and it felt as though there was space to breathe. Seville was beautiful, but already I could see that Lisbon was too. It was, though, a total contrast; perfect for someone who wanted to cast off memories and make a fresh start in a completely different environment.

As Vanessa hadn't contacted me, I assumed she was still tunnelling out from underneath a mountain of paperwork. I thought I might do some sightseeing and set off on a route which took me through the park and to the top of the Avenida da Liberdade. An archway of trees framed the lanes of traffic and pavements. As I walked down the avenue, I took time to appreciate the little cafés, fountains and monuments and the exquisite designs of the black and white pavements along the way. It was easily possible to forget the traffic which continued to whir past.

Noticing a side street on the right leading up to what looked like a park, I headed in that direction. One of my favourite things to do in a new place was simply to wander around and see where the path took me. I walked uphill and found a small square with a market in full swing. I had a look around and started to feel as though I was actually on holiday.

I found my thoughts drifting to Vanessa and pulled out my phone and tried to call her again. There was still no reply, and a vague feeling of uneasiness started to grow in the pit of my stomach. I wasn't sure whether it was because she had not replied or whether it was due to wondering what would happen when we did finally meet again.

Retracing my steps back to the main street and continuing down it finally brought me out into Restauradores Square with the Monument to the Restorers, a soaring limestone obelisk, pointing to a brilliant blue sky. I heard my phone buzz and found a message from Vanessa.

Hi. I'm sorry I didn't get back to you more quickly. Work has been crazy! I'm so pleased you're here. I'm going to send you my address. When can you come by?

She followed her message with a link to an address on the map. I consulted my phone and found a bus that would take me from close to my location to a stop which looked to be near to her home.

How does twelve sound?

Perfect. We'll chat when you get here. I think that's better.

Whether I would have agreed with her or not didn't matter as she had hung up, and I needed to get to the bus stop.

* * *

With the help of my fellow passengers, I managed to get off at the right stop. I looked at the steep hill rising in front of me and checked on the map that I did indeed need to climb to the top of it. I hadn't considered Lisbon's hills when looking for a stop close to Vanessa's flat. There could be no doubt so I trudged up it. 'I hope this will be worthwhile,' I said under my breath.

Arriving at the top, I turned right into a street lined with pastel pink and blue buildings fronted with modest wrought-iron balconies. Clothes lines were strung along the exteriors of the balconies, many of which were draped with washing floating in the breeze.

The entrance door to the building which housed Vanessa's flat was open and as I went inside, I blinked rapidly as my eyes adjusted to the low light. Old-fashioned metal post boxes were fixed to the wall to the left. I looked at them but they only had the numbers of the flats; there were no names. Straight ahead were the stairs, and I sighed as I realised there was no lift. I checked the address again – fourth floor, flat B. I plodded up flight after flight of stairs until I arrived at the fourth floor and found the door marked B.

I was about to knock on the door when I realised it was slightly ajar. 'Vanessa? Are you there?' I called out, looking cautiously round it. There was no answer except the distant barking of a dog somewhere. I opened the door and called her name again. I phoned her, but there was no answer and no sound of a phone ringing in the flat. I sent a message. *Vanessa, I'm here at your flat. Your front door is open. Where are you?* Staring at the screen, I became irritated as I noticed for the first time that there was no way to tell if she had read the message or not. In the continuing silence, I swore under my breath as I wondered what was going on.

I stood at the entrance, trying to decide what to do for the best. Then, telling myself to snap out of it, I went in and closed the door behind me. The front door opened directly into a small sitting room with an even smaller kitchen off to the right, separated from the sitting room by a modest breakfast bar. To the left was another door, leading, I assumed, to the bedroom and bathroom.

Every part of me said that it was wrong to go snooping about in someone else's flat, but these did not feel like normal circumstances. I checked my phone in case I had somehow missed a call or message, but there was still nothing.

I looked around to see if she had left a note. Perhaps the battery in her phone had died. Perhaps she had popped out to the supermarket for something and had forgotten to close the door. Those possibilities seemed unlikely, but they would at least explain the situation. There was nothing, not only no note, but nothing which betrayed Vanessa's personality. It was also extraordinarily tidy for her. I ventured further into the room, and then I noticed the table in the far corner by the window and the array of framed photos on it.

I went over and crouched down in front of them, somehow reluctant to pick them up and worked my way along the row. The first one was of Vanessa on her own in a location I didn't recognise; her blonde hair caught the light and her pale blue eyes stared intently into the lens, her expression enigmatic. The next was of the two of us together in front of the Neptune Fountain in Gdansk, bundled up in bright hats and scarves, with a soft flurry of snow falling around us. The third was also of us, this time at a pavement café in Seville, wearing T-shirts and shorts, two glasses raised to the camera. I remembered the people at the next table taking it for us.

I moved on to the next one and stopped, taken aback by what I saw. It was a photo of Vanessa and Javier. She was kissing him on the cheek but with one flirty eye on the camera as he smiled broadly while taking a selfie of the two of them. I sank back on my heels. Vanessa had surely intended me to see those photos but why? She didn't know Javier and I had split up or did she? I wondered if I was supposed to read some meaning into the photos, which I felt had been carefully selected for my benefit. I looked at them in turn again. Whatever meaning there was, if indeed there was one, was lost on me.

As the white muslin curtains caught on the breeze, I realised for the first time that the windows to the balcony were not fully closed. I went out onto the balcony and took in the scene. The smell of freshly laundered clothes wafted up towards me. The façade of the building opposite was covered with blue and white tiles so typical of the photographs I had seen of Lisbon. Between a jumble of terracotta rooftops, I saw the Tagus sparkling in the distance in the bright Atlantic light. One of the little sunflower yellow trams for which Lisbon was so famous screeched as it rounded the corner and then rumbled down the street. I heard the grinding noise of metal against metal as it came to a stop and then the sigh as it set off again, contrasting with the absolute silence inside the flat.

I went back inside where it was a little darker and easier to see the screen of my phone. I called Vanessa. Once more, when there was no reply, I sent a message. I checked my watch as if not trusting my phone to tell me the correct time. I had seen a small supermarket on my way to her flat; if she had gone there, she would have been back by now.

I got up and reluctantly went through the other door. I found the bathroom and one bedroom, but they were strangely impersonal and could have belonged to anyone. My respect for personal space meant I was not about to start going through drawers and cupboards. The stillness was starting to unnerve me. Perhaps I had just grown more accustomed than I had realised to the almost constant noise which was an unfortunate consequence of sharing a flat with four other people, two of whom could not stand each other and regularly engaged in shouting matches.

Going back out into the sitting room, the photos caught my eye once more. I went through them again more carefully, searching for the clue they contained which would make everything clear to me, still half expecting Vanessa to burst through the door at any moment, a bag full of shopping in her arms, full of breathless apologies and explanations. Ones which would make my current anxiety seem laughable. We would resolve our differences and joke about how jumpy I had been.

I started to pace the room, checking my watch so often that time seemed to grind to a halt. Any moment now, she'll be back, I told myself. I checked my phone again and sent another message. *Where are you?*

Somewhere in the building, I heard a crash as someone dropped something followed by muffled shouting in a tone which sounded like someone swearing. I jumped and felt my heart rate accelerate. Suddenly, I wanted to be anywhere rather than in that flat. I hurried out and raced down the stairs. I broke out into the fresh air, feeling as though I had been released from some kind of captivity.

I had been so preoccupied by the photos and the unnatural silence in the flat that it was only once I was outside again that it seriously occurred to me Vanessa might not be going back to the flat and could be in some sort of trouble. I phoned her again. I sent another message. *Are you OK?* I thought about phoning the police, but my aversion to them made me think twice.

My experience with the police after Finn's death had not left me keen to have any further dealings with authorities of any type. Even the immigration police I had had to deal with in various countries had made me anxious, however pleasant they had been. It also seemed like an over-reaction. I couldn't imagine what could possibly have happened to Vanessa in the short length of time between her messages and my arrival at her flat, but it surely couldn't have been anything which would warrant involving the police. Knowing Vanessa, she had probably got sidetracked by something or someone. She had always hopped from one task to another, distracted by whatever or whoever crossed her path.

Consulting my phone again, I realised I could get the tram from across the road to go back into the centre. I crossed over and at the tram stop tried to decide what to do for the best. I had a week in Lisbon, which would give Vanessa plenty of time to get in touch again. We would sort things out, or we wouldn't, and I would enjoy Lisbon before heading back to Seville or off somewhere else. I had the car for three weeks so I had time to work with. The thought of a road trip appealed and as I got on the tram, my spirits started to lift.

I took a seat on one of the benches and as the tram set off, something made me glance up at the building. I saw a glint of sunlight strike a window as it closed and had a fleeting impression of blonde hair. The image was gone again before I could really register what I had seen. It had been on the fourth floor, I thought, but I wasn't sure.

I got up, but the next stop was still some way off. I drummed my fingers against the handrail and, under my breath, I urged the driver to hurry, but nothing was going to speed the old tram up as it trundled on its way.

As soon as it juddered to a halt, I jumped off and jogged back the way I had come, lamenting how much I had neglected my fitness over the years along with so many other things. At the entrance to the building, I paused to catch my breath. Taking in a few more gulps of air, I made my way up the stairs again. When I arrived at Vanessa's door, it was shut. I wasn't sure if had closed it behind me when I had left or not. I tried to think, but I had been in such a rush to get out of there that I couldn't picture the moment clearly.

I raised my hand to knock on the door and then thought better of it. I took my phone out and called Vanessa, my ear close to the door, listening for the sound of the phone ringing on the other side. I could hear nothing. Frustrated, I hung up and banged my fist on the door, calling Vanessa's name. If she was inside, she chose not to respond.

A door further down the hallway opened, a woman appeared, and I heard a flood of Portuguese. I had no idea what she was saying, but it was clear I was making too much noise. I put my hands up in a gesture of surrender which seemed to placate her, and she disappeared back into her flat.

I sent another message. *Where are you?* It stared at me. There was no reply. It seemed pointless to stay there any longer so I went back down the stairs and caught the next tram, thinking perhaps I could try to do some sightseeing and take my mind off whatever was going on. I still wasn't sure whether I was worried or annoyed. The thought that she was playing some sort of game with me crossed my mind, and I immediately felt ashamed for thinking the worst of her and dismissed the idea.

The tram deposited me back in the centre, and I spent the afternoon wandering aimlessly through the city, seeing it but taking in nothing. I started to become obsessed with my phone, checking it with increasing regularity in case I had missed any calls or messages from Vanessa.

After a while, I found myself walking under the Rua Augusta Arch into a vast, imposing square. The light reflecting off of the white paving was blinding and the sight of the Tagus, now much closer, slowed me down. Instead of walking out into the square and down to the waterfront, I turned and walked under the arcades surrounding the square. Occasionally, I sensed Vanessa was behind me but, when I turned to look, it was not her. Once when I turned, there was nobody there at all. Vanessa had become a shadow; elusive, mutable and impossible to pin down.

Back in my hotel room, I rang Vanessa yet again, but there was no answer. I wasn't sure what to do. I brooded over the scene which had confronted me at her flat and the fleeting glimpse I thought I had caught of someone at her balcony, shutting the windows. The impression had been almost imperceptible, and I started to wonder if my imagination had simply been working overtime.

Frustrated by my inability to contact Vanessa or make any sense of the situation, my thoughts turned back to the photos. Could they have been intended to convey some kind of message? Or did I simply want to believe that to give me something to occupy my mind?

Had the one of her in a place I didn't recognise been intended to convey I didn't know her? I wasn't sure what could be read into the two photos of us together. And the one of her with Javier? One of the reasons we had fallen out was due to him. She had insisted that he had liked her, and they had been getting close until he had met me. I had known nothing about that back in early April when he had suggested a date, but I had soon found out about it at Easter along with a few other things.

Had there really been something between them? I decided that was one thing which I could at least try to find out. If I could, perhaps it would help me to make some sense of the situation. With nothing else to go on, I reluctantly called Javier.

'Isabel?'

'Yes, I'm sorry to call you,' I said, kicking myself for starting with an apology.

'It's OK.'

'It's just that … I know this sounds strange … Did you and Vanessa ever go out together? On a date, I mean.'

'Vanessa? I haven't heard that name for a while. No. Why do you ask?'

'I found a photo of the two of you together.'

'Where are you?'

His change of tack instead of sticking to the point irritated me. 'Lisbon.'

'Lisbon?' Javier echoed. 'What are you doing there? And what's this photo you're talking about?'

'It's a long story. Forget it.'

'Why don't you send it to me so I can tell you when it was taken?' He sounded unusually conciliatory. Or perhaps he was humouring me.

'I don't have it on my phone. It's you and Vanessa, in a park I think, and she's kissing you on the cheek.'

'So you want me to tell you the story behind a photo that I can't remember, and that you don't have a copy of?'

I hated the way he managed to make me sound unreasonable whilst being eminently logical himself. It wasn't the first time. 'Look, it doesn't matter.'

'It doesn't sound like it doesn't matter.'

'Really, forget it. You've answered my question anyway. You and Vanessa didn't have any sort of relationship, right?'

'Right.'

'OK, well, that's that. Bye,' I said, clumsily.

'Bye,' he said, and I heard the line go dead straight away as if his finger had been hovering over the screen, keen to finish the conversation as quickly as possible.

I phoned Vanessa again, but she didn't pick up. I wondered if I should have gone straight to the police as soon as I had discovered she was not at home and her front door was open. Earlier in the day the idea had seemed like an over-reaction, but as the night crept in I was no longer so confident about that. I looked up the procedure for reporting someone missing in Portugal. I switched back and forth between dialling the number and waiting it out.

Finally, deterred by the thoughts of dealing with the police and creating a huge fuss about what was probably nothing, I decided to wait it out. There had been no sign of a struggle at her flat, no sign anything was amiss except the continuing silence from her end. I resolved to get to Vanessa's flat early the next day. She knew me well enough not to expect me to turn up at any time before about ten. If she was playing some sort of game, I would be arriving early enough to take her by surprise. If she was not there, I would grit my teeth and go to the police. I would still be reporting her disappearance, if that was what it was, within twenty-four hours.

The night was another restless one, but I knew I managed to sleep at some point for I remembered a fragment of my dream; a brilliant red kite flying high before floating back down to Earth and landing in the sea where the waves rolled over it, leaving it shattered and broken.

Chapter 5

I arrived at Vanessa's at eight the following morning. It had meant getting up at a horribly early hour for me and only the prospect of establishing she was safe had encouraged me to crawl out of bed.

Arriving at her flat, I knocked at the door and heard footsteps inside. I felt relieved she was at least there although I was also annoyed. I told myself not to dwell on that. I was there to make up with her, not to fall out all over again. I played out what I might say when we finally came face to face. The door opened, and I found myself adjusting my gaze from the tall, fair-haired Vanessa I had been expecting to a shorter woman with light brown hair in her late thirties or early forties. I took a step back to check I had the right flat. The woman peered round the door at me, apparently reluctant to open it fully.

We continued to stare at each other, a wary look on her face and one of incomprehension on mine. As she didn't seem inclined to say anything, I began. 'Do you speak English?'

'Yes. Who are you?'

The four words made it clear that not only did she speak English, but she almost certainly was English.

I'm looking for a friend of mine. Her name is Vanessa. Vanessa Taylor.'

An indecipherable look passed across her face. 'Who are you?' she repeated.

'My name is Isabel Foster. Vanessa is a friend. She asked me to meet her here yesterday. I came over, but nobody was here.' I decided the fewer details I gave away about my previous visit, the better.

'Oh.' She appeared to be wrestling with a decision. 'I suppose you'd better come in.'

She led me into the familiar room. 'Have a seat.'

'Thank you.' I perched on the edge of an armchair, feeling I should not appear to make myself too comfortable. 'What's your name?'

'Lou.'

Lou sat down and there was a long silence, which she eventually broke. 'You said you're a friend. How long have you known Vanessa?'

'Nearly two years. Not that long, I suppose but we are – or were – good friends.'

Too late, I realised my mistake, but Lou picked up on it straight away. 'Were?'

'We had a bit of a disagreement. She contacted me a few days ago and suggested that I come here so we could clear the air.'

Lou inspected her surroundings as though a suitable

response might be found on one of the walls.

'How do you know her?' I asked, keen to break the silence.

'We work together.'

'You're a teacher too?' I was hopeful we might find some common ground, which would make the conversation less strained.

'A teacher? No. What makes you say that? We're tour guides.'

My confusion was mounting. Vanessa had always said teaching was her vocation, and she couldn't imagine doing anything else. She hadn't said anything about having stopped teaching in her messages. 'Do you know her well?' I asked as I tried to make sense of Vanessa's sudden career change.

While I waited for a reply, I looked out at the same view I had seen the day before of the Tagus. It looked different somehow, but then everything seemed different; slightly off. I wondered if it was just the lack of sleep.

'I'm not sure anyone can know her well.' Lou glanced at her watch and back at me.

Unsure how to respond to that, I asked another question. 'Did she mention anything to you about meeting me here?'

'No. I don't know anything about that. She was staying here for a few days because she offered to cat sit for me. I didn't know she was planning to have visitors.' Lou gave me a suspicious look and resumed. 'I only got back late last night.' She gestured at a suitcase in the corner of the room.'

'You mean this isn't where she lives?'

'No.' Lou cocked her head to one side. 'Why would you think that?'

'As I said, she told me to meet her here. I understood this is where she lives.'

'No,' Lou repeated once more. I was getting tired of no. I looked at the room properly for the first time and noticed the framed photos I had seen the day before had gone. I felt a cold line of sweat work its way from my hairline down my neck and back.

'Was she here when you got back last night?' I asked.

Lou shook her head. 'She'd gone by then.'

'Have you spoken to her since?'

'No, as I said, I got back late and it's,' she broke off to consult her watch again, 'not even eight-thirty yet. I would consider phoning someone so early to be rather … unnecessary unless there are extenuating circumstances.' She gave me a less than amenable look, which I could understand.

'I really am sorry to disturb you at this time of day,' I said, trying to ease the tension. 'I'm just worried about Vanessa. I can't get hold of her.'

'I shouldn't worry about her. No doubt she'll turn up. She's very capable.'

There was something acidic about the way she had said the last word, but I didn't pursue it. 'Yes, I suppose so. Could I give you my phone number, though? If … when you see her, would you let me know?'

Lou gave a non-committal shrug. 'Sometimes we don't see each other for days. It depends which tours we're leading.'

I wrote my number down and went to give it to her. When she didn't extend her hand, I dropped the paper on the coffee table between us. 'I'd appreciate it. I am actually quite concerned about her.'

Lou inclined her head slightly and checked her watch again.

'Would you give me the name of the company where you work?'

'Why?'

'I could check to see if she's there.'

Lou seemed to hesitate but then scribbled a few details on a piece of paper and slid it across the table.

I retrieved the paper as it fluttered to the floor and then got up. It was clear Lou had no intention of saying anything else and wanted me to go. 'I'll see myself out then.'

I reached the door and realised I had seen no sign of a cat since I had been there or during my visit the previous day. I glanced at the kitchen. There were no food bowls on the floor. 'Where's the cat?'

'Asleep probably.'

Closing the door behind me, I leaned against the wall, trying to make sense of the strained conversation I had had with Lou and what I had learned about Vanessa. I couldn't decide if Lou was keeping something from me or was simply tired and not in the mood for early morning calls from complete strangers.

Once outside, I found a patch of shade and looked at the address on the piece of paper in my hands. I mulled over whether I should go there to try to catch up with Vanessa, wondering why she had not told me she had changed careers and trying to anticipate how she would react if I turned up at her workplace. I found the location on my phone and decided there was nothing to be lost by heading over there. I searched for bus routes and once I had discovered where the bus stop was, I walked back past Lou's building.

Just after that, there was an entrance to a garage. I saw the doors start to open and waited for the car to pull out. The car drove away and as I started to move on, I glanced to my left to make sure there was not another car on its way out as well. Parked just inside I could see a matte green SUV.

Without stopping to think about how I would get out again, I ran into the garage, squeezing between the doors as they started to close. I stood there facing the car. It was so distinctive I was sure it had to be the same one which had been following me and yet … I swore under my breath for not being able to recall the number plate. Looking around and seeing that the garage was deserted, I switched on the torch on my phone and approached the car. I tried to see through the windows, looking for something which might give away the owner's identity, but it was as impenetrable as the armoured vehicle it so closely resembled.

I heard a door scrape open in the far corner and moved out of sight behind a concrete pillar. I chanced a brief look and saw a man walking in my direction, his footsteps echoing around the garage. As he approached, I sidled round the pillar, trying to watch him without being seen. He reached the SUV, checked something on the piece of paper he was holding and fished some keys out of his pocket.

If I were to stand a chance of learning anything about who had been driving the car, I would have to approach him. I tried to assess him. He had a slight build and didn't appear to be threatening. I moved out of the shadows. 'Who are you?' I asked, trying to sound confident while feeling anything but.

The man turned around, looking surprised rather than startled.

'Who are you?' I repeated.

'No English,' he said, waving his hands as if to ward me off. He went to the wall by the doors and flicked a switch. I saw the garage doors begin to open as he got into the car and started the engine. He turned the car towards the exit, and I ran out in front of it to stop him. He had been going slowly, and he managed to brake and avoid hitting me.

I pressed my hands flat on the bonnet and stared at the windscreen, aiming for where I hoped his eyeline might be. I must have looked completely crazy, but at that moment all I could think about was trying to get some information about the owner of the car. I heard him revving the engine. I stared at the windscreen a little longer and realised it was a battle I could not win. He revved it again, and I hesitated and then moved to one side and watched him drive away.

Remembering the door the man had come through, I ran to the back of the garage and found it led into the hallway of Lou's building. It came out under the staircase, which was why I hadn't seen it before. I took the stairs two at a time to Lou's flat, convinced it could be no coincidence I had seen the SUV there. I banged on Lou's door, still panting, and as she opened it, an expression of annoyance turned to something altogether less easy to read when she registered that it was me.

'What are you doing here again?' Lou asked.

'Tell me about that green SUV,' I demanded.

'What green SUV? What are you talking about?'

'The one in the garage which belongs to this building. I've just seen it being driven away. It followed me to Lisbon the other day, and now it's in your garage. Or it was until a few minutes ago. That's a bit of a coincidence, don't you think?'

'What I think is that you need to calm down and get a grip of yourself.'

'I am perfectly calm, 'I said, fully aware I didn't sound that way. 'Just tell me about that car. Was it you who followed me from the Algarve Welcome Point?'

'I have absolutely no idea what you are talking about. Why would I want to follow you anywhere? I'd never even met you before this morning. And I have been nowhere near the Algarve or this Welcome Point you're going on about.'

'Yes, but just listen for a moment.'

'No, I don't want to listen to you ranting on about some car.'

'Please listen to me.'

'No. You listen. Unless you want me to call the police, you'd better go away. Now.' She started to close the door, and I considered putting my foot in the way to stop her before thinking better of it. She slammed it shut in my face, also closing the door on any chance that I would hear from her again. I couldn't have made the situation worse if I had tried.

* * *

Feeling thoroughly disheartened and realising there was nothing to be gained from hanging around any longer at Lou's building, I retraced my route back down the stairs and walked to the stop to get the bus to the agency. It was the only step left which I could take to find Vanessa.

I waited my turn patiently in the queue of people eagerly booking tours and gathering information about Lisbon. I gazed out of the window, watching the world go by. I felt Finn's presence and thought for a moment I had seen her but knew that was impossible. It had happened a lot in the early days but as the years had passed, not as often or with the same conviction. She was no less with me though despite that. I moved to the top of the queue and up to the desk on autopilot, my mind still on other things.

'Excuse me. Can I help you?' The harassed young woman at the desk glanced behind me, no doubt hoping my query would be brief as she assessed how long it would take her to deal with the ever-growing queue of people.

'Yes. I'm looking for my friend Vanessa Taylor. I understand she's a guide here.'

Her previously open if rather stressed expression changed. 'I'm sure you'll understand I can't tell you anything about who works here –'

'I don't want any personal information. I'd just like to know when she's due in again.'

The woman's eyes slid around me and eyed the queue again. 'I'm sorry I really can't tell you anything about staff.'

I rummaged in my bag and pulled out a pen and a piece of paper. I jotted down my name, phone number and the hotel in which I was staying, painfully aware of her growing impatience. 'Would you at least give her this and ask her to contact me if you see her?'

She took the piece of paper and bit her lip. I thought she appeared to be softening.

'Please.' I said, hoping to appeal to her better nature. 'It's important.'

'I'm afraid you'll have to go.' Whatever vulnerability there might have been in her defences had been shored up. She looked past me and called out in her brightest, most professional voice. 'Next, please.'

The queue shuffled forward obediently, leaving me sidelined. I traipsed back out of the door and wondered where to go from there. I phoned Vanessa and then, when there was no reply, followed the familiar yet apparently pointless routine of sending her a message. *I'm trying to find you. Where are you?*

I waited for a while, hoping she might respond, and then shoved my phone in my bag and set off back to the hotel, no longer in the mood to even attempt any sightseeing.

Chapter 6

I looked out over the sea of crisp, white linen tablecloths in the hotel dining room; most now littered with the debris of breakfast but a few others still untouched and pristine. My gaze then reverted to my phone. I had woken several times during the night and reached for it in case I had missed a message. Before leaving my room, I had made my habitual phone call and sent the usual follow-up message. There had, of course, been no reply.

Over breakfast, I tried to decide what to do. I knew I always felt better when I had a plan, no matter how weak that plan might be. My inability to track Vanessa down, the sight of the green SUV in Lou's garage and her strange attitude towards me, even before I had gone charging in with accusations about her following me, had left me unsettled. Part of me was inclined just to leave Lisbon and set off on the road trip I had been considering, which would eventually lead me back to Seville. I would have plenty of time on the road to think and that was something I needed as I contemplated whether to stay in Seville or move on.

On the other hand, the idea that Vanessa might actually be in trouble was still a possibility which was playing on my mind. However badly we had left things, I didn't want to walk away if she really needed help. Looking again at the map of Lisbon and the information I had been given at the reception desk at the hotel, I decided I would spend the day exploring Lisbon, interspersed with regular attempts to contact Vanessa. If I had still not managed to get in touch with her by late afternoon, I would go back to the agency and ask someone in authority there if she should be reported as missing. If I was told she had been going to work as usual, I would concentrate on enjoying the city for a few days before setting off on my road trip, and I would put Vanessa out of my mind for good. It occurred to me that perhaps I could book an excursion or two; I thought how ironic it would be if either Vanessa or Lou turned out to be my tour guide.

I left the hotel and as I walked down the Avenida da Liberdade again, I tried to distract myself by taking some photos and stopping for coffee at one of the kiosk cafés, but I wasn't really taking in my surroundings. I phoned Vanessa again and sent her another message. With every unanswered phone call and message, the flame of anxiety which had been lit on my journey to Lisbon was growing stronger.

I got as far as Rossio Square before I gave into my urge to phone her again. I stared at the screen, willing her to answer. I sent another message. It was only midday, and I had decided I would wait until later in the afternoon to go to the agency. But what if she was in trouble and that would be too late? What if it was already too late?

Feeling a rising sense of panic, a feeling I might have failed another person, I abandoned my sightseeing plans and rushed over to the agency as quickly as I could, anxiety gnawing at me as I waited my turn in the queue again. I saw two people at the counters; the woman I had spoken to before and an older man. There was only one queue so I hoped I would get the man. He could hardly prove to be less helpful than the woman had been.

As my turn came, I realised I would have to go to the woman's counter. I tried to indicate to the couple behind me to go ahead and take my turn, but they were insistent that they should not jump the queue. People behind us started to grow impatient and there were the first murmurs of discontent so I gave in. I sighed and approached her, noticing her fixed smile flicker as she recognised me.

'Why are you here again?' she asked, lowering her voice.

'I'm worried about Vanessa.'

'And I told you I cannot talk to you about our staff or whether we even have a member of staff called Vanessa. You could be anyone.'

'OK. I understand that, but let me put this to you. I cannot contact her. She isn't answering her phone or replying to any messages.'

'Perhaps she simply doesn't want to talk to you,' she replied with the pained smile still in place for the benefit of those behind me in the queue.

'As she asked me to come to Lisbon to meet her, I find that somewhat unlikely.' I returned the same artificial smile.

'What do you expect me to do about it?'

'I know Vanessa works here so you can cut that line out. I have no idea whether she is missing or not but, as I said, I cannot contact her. You will know if she is missing as she works here. If she isn't turning up for work, I expect you to report that to the police.' I added a lie. 'It's not entirely clear to me how to report a missing person. That is something you will be able to find out more easily than me. I cannot speak Portuguese whereas, I assume, you can. In short, it's on you if she's in trouble and you do nothing.'

The woman took a step back. Her smile had vanished, and a look of something closer to alarm had replaced it. 'You have made your point. Now please leave.'

'Fine,' I said and walked out, phone in hand, preparing to phone Vanessa yet again.

* * *

To try to burn off some of my nervous energy and annoyance, I walked and walked, again not really appreciating the city. What had been supposed to be a break and a chance to put things right had proved to be anything but relaxing or constructive so far.

My phone buzzed. The light was so bright I had to find some shade to read the message which had arrived.

It was from Vanessa. *Hi. Can you get to the Café Bar Jardim in Chiado?*

Relief flooded my body, swiftly followed by the rather less positive feelings of confusion and irritation. *Where have you been? What's going on? I've been trying to get hold of you ever since I got here. I've been so worried.*

Sorry. I've had some problems. Can you get to that bar?

Yes, but what's happened? Are you OK?

Not really, no. Please just come. Can the questions wait?

My frustration at being unable to get a straight answer out of Vanessa was outweighed by my concern. I had never known her to be so cryptic before. I looked around me, unsure of my exact location, and then, as I arrived at the next corner, saw the striking Gothic wrought-iron tower of the Santa Justa Lift at the end of the road to my right.

I'm near the Santa Justa Lift. Not sure how long it will take me, but I'll get there as soon as I can.

Thank you.

Checking my phone, I found the café, mapped the route and sent another message. *I'll be there in 10 – 15 minutes, more or less.*

Ignoring the fact I was already hot and thirsty and more than ready to stop for a drink, I picked up my pace. Somewhere in the winding streets, I took a wrong turn, but after some enquiries in a shop, I found the street I needed in just under fifteen minutes. I didn't want to get there late and risk missing her.

Once I had found the street, the Café Bar Jardim was hard to miss. It had a glass frontage and proudly displayed its name in bold, gold-leaf lettering in an ornate script over the door. Inside it was lined with floor to ceiling mirrors, some fogged and spotted with age, others brand new. It was lit with ornate glass and brass chandeliers. The floor was laid with black tiles so highly polished they reflected the people, tables and chairs of the world which rested on them. Just going through the door was a disorientating experience.

I walked round the bar, slowed down by the strange experience of my reflection accompanying me from below and the sensation that I might slip on the highly polished floor at any moment. Vanessa was nowhere to be seen. I got my phone out and sent her a message. *Just got here. Can't see you, though.*

Unable to wait any longer, I ordered a drink and carefully made my way to a table near the back of the café. I would have taken a seat on the terrace or by the windows at the front to be sure I would spot her, but they were all taken. As I sat down, I phoned her. There was no reply. I sent another message. *I'm here. You said it was urgent. Where are you?*

People came and went, drifting through an idyllic summer's day, but my phone remained silent. A soft breeze floated through the door and the glass chandeliers responded, tinkling softly. I sipped my drink, the ice clinking gently against the glass, and despite my concerns, I felt myself being lulled into the alternate reality the café induced.

I was about to ask for another drink when I got a fleeting impression of something familiar, something which tugged at memories. I had seen that long, pale blonde hair and that emerald green dress before. Vanessa. With all the reflections, I struggled to place exactly where she was sitting at first. I turned round, and she disappeared. I turned back, and I could see her again. It took me some moments, but finally I placed her location. She was at a table close to the door. I was convinced she had not been there when I had arrived; I would have had to walk straight past her; it would have been impossible to miss her.

I felt relief but also anger at seeing her sitting there looking carefree whilst I was fretting over what had happened to her. She certainly didn't look like someone going through a bad time. I was about to get up and go over to confront her when a better idea occurred to me. I would phone her first so I would have the chance to see her reaction. I would know then if she was simply ignoring me and was no longer worth expending any energy on. I shrank back against my seat, and propped up the large menu in front of me.

Phoning Vanessa, I looked cautiously over the top of the menu. I saw her look at her phone, which was on the table, smile and then ignore it. The smile unnerved me; it wasn't a warm, genuine one. There was something calculating and cold about it. I waited, trying to give her the benefit of the doubt, and then I hung up and followed my normal pattern of sending a message. I didn't want her to know I was still at the café so I decided to be less than completely honest.

Hi. I'm really worried about you. I don't understand what's going on. You asked me to meet you at your flat in Lisbon, but you weren't there. Then you said that it was urgent to meet at that bar, but you weren't there either. I'm on my way back down to the Santa Justa Lift. If you want to see me, I'll be waiting in the queue to take it so I'll be there for a while. If you've changed your mind about meeting up that's fine, but just contact me to let me know you're OK. You said you'd been having some problems.

I watched carefully and saw Vanessa turn her attention back to her phone as the message presumably arrived. Her finger moved across the screen, and I supposed she must have been reading my message. I waited and wondered and then saw a raised eyebrow as if something I had written had surprised her; it was followed by that smile again. I waited, willing her to reply. Her hand lingered over the screen. She picked the phone up.

'Come on,' I urged her under my breath. She chewed on her lip and turned the phone over and over as though debating what to do. 'Go on, phone me,' I muttered. She raised her hand to the screen, and I realised I was holding my breath. I waited for my phone to ring, but it was not to be, and I watched as she slipped the phone into her bag and took a sip of her drink.

Enraged by all the anxiety she had caused and the fact it was now obvious that she was playing some sort of game with me, I threw the menu down on the table and pushed my chair back, scraping it noisily over the tiles. The sudden disturbance made those closest to me turn and caused a ripple effect as other people looked round, Vanessa amongst them. I had a moment of grim satisfaction when I saw the startled look on her face. However, she had the advantage of being far closer to the entrance and was outside before I had even reached the door. I had one foot on the pavement when I felt a hand on my shoulder and turned to find a waiter asking for payment for my drink.

I saw Vanessa vanishing into the crowd and with a hurried apology, I pushed a five euro note into the waiter's hand. I ran out of the door and pursued her down the hill, nearly colliding with a group of tourists, who were forced to scatter and then yelled at me to watch where I was going.

Vanessa stopped to look back at the commotion, and I paused as well. It would have been my opportunity to gain on her, but it was as though my actions were no longer under my own agency but dictated by hers. If she stopped, I had to. If she ran, I would follow. She made eye contact with me and a flicker of a smile appeared on her face, and then she set off again, setting a pace which I struggled to follow. I pushed past another group of tourists, who had just emerged from a side street and were taking up the width of the narrow pavement.

We continued downhill. It should have been easier than going uphill but trying to stay upright on the slippery cobbles made it far more challenging. Gradually, the road became wider and flatter. Vanessa turned a corner, and I followed her as fast as my body would allow. My lungs were starting to burn, and the muscles in my legs had begun their own protest, but I was determined to catch up with her. We rounded another corner and after another short, flat stretch, we came out onto the main coastal road.

Vanessa dodged across the first two lanes of traffic without missing a beat, and I followed with my heart in my mouth. Disregarding cars and blaring horns, we crossed the other carriageway, and I thought I was finally catching up with her. We continued along the pavement, and I would have called out to her, but I barely had enough breath left to run. I became aware of one of Lisbon's new trams gliding past me and coming to a stop a short way ahead.

A man stepped backwards, and I crashed into him, unable to control my momentum. I span past him, incapable of even panting an apology. He had blocked my way just long enough for Vanessa to regain the advantage, and I watched as she stepped on board the tram as if nothing had happened. She looked completely composed, not a hair out of place. She didn't even glance round at me to check how close I was. I started to run again, and my fingertips brushed the back of the tram as it moved away from the stop. I doubled over, trying to get my breath back as she was spirited away, leaving me helpless in her wake.

I had no idea where she was going and as I stood in the middle of the pavement, with the man I had jostled berating me, I realised I could say the same for myself. After I had managed to apologise enough to calm him down, I went into the nearest café, grateful to have a chance to sit down and collect my thoughts. As my adrenaline stopped pumping and my lungs and legs stopped burning, indignation took over. Vanessa had dragged me all the way to Lisbon and was now taking pleasure in … in what? That was what I couldn't fathom. I was like a puppet having its strings pulled with no understanding of what was happening to me.

I picked up my phone and contemplated calling Vanessa but thought better of it. There was no point. She probably wouldn't answer but if she did, she would only tell me a lie. I got up, paid and walked back along the main road, under the Rua Augusta Arch, through the old town and up the Avenida da Liberdade, the incline seeming steeper than it had before. Back in my room, I packed my bag. I would leave the following morning, taking the loss on the cost of the hotel room. From what I had managed to see, Lisbon was a gorgeous city, but at that moment, I wanted to be somewhere else; anywhere where Vanessa was not.

* * *

Another restless night was brought to a definitive end by my phone ringing and in my hurry to get to it, I knocked it onto the floor. I waited for it to switch off, irreparably damaged, but it was undeterred and continued to ring as I scrambled to reach it. 'Don't ring off,' I shouted at it. I answered on automatic pilot, my mind still replaying the events of the previous day. 'Vanessa?'

'No. This is Lou.'

'Lou?'

'Yes, we met the other day when you came to my flat.' She sounded as though she thought she was talking to an idiot.

'Yes, yes, I remember. Sorry, I was asleep.'

'I suppose it is quite early.' There was a slight edge to her voice which sounded suspiciously like satisfaction.

I squinted at the screen. Eight. The time I had turned up at her flat.

'Are you there?' Lou asked.

'Yes.' The realisation dawned on me that given the way our last encounter had ended, Lou would not have called me unless something significant had happened. 'Have you spoken to Vanessa?'

'No, unfortunately not. The thing is she hasn't turned up for work.'

I was fully awake by then and sat up in bed. 'What? Has she ever done that before?'

'No, never. She's very reliable.' Lou paused. 'And she isn't answering her phone. I'm at the agency getting ready to meet my group, and her group is short of a guide. The boss looks set to start throwing things at any moment.'

Lou's boss was the least of my concerns. 'Lou, I think you ought to know that I saw her yesterday.'

'What? Where?'

'At a café in Chiado. Café Bar Jardim. An expensive place; all glass and chandeliers.'

'Yes, I know it. What did she say to you?'

'Nothing.'

'I thought you said you'd seen her.'

'Yes, that's the thing. I saw her, but I didn't get to speak to her. She sent me a message saying she'd been having some problems and it was urgent and I had to meet her there, but when she saw me, she ran out of the café. I tried to catch up with her, but she got on a tram before I was able to get close enough to her to say anything.'

'It seems she's keen to avoid you,' Lou remarked. 'After your behaviour the other day, I can't say I entirely blame her.'

I didn't care for Lou's comment or tone of voice, but it wasn't the moment to start an argument. 'As I said, she did ask me to meet here there, but my point is that as of yesterday she was absolutely fine.'

'Yes, but that was yesterday. Anything could have happened since then.'

I fell silent, knowing it was a possibility yet not really believing it. 'Well, I hope you find her, but it's not my problem anymore.'

'What do you mean?'

'I'm leaving Lisbon. Vanessa got me to come all the way here, only to start playing silly games with me. She either wants to see me or she doesn't and after yesterday, I can only conclude she doesn't so I'm off.'

'I don't think you should be so hasty,' Lou said, sounding alarmed.

'Why not?'

'Because there's obviously something strange going on with her after what you said about yesterday and now she's not here today. I don't think you should leave until you know for sure that she's OK. How would you feel if she was in some sort of trouble and you'd walked away? You'd feel terrible, wouldn't you?'

'I suppose so.'

Someone shouted in the background and then Lou spoke again. 'Look, I've really got to go. I'll let you know if I hear anything.' She paused for effect. 'But I really do think you should stay here until she turns up. Promise me you'll sit tight. At least for a day or two.'

I hesitated; an extra couple of days in Lisbon wouldn't do me any harm. 'OK, and I'll let you know if I hear from her.' The line went dead, leaving me staring at the screen as though it would provide me with some insight into Vanessa's whereabouts.

Lacking inspiration, I slumped back into the pillows trying to make sense of what had happened. Vanessa had clearly told me she wanted to meet me in Lisbon and had given me to understand that Lou's flat was actually her own although I realised that had been implied rather than actually stated. Rather like the fact she was still teaching. I had made some assumptions, but Vanessa hadn't chosen to disabuse me of them either. I thought about the photos which had been placed in Lou's apartment and which had then disappeared. I thought about the green SUV in the garage and her emphatic denial that she knew anything about it. I wondered if Lou, like me, was caught up in something she didn't understand or if she knew more than she was letting on.

Picking my phone up again, I looked over the messages Vanessa and I had exchanged. She had seemed so keen to see me. I called her again and tried to imagine what was going through her mind. She hadn't missed a day at work in the time I had known her, even when she had been sick. I rang off and, as usual, sent another message. *Please contact me. I don't know what happened yesterday, and it doesn't matter. Just call me.* I deliberately didn't mention Lou or the fact I knew she had not arrived at work. Not for the first time, I cursed the fact I had no way of knowing if she had read a message unless she replied.

I wondered if the woman I had spoken to at the agency had mentioned my visits there to Vanessa, and then I wondered why it would matter if she had. Had my visits to the agency been the catalyst which had led to her disappearance? Why would they have been when Vanessa had been the one who had invited me to go to Lisbon? What had been behind her behaviour the day before? None of it made sense. My head was starting to swim, and I went to stand under a shower just cold enough to take my mind off of the situation for a few minutes.

Hearing the phone in my room ringing as I turned the tap off, I grabbed a towel and rushed to answer it, sliding across the floor, colliding with a chair and stubbing my toe.

'Yes?' I said, sitting down on the bed and rubbing my foot.

'Hello Miss Foster. This is Mariana at reception. When you made your booking, you indicated that you might wish to extend your reservation. You still have a few days of your original booking left, but I was wondering if you know yet if you would like to extend your stay.'

'Oh.' I was deflated, having hoped it would be Lou saying Vanessa had just been late, and it had all been a false alarm. I wondered what to do. Before Lou's call, I had been sure about cutting my visit short; I certainly hadn't been planning to stay longer. But now I had made a promise of sorts to Lou.

'Miss Foster, are you there?'

'Yes, I am. I was just thinking about what to do.' Lou's words echoed in my head. *I don't think you should leave until you know for sure that she's OK. How would you feel if she was in some sort of trouble and you'd walked away? You'd feel terrible, wouldn't you?*

'I'm sorry, Miss Foster, but I do need to know. We have

other people asking about availability.' She hesitated, sounding uncomfortable about pressing me on the issue. 'It is high season.'

'Of course.' I sighed. Vanessa's failure to appear at work had changed the situation. The idea of a road trip I hadn't even thought through properly was no longer uppermost in my mind. I wanted to know what had happened to Vanessa and find out why she had got me to go to Lisbon for no good reason. 'Could I extend my reservation by another week, please?'

'Certainly. Thank you.'

I put the phone down and walked over to the window, watching the cars pass by far below. I realised that it was over a week since Vanessa had first contacted me. The chance to put things right with her, which had moved closer, now seemed to be further away than ever.

Chapter 7

I jumped as my phone rang. 'Any news?' I asked Lou, dispensing with the social niceties which she seemed to have no time for anyway.

'Not from Vanessa, but our boss has filed a missing person's report.'

'What?'

'She's been missing for over twenty-four hours now. She's still not answering her phone or replying to any messages.'

It occurred to me that while her boss had probably done the right thing, it had transformed the whole situation from Vanessa playing some sort of game to Vanessa potentially being in serious trouble. Perhaps she hadn't been playing a game with me when she had avoided me the other day, and I had completely misinterpreted the situation. 'Is there anything I can do?'

'Not unless you can give guided tours of Lisbon without any preparation,' Lou replied drily.

I bit my tongue. 'I meant anything I can do to help to find Vanessa.'

'I know. I suppose you could go to the police station.'

'What for?'

'To tell them what you know.'

'But that's the problem. I don't know anything.'

'You told me you know Vanessa well. Perhaps you can give them some insight into her that would help.'

I reflected on that. I wasn't sure what, if anything, I could tell them that would be useful, but if there was a chance I could help, I still felt I owed it to Vanessa to do so.

'Hello?' Lou's impatience cut across my thoughts.

'Yes, I was just thinking about what you said. Can you give me the address of the police station I need to go to?'

'Hold on.' There was a pause and a message came through. 'Sent.'

'Thanks. I'll let you know what happens.'

'As you wish.' With that, Lou was gone.

I mulled over the idea of going to the police. I walked down the Avenida da Liberdade and stopped at another small kiosk café and made a mental list of the pros and cons. The trouble with those lists was that they never allowed for any weighting of the pros and cons. The only con was my dread of having anything to do with the police, but that was a big one. On the other hand, the pro was doing something which might help Vanessa if she really was in trouble. That was tempered by the fact I knew nothing which I felt could be useful. If I could avoid the police, I would rather do so.

I phoned Vanessa. 'Come on, pick up,' I muttered. If she would only answer, we could get everything sorted out, and there would be no need to go. I tried her three times and then set my phone down on the table, feeling defeated.

The bangle on my wrist caught in the light as I picked up the tiny cup and sipped the coffee. I knew I was procrastinating, but I decided I would leave it until the next day. After all, I genuinely didn't know anything which could help. Vanessa might still make an appearance. Even so, a part of me was not convinced, and I had a horrible feeling I would find myself going to the police station the following day.

* * *

As I approached the police station the next morning, I began to have second thoughts. After all, I knew nothing that could help them. Hearing my phone ring, I pulled it out of my bag.

'Lou?'

'Have you been to the police yet?'

It occurred to me that it was just as well I was getting used to her abrasive nature. 'I'm on my way there now. But actually I was just thinking there's really no point.'

'Why?'

'I don't know anything about her disappearance.'

'We went through this yesterday,' Lou said, sounding weary. 'You might be able to tell them something that is helpful. You never know what information could be useful.'

'Yes, but –'

'And think how awful you'd feel if …' Lou lowered her voice. 'If something has happened to her. And you hadn't done everything you possibly could.'

I sighed. 'Look, Lou. I'm almost outside the police station now. I'll go in and talk to them. I promise. But what I can't promise is that it will do any good.'

'It's the right thing to do.'

'Hope so,' I replied, but she had already gone.

I walked up the steps and into the police station. For a moment I felt as I had back on the road to the border, at a point where I could still turn round, still go back, and then it was too late, just as it had been when I had seen the Guadiana Bridge ahead, and I was inside with a police officer speaking to me in Portuguese.

'I'm sorry, I don't understand. Do you speak English?'

'Moment please.'

I resisted the urge to take the opportunity to run, helped by the fact I didn't trust my legs to support me.

Another officer approached me. 'Good morning. May I help you?'

'Yes. I need to speak to someone about Vanessa Taylor.' I said her name as though hers was the only case they had, and everyone would be familiar with her name.

'I'm sorry, I don't know this person. Who is she?'

I finally pulled myself together enough to explain who Vanessa was, who I was and why I was there.

'Take a seat over there, please.'

I sat down, grateful for the chance to do so. I stared around me – the institutional feeling of the building, a place where the force of authority met the powerless individual washed over me. I remembered sitting in a similar place before, shortly after what had happened at Woolacombe

Sands. Waiting. Helpless. Hopeless.

'Miss Foster?'

I looked up. 'Yes?'

'Will you come with me, please?'

I got up and obediently followed the officer, just as I had done ten years ago. The images of past and present were colliding, pushing each other aside and clamouring for my attention. I felt as though I was choking again. Then my memories took me to the retreat I had been to in Thailand. I remembered the small collection of cabins in a remote, forested area. I thought of my mentor there, teaching me to control my panic attacks. Take regular, deep breaths. Clear your mind and focus on your breathing. I tried to follow that advice and pulled at my top, which felt sticky against my skin.

'Sorry, what did you say?' I realised we had stopped halfway down a corridor and the officer was speaking to me.

He looked at me curiously, and I tried to force a polite smile, one which I was sure made my behaviour seem stranger still.

'Are you feeling unwell?'

'No, not at all. It's just the heat. I'm fine, thank you.'

'Very well.' He knocked at the door, and we waited for a response. After what felt like an eternity, we heard a voice within and the officer opened the door and led me in. He said something to the man at the desk, who replied and dismissed him. The language barrier made me feel like a confused child; the only thing I had caught was my name. I stood by the door, unsure whether to approach the man standing at the desk.

I was saved from having to make a decision as he strode across the room to shake my hand. His grip was hard, designed, I felt, to demonstrate power. He was wearing a navy suit which was well cut and looked expensive and his dark hair was cropped close and shot through with the first streaks of grey at the temples. He exuded a confidence which did not cross over into arrogance but seemed to teeter dangerously close to it.

'Good morning Miss Foster. I am Inspector Mendes Silva. Come in. Take a seat.'

'Thank you.'

I perched on a chair and watched him as he took his seat on the opposite side of the large mahogany desk. It had a dark green leather top, embossed with gold and seemed strangely out of place there yet absolutely in keeping with the image the man projected.

'I understand you have some information about the disappearance of Vanessa Taylor?'

'No, not really. Well, that is to say, I know her, but I don't know what has happened to her. Someone suggested I come in to speak to the police because I know her, and they thought I might be able to help.' What had sounded perfectly plausible when Lou had suggested it to me, now sounded faintly ridiculous.

Mendes Silva reached for a notepad and fountain pen. 'How did you know she had been reported as missing?'

'Lou told me.'

'And does this Lou have a surname?'

'I only know her as Lou. She works at the agency with Vanessa.'

And how did you meet her?'

'Lou or Vanessa?'

Mendes Silva made an expansive gesture. 'Why not both?'

I started to explain that I had visited Lou's flat because I thought Vanessa lived there but dried up when I met his eyes. He was already looking at me as though I had the word unreliable written all over me. 'That's how I met Lou,' I said, stumbling to the end of my poor explanation. I realised I should have prepared myself better.

'How do you know Vanessa and what do you know about her which you think might help us?'

I shrugged. 'We worked together for nearly two years, and we were friends. I thought perhaps I could tell you something about her that would help you. I don't know …' I trailed off, wishing I were anywhere else. 'It was a stupid idea.' I got up. 'I'm sorry to have wasted your time.'

'Not at all. I'm actually glad you're here. Sit down, please.'

'Why?' I had a sudden vision of having to identify Vanessa. She had died, and I would never get the chance to make things right with her. I wondered how I would live with more guilt. 'Have you found her?'

'No.' He paused and assessed me. 'You look relieved.'

I realised this was a man who would not miss a flicker of emotion. 'No, well, yes. For a terrible moment I thought you might have found her …'

'Her body?'

I nodded, unable to speak and unsettled by his apparent ability to read my thoughts.

'No, we have not found her body. Why would you think that?'

'I don't know. I seem to be inclined to think the worst.'

'There is no body. In fact, we have found no trace of her. She presents us with something of an enigma.'

'Have you searched her home?'

He gave me a look which told me all I needed to know about how he felt about being asked such a question. 'Obviously we would search her home, but we don't know where she is living.'

'But there must be records?'

'Yes, of course there are records, and we have been to the address we have for her. Unfortunately, it appears she moved a week ago and has so far neglected to inform the authorities of her new address. Nothing of hers remains at her old address, and the people she was living with did not know where she had gone so we have not been able to make progress on that front.'

'Oh.'

'Quite. We have checked hotel records and contacted all the hospitals – nothing. So we are at something of a loss. It feels as though we are chasing a shadow. It is rather frustrating. Therefore, any information you can provide would be most welcome.'

'What would you like to know?'

'Tell me about her character.'

'Vanessa is spontaneous and fun, but she's serious about her work. She wouldn't just not bother to turn up for work and not tell anyone unless she … unless she couldn't. I suppose that's why I'm worried.'

He made a note on his pad. I watched as the ink bled into the paper.

'I've been here in Lisbon for days, trying to get in touch with her.'

He looked up, and I felt a jolt of fear. 'She was reported missing yesterday. You are now telling me she has been missing much longer than that?'

I thought of what had happened at the café. 'No, well, not really.'

'When did you arrive in Lisbon?'

The days since my arrival had blurred into one. I counted back, acutely aware of the expression on Mendes Silva's face. 'This is my sixth day here. Is it six?' I counted back again. 'Yes, six. I came here to visit her, but then I couldn't get hold of her. I was worried at first, but then I thought perhaps she was playing games with me or had changed her mind about seeing me because after she had contacted me, she went quiet. And then after what happened at the café, well, I didn't know what to make of anything after that.' With every sentence, I felt the hole I was digging for myself getting deeper.

'Excuse me, but I am finding this rather confusing. Perhaps you could go back to the beginning and explain more clearly.'

I pulled my phone out of my bag, found the chat with Vanessa and scrolled back up to her first message.

Hi Isabel. It's me, Vanessa. I really don't know where to start, but I was wrong about everything. I realise that now. I'm so sorry. I feel terrible about what happened. I wish we could meet and talk everything through.

'She asked me to come and see her. Look.' I handed the phone over.

He looked through the messages, and I knew he was reading about my agreement to meet her; that he was looking at the map giving directions to what I now knew was Lou's flat and at all the messages I had sent asking her where she was and then Vanessa's request that I should meet her urgently at the café in Chiado.

'You parted on bad terms. Your friendship was strained.' It was a question rather than the statement it was framed as.

I shifted in my chair. 'Yes.' I reached out for my phone, but he didn't give it back.

'This is not the address we have for Miss Taylor. Whose is it?'

'That's Lou's flat. Her colleague. The person I was telling you about earlier.'

The silence filled the room. I had read somewhere that silence was an interrogation technique used to make a person feel uncomfortable and prompt them to start talking so the smart thing to do was to keep quiet. I knew that, just as I knew you were supposed to turn on your back to stop yourself from drowning but, as I also knew, theory and how someone reacted under pressure didn't always bear much resemblance to each other.

'We had a big falling out around Easter, and then she disappeared. I didn't hear from her again until that first message you can see there.'

'A falling out?'

'An argument. And then, as I said, she disappeared.'

'So she has done this before?' Mendes Silva seemed keen to seize on that angle.

'No, not exactly.'

'But that's what you said. Did I misunderstand?'

'I did say that, but what I meant was that she left. She resigned from her job, and she packed her things and left. She didn't simply vanish without any notice.' The silence continued to echo around us. 'I meant she disappeared from my life.'

'And you obviously weren't happy about that.' Another question. I watched as he worked the fountain pen through his fingers, and it came to rest on top of the notepad.

I fought to reverse my fortunes and rescue the situation. 'Naturally I was sad she had left without us having a chance to sort out our differences.'

'Naturally. So you were pleased you would have the opportunity to come here and resolve everything. What did you argue about?'

'It was something stupid.'

Mendes Silva waited. My reply clearly wouldn't do.

'I got a promotion which she thought should have gone to her.' I didn't mention Javier, imaging how childish it would sound to someone like him.

He picked up his pen again and tapped it on the pad. 'Where have you come from, by the way?'

'Seville.'

'That's where the two of you worked?'

'Yes.'

'But you are British.'

'Yes.' I almost added that I had a French passport as well but thought better of it.

I watched as he made a note. 'Seville is quite a long way from here. You must have been very eager to resolve your differences.' He let silence take over for a while and then started to speak again. 'You haven't told me about the café yet.'

The sudden change of tack took me by surprise. I recounted the story.

'When was this?'

'Three days ago.'

'And she was reported missing yesterday.' He looked out of the window. 'Who suggested that you come here? You didn't say.'

'Lou.'

'And when did she suggest that?'

'Yesterday when she told me that Vanessa had been reported missing.'

'So it has taken you another day to come here since she suggested that you should offer your assistance.' Another statement and all the more intimidating for it.

'Yes,' I said warily.

'Do you not understand, Miss Foster, that in the case of a missing person we are working against the clock?'

'Yes, of course. But I don't know anything about why she's missing.'

'Do you not think that is for us to decide? How do you know what is important or significant and what is not? We have now established she was definitely in Lisbon three days ago, which is something we did not know before.'

'I really am sorry. I suppose I didn't come here before because I didn't want to waste your time.'

'Inadvertently, you have wasted our time by not coming forward more quickly.' He tapped his notepad again. 'Perhaps there are other things you would like to tell me.'

'No, there's absolutely nothing else I can tell you.'

'Think carefully. It is always best to be sure.'

'I am sure.'

'I urge you not to withhold anything.'

'I'm not,' I said, as evenly as I could manage.

Mendes Silva sighed and sat back in his chair. He gave me the impression he had to deal with obstructive people such as me far more often than he cared to remember.

Aggrieved by the turn the interview had taken, I was seized by the desire to get out of there. 'May I have my phone back, please?'

'Of course.' He leaned forward and passed it over the desk to me.

'I came here to try to help in whatever small way I could. There's nothing more I can tell you so I'll be on my way.' I got up, waiting for him to tell me to sit down again, but he said nothing.

As I reached the door and felt safety beckoning, he spoke again. 'We will need your passport and Spanish Identity Card numbers, your telephone number and the name of the hotel where you're staying. We may well need to be in touch again.'

'I assume I would be free to leave Portugal if I wanted to?' The thought of any restrictions being placed on my freedom was unbearable.

He made a gesture which was indecipherable. 'Are you in a hurry to go somewhere?'

I shrugged, sure that whatever I said would do me no favours. I waited, hoping for clarification.

When none was forthcoming, I spoke again. 'I live in Seville. I'm not planning to stay here indefinitely.'

'You will need to contact us if you wish to leave Portugal. Our decision will depend on where we are in the investigation.'

I opened the door and walked into the policeman who had escorted me to the room. 'This officer will take all your details, Miss Foster.'

* * *

I was finally released into the pure, clear sunlight of Lisbon. I walked and walked, trying to burn off the agitation which had consumed me during my interview with Mendes Silva. I continued walking and found myself outside the botanical gardens. I paid and went in. Being away from traffic in a tranquil garden soothed me slightly. I found a bench in the shade and tried yet again to make sense of events.

Vanessa had wanted me to visit her, but the place she had sent me to was not her address. She had not been answering anyone's calls or messages, not just mine. The bizarre incident at the café had led me to believe it was all some strange game, but then she had failed to turn up for work. She had been reported missing to the police, who had no idea where she was. Their only lead, as I could almost imagine it being viewed, was the appearance of her friend Isabel Foster in Lisbon, coinciding more or less with her disappearance. My summary of the facts was interrupted by my phone ringing.

'Hello Lou.'

'How did it go at the police station?'

'Not very well. I couldn't think of anything helpful and instead I seem to have got myself into trouble. The police said I can't leave Portugal without checking with them first.'

There was silence at the other end. 'Lou?'

'Yes, I'm still here. That's unfortunate, isn't it?'

'I suppose "unfortunate" is one word for it although I can think of others.'

'Yes, I imagine you can. So no news?'

'None at all. What about at your end?'

'No, nothing new here.'

'You'll contact me if you hear anything, won't you?'

'I guarantee you'll be the first to know.' As was her habit, she hung up before any goodbyes could be said.

* * *

Later that afternoon, back in my room, I debated what I could do to try to find Vanessa. The need to do so was now driven not just by my desire to put an end to my worries and satisfy my curiosity, but the more pressing requirement to get Mendes Silva off my back. The phone in the room rang, and I grabbed it, hoping for news.

'Hello. This is Ana at reception. There is someone called Carolina here to see you.'

'Carolina? I don't know anyone by that name. I think you've got the wrong room.'

'Just a moment.' I heard a muffled conversation as though someone had put the receiver down on the desk and then she came back to me. 'This is Isabel Foster, isn't it?'

'Yes.'

'She says she is definitely here to see you.'

'OK. I'll come down.'

I found a woman who I assumed had to be Carolina hovering around the reception desk, biting a nail and looking as though she would rather have been anywhere else. I thought she looked familiar, but it took me a moment to place her; she was the woman who had sent me away from the agency where Lou and Vanessa worked.

'Isabel.'

'Carolina?'

She stared at me but said nothing.

'Do you have some information about Van–?'

'Not here.'

'Outside?'

'No,' she said. 'Is there a meeting room we could use?'

Ana, who had made no secret of the fact she was listening, reluctantly said, 'The dining room is free.'

I ushered Carolina into the empty room, and she took a seat as far away from the windows as possible. I waited and watched as she picked at a loose thread in the tablecloth and started to twist it round her fingers. I resisted the temptation to speak. I would try to learn from Mendes Silva and be patient like him.

'I didn't want to come here,' she started, the sound of protest in her voice.

I refrained from observing that much was clear and continued to wait. I could see the silence was close to becoming unbearable for her.

'You asked me about her,' she ventured.

'About Va–?'

'Yes,' she interrupted quickly. 'You don't need to say her name.'

'OK. You must know by now that she's missing. It was your boss who reported it.'

'There's talk of little else at the agency at the moment.' Carolina looked around the room as if wondering how she had ended up there and whether there was any means of escape.

My resolve not to prompt her began to crumble. 'Why are you here?'

She leaned forward and spoke so softly it was a struggle to hear her. 'Before she disappeared, she told me you'd probably turn up asking questions. She also told me that if I valued my job, I wouldn't answer them.'

'How could she jeopardise your job?'

'She has a way of getting things out of people and then using that information to get what she wants.'

I thought about Vanessa and could not reconcile what Carolina had said with the person I knew. And yet, there was a doubt inside me. Fleetingly, I wondered if Vanessa had ever got anything out of me that I was not yet aware of and if so, how she would choose to use it. 'So why are you here?' I repeated.

'Because for a while I've been thinking of moving on, and now I've just found out that I've got another job so she won't be able to cause me any more problems. I'll finally be able to get away from her and … everything. I can't help you to find her, but I came here to say that if you take my advice, you won't try. I don't like her, I don't trust her, and you shouldn't either.' Carolina broke off and picked at the tablecloth again. 'Be careful of Lou as well. I used to think she was OK, but after she got so friendly with her … well, they say you can tell people by their friends, don't they?'

'Why are you telling me this?'

'Because I think you genuinely want to help Vanessa, and she doesn't deserve it. And I don't see why anyone else should get dragged into her web.' Carolina got up.

'Wait a moment. What else do you know? There must be more to it than that. You can't just tell me that and then walk out.'

'Good luck, Isabel. You'll need it to find her. And I think you'll need more than luck if you actually do.'

I watched her go, wondering if she was genuine or another puppet in Vanessa's game. It was becoming hard to know who to trust.

Chapter 8

'Hello,' I said, retrieving my phone from under the sheets where it had ended up at some point during the night.

'Hi Isabel.'

'Vanessa? Where the hell have you been?'

'Please don't be angry. Things have been … complicated.'

I pushed myself upright. 'They've been complicated for everyone since you did your vanishing act. Would you care to explain what's been going on? People have been worried sick. Did you know you've been reported to the police as missing? There's an investigation going on.'

'No, I didn't. I suppose I should have thought of that,' Vanessa said as casually as if she had been reminded that she had forgotten to buy a carton of milk.

'Well you ought to contact the police so they don't waste any more time looking for you.'

'I can't do that yet.'

'Why not? Don't you think it's time to tell me what's going on?' I forced myself to soften my tone. 'If you're in some sort of trouble, perhaps I can help you.'

'No, it's nothing like that. I will explain everything, of course. But when I see you.'

I sighed. We were back to that again. 'And when will that be? Don't suggest we meet at your flat. I already know you don't live there.'

'Oh yes. Sorry. I'm between places to live at the moment, but I was too embarrassed to tell you so Lou's place seemed ideal as she was away.'

I recalled what the police had said to me about not having a current address for her. 'OK, I'll go along with that for now, but why weren't you there when you said you would be?'

'Something came up.'

'Did it really? Did something come up every time I called you or sent you a message? Did something come up when we were at that café? In fact, scrap that. I saw you ignoring my call and my message. Speaking of which, why *did* you run off after getting me to go there? Where are you staying? Why haven't you been to work? And why are you working as a tour guide when you told me you could never do anything other than teaching?'

'For pity's sake, slow down, Isabel. I've told you I'll explain everything, but I really need to see you. To be able to tell you everything face to face.'

'This is your final chance, Vanessa.'

'Yes, I understand. Do you know the Panorâmico de Monsanto?'

'Never heard of it.'

'It's an abandoned restaurant.'

'It sounds delightful.'

'Relax, Isabel. It has incredible views of the whole city. It gives you an amazing perspective. You can see so much from there. '

'Where is it?'

'In Monsanto Park.'

As she spoke, I spread my map of Lisbon out on the bed and spotted the vast expanse of green to the west of the city. 'Couldn't we meet somewhere more convenient?' I asked, thinking of the numerous bars, restaurants or parks in the city centre, which would be more appealing and easier to reach.

'It would be a bit of a pain to get there by bus, but it's easy with a car. It's not as far as it looks. I'll see you there at four tomorrow.'

'Yes, but …'

'The buts can wait. There is one thing, though. Don't tell the police. Please. If I see any police, I won't meet you. I'm relying on you. Don't let me down.'

She hung up, and I dropped the phone on the bed and started massaging my forehead. I had no idea what I thought about Vanessa and her motives anymore. I wearily got up and made a cup of coffee and then looked up the place where Vanessa wanted to meet me. Whatever I had expected, a desolate, graffiti-covered building had not been it. Online guides raved about the amazing views and the beauty of the area, but I had my doubts.

I resolved that I would go. If she was there, I would convince her to contact the police. If she let me down again, that would be the end of it. I would go to the police myself and tell them she was not missing. Somehow I would get them to lift the cloud of suspicion which seemed to be hanging over me and get them to give me permission to leave Portugal. By the following day, one way or another, I would have my freedom back.

* * *

The next morning, I opened the curtains to a day which was overcast and unwelcoming. The drizzle turned to a downpour which spat against the windows with force and then, as if the supply of rain had been almost completely exhausted, turned back to drizzle. I had no desire to go exploring in that weather. I managed to sleep on and off for a while longer and once I had got up, found a sad-looking sandwich and a can of drink in a vending machine near reception.

Having taken what passed for lunch back to the room, I read more about the meeting point Vanessa had chosen. Among all the glowing reviews and photos on the Internet, a few lines caught my eye. *The Edifício Panorâmico de Monsanto is abandoned and in a run-down state. Some people believe that the building is haunted by bad luck that doesn't allow any project to move forward.* It felt like an appropriate meeting place, and I wondered if Vanessa had also heard that legend. I checked my watch and threw the remnants of the sandwich in the bin; it was time to go.

I collected my car from the hotel's underground car park and headed out into the city. The drizzle had finally stopped, but the afternoon skies were no less grey for that. I navigated the Marquês de Pombal roundabout with some trepidation, trying to ignore the blaring of horns, which I thought might have been directed at me due to my slow progress, and I took the exit which would lead me to the park. Somewhere along the way, I became aware that the city had fallen away behind me and ahead I saw the thickly forested slopes of what had to be Monsanto Park. It looked dark and forbidding and not a place I would have chosen to visit, particularly not on such a dismal afternoon. The same feeling I had had when I was about to cross the Guadiana Bridge and when I was on the steps of the police station filled me; the sense that I had no option but to go forward, that it was too late to turn back, however much I wanted to.

I continued the drive up into the park. From there, the suburbs of Lisbon were clearly visible but seemed oddly distant. Climbing ever higher, the road narrowed and the trees began to obscure the view, cutting me off from the city completely. As I continued around the tight bends which seemed to lead nowhere, I could easily have believed this place to which Vanessa was leading me didn't actually exist if it hadn't been for all the articles dedicated to it. I drove on through tunnels made by the trees as they arched overhead to meet each other.

According to the GPS, I was almost there, but I couldn't see anything. I was about to give up and look for a place to turn round when I caught my first glimpse of it. The trees had given way to a steep bank of earth, topped with railings. Through them, I finally saw the top of the building. From that angle and only able to see a part of it, it had the appearance of a carousel. Images from horror films I had seen involving abandoned fairgrounds flashed through my mind as I slowed down and drove further on to get to the entrance.

Parking was easy as the place was deserted. Clearly nobody thought it was a good day to go there, and I was in wholehearted agreement with them on that point. I checked my watch; I was a little early so there was still time for Vanessa to get there. I sat back and surveyed the place. I imagined it could have been spectacular at one time, but in its current condition just the look of it filled me with despondency. I tried to tell myself that on a sunny day it would look so much better and it was just the weather which made it so depressing, but I remained unconvinced.

Fine drizzle misted the air again and showed no sign of clearing. I waited as four o'clock came and went. I phoned Vanessa, urging her under my breath to pick up. There was no response. With no other option, I sent her a message. *I'm here. Where are you? I told you this was your last chance.* I stared at the screen, willing her to reply, just as I had willed her to answer my call. It seemed my wishes were not to be granted.

Reluctantly, I got out of the car and walked slowly towards the shell of a building. It occurred to me that Vanessa might have gone there by bus and could be sheltering inside from the rain. The fact there were no cars around, didn't mean she couldn't be there. I had no desire to go into the building but if I didn't, I would never know for sure. And I needed to know. I needed my freedom back.

Out of other options, I went inside. The smell of decay from years of neglect seemed to soak into me and made me feel grimy, but I carried on into the heart of the building, the only noise the dust and rubble crunching underfoot. Alongside outright vandalism, the quirky, the poignant, the eerie, the grotesque and the banal were all represented in the artwork within the building. I tried to focus on the more thoughtful pieces of work and not the vaguely menacing atmosphere of the place.

Continuing further and despite my misgivings, I went up the imposing spiral staircase and then further into what had at one time been the restaurant. On the panels under the windows, once exquisite tiles indicated the buildings which could be seen from each viewpoint.

The air of desolation was unnerving me more with every passing minute. I pulled out my phone, hoping I had simply missed a message or call, but there was nothing. I checked, and I still had a signal. 'Where the hell are you?' I said to myself. I considered calling her name in case she was in another part of the building, but to have made any noise which would have broken the silence and betrayed my presence there seemed inconceivable. My mouth went dry at the thought of it.

I gazed out of the window through which I could see the 25th of April Bridge, so reminiscent of the Golden Gate Bridge, winding away into the distance; the bridge which had brought me to this city and this situation could also take me away from it. It seemed to beckon me, and, as stressful as it would be to cross it again, I realised I could get into the car and just go. By late that night, I would be back in Seville and my old life – such as it was – would be there waiting for me, and I could pick it up as best I could. Or prepare to leave it and move on. I wanted to get out of the city with a desire that was visceral. I wanted to be running away again. I felt exhilarated just at the thought of it. Then I recalled Mendes Silva's words and felt an invisible cage close around me.

I remembered Vanessa's words as well. *It gives you an amazing perspective. You can see so much from there.* It was like the photos in Lou's flat all over again. I felt I should be able to read the subtext, but I had no idea what it was or even if it truly existed at all.

I went downstairs again and from my vantage point, I could see a short stretch of the road beyond the turning for the car park. I froze as I saw a car slowly cruise past. It was a matte green SUV.

Desperate not to be alone there any longer, I fumbled in my bag and found the keys, dropping them twice before I finally got hold of them. I clutched them in my hand and felt the metal digging into my skin as I tried to calculate whether I would be able to get to my car before the SUV could turn round and come back. I couldn't remember where the last turning point on the road had been and the more I tried to remember, the more time I was wasting.

Taking a deep breath, I ran to the car and heard the reassuring click indicating it had unlocked. I got in, locked the doors again and tried to stop trembling. It was going to be fine, I told myself. All I had to do was get back to Lisbon.

I would stop at the police station and plead some compelling reason to have to leave Portugal. A sick relative; a funeral; anything to get me out of there. They would let me go. I would make a quick stop at the hotel to pick up my bags and pay the bill, and then I would be on my way. I turned the key, relieved to hear the engine come to life and started to steer back towards the road. Or more accurately, I tried to because I felt the car veer sharply to the right and then there was a juddering sensation which seemed to come from both the back and the front of the car. The tell-tale sign of a flat tyre. Or two.

I stopped the car and thumped the wheel in frustration. 'Stop panicking, breathe slowly, think,' I repeated to myself until I just about managed all three. I couldn't drive back to Lisbon with the car as it was. I would have to get out and investigate the problem, but getting out of the car was the last thing I wanted to do. I glanced round, expecting to see the green SUV pull up behind me. But there was nothing there and as I forced myself to focus, I heard a tap on the window.

The adrenaline was already pumping painfully through my body, and a knock on the window was the last thing I needed to hear. I whipped my head round and saw a man of about my age peering through the window at me. He was gesturing for me to wind the window down, but I wasn't about to trust anyone; certainly not in that desolate spot. I shook my head and tried to move the car on but, as before, it veered off course.

I turned the engine off but kept the doors locked as I saw

the man approach the car again. In the corner of the car park, I saw a bright blue car. There was no sign of a green SUV anywhere. I tried to calm down and think more rationally.

The man knocked on my window again. I checked that the door was locked and cracked the window open just far enough to make conversation possible. He spoke to me, but I couldn't understand a word.

'I'm sorry. I don't speak Portuguese.'

'English?'

'Yes.'

He switched to perfect English. 'Can I help you?'

'There's something wrong with my car. I think I might have a puncture.'

'Would you like me to take a look?'

'Yes, please.' It occurred to me that the normal thing would probably have been to get out of the car and have a look with him, but my guard was still up. My eyes kept sliding towards the road, looking for the green SUV.

'Hold on,' he said amiably and went round to the front of the car and crouched down. He stood up and then, apparently noticing something else, he frowned and walked round to the back of the car.

He came back to the window. 'You've got two flat tyres.'

I swore under my breath.

He continued. 'You could change one of them, but it's not safe to drive far even with one flat.'

'Well I can't stay here,' I responded, sounding more irate than I had intended to. 'Sorry. You're being very kind. It's just … I really need to get back to Lisbon.'

'My cousin has a friend who runs a garage. I can call him if you like.'

'I suppose I should phone the car hire agency.'

'OK. My cousin's friend would be quicker, though.'

Thoughts of phoning the agency and hearing how important my call was while I waited in an interminable queue crossed my mind. 'Thank you. I would really appreciate that.'

'No problem.' He made a phone call and then looked through the window again.

'Do you think your cousin's friend would be able to take me back to Lisbon?' I asked.

'I'm not sure about that. His garage is on the other side of the city. I can give you a lift, though.'

I heard the voices of every responsible adult I had ever known warning me never to accept lifts from strangers. 'There's really no need. I could get the bus.'

'The nearest stop is about a ten-minute walk from here. In this weather you're going to get very wet.'

I noticed for the first time that it had started to rain more heavily, and he was standing there getting drenched himself.

'I can get a taxi then. Please go back to your car. You're getting soaked.'

He shrugged. 'I'll wait until they've picked your car up. I don't think anyone who works with him speaks English.'

I watched him walk away and felt guilty. He had been helpful, and all I had done was treat him with something close to hostility. I got out and caught him up.

'I'm sorry. I've not had a very good day. Days really …'

I shook my head. 'Anyway, I really am sorry. And thank you again for your help.'

'Would you like to sit with me while we wait?'

I hesitated, thought of the green SUV again and realised I wouldn't mind some company. 'Yes, please.'

'My name's Nuno,' he said.

'Isabel.'

We sat in his car, watching the rain run down the windscreen. Between each flick of the windscreen wipers, I looked for the SUV, but it didn't make a reappearance. A breakdown truck was the only vehicle which turned up, and we got out to meet the driver. Another conversation which I couldn't understand took place. Nuno turned to me. 'He doesn't speak English so he's going to call me when it's ready to pick up. I'll need your phone number to let you know when it's fixed.'

There was no choice but to give him my number. I signed some paperwork, which Nuno assured me was routine and watched apprehensively as the car disappeared from view.

'What would you like to do, Isabel? I can drive you to the bus stop if that's what you want.'

It occurred to me that if Nuno had been going to do something to me, he could have done it while we were waiting for the breakdown truck. It also made no sense to accept a lift as far as the bus stop but not to Lisbon. Nuno was either dangerous or he wasn't. The thought of waiting for the bus and then trudging back to the hotel in the rain didn't appeal. 'Is the offer of a lift to Lisbon still available?'

'Yes.'

'In that case, can I take you up on it?'

'Of course.'

We set off and, at first, I said nothing, tense and alert for anything which would raise my suspicions.

Nuno was the one who broke the silence. 'What brought you out here in this weather?'

'It's a long story.'

'Are you on holiday?'

'Yes,' I said, opting for a simple version of the truth. 'I live in Spain, but I'd never been to Portugal so I thought I'd come over for a visit.'

'Where have you been so far?'

'I drove up here via the Algarve, but I only stayed there overnight. Other than that, I've only seen Lisbon.' To say I had seen Lisbon was stretching the truth; events had meant I had not had a chance to appreciate the city. 'When I say "only" … you know what I mean.'

'Yes, I know what you mean. Do you like it?'

'From what I've seen, yes, I do.' And that much at least was true. Under different circumstances, I felt I could have fallen in love with Lisbon. It had a spirit which was captivating. 'Are you from Lisbon?'

'No, Évora. It's about an hour and a half from here. But Lisbon is my second home. I went to the international school here and stayed with my aunt and uncle in the week. I'm visiting them and my cousins at the moment.' He glanced at me and smiled. 'That and escaping the heat in Évora.'

'Yes, I was glad to get away from the heat in Seville.'

'Is that where you live?'

'At the moment.'

'You're lucky. It's a beautiful city. What do you do there?'

'I'm an English teacher.'

'Do you enjoy it?'

I considered the point. 'It has its highs and lows.'

'How long have you been there?'

'Only since last August.'

'Where were you before that?' Nuno asked.

'I've lived in a lot of different countries.'

'So where's home?'

It was a question I had been asked a few times, but I had never had an answer. 'Everywhere and nowhere,' I said and heard the regret in my voice. Anxious not to allow Nuno to pursue the point, I added a question of my own. 'Where do you feel more at home?'

'I love Lisbon, but Évora is home. My parents are there and …'

I saw Nuno's face tense and recognised the signs. He had found himself in a verbal cul-de-sac and didn't know how to get out. I knew how that felt and wanted to help him. 'What do you do there?' I asked.

'I'm a graphic designer, which I imagine is a lot less stressful than teaching.' I saw his face relax, and he smiled at me.

I felt I would have liked to continue the conversation, but I had never been a great one for small talk and my predicament was not conducive to putting me in a particularly sociable mood. I fell silent but chanced a few looks at Nuno while he was focusing on the road.

He was undoubtedly attractive, but he gave me the impression it was not something he was aware of and certainly not something he played on, which was refreshing. Javier had always been acutely aware of the fact his looks got him noticed. It had been one of his less appealing traits. My thoughts switched back to Nuno and as I considered him, I realised I also liked the air of kindness and unflappability he had about him. My earlier worries about being safe with him seemed absurd, and I felt guilty for having been suspicious of him.

The outskirts of Lisbon appeared, and I began to think about what I would do once I was back in the city. I wouldn't be able to even think about going any further than Lisbon until I had the car back. And then there was Mendes Silva to contend with. The thought of another encounter with him only served to lower my mood further.

Nuno spoke, waking me from my deliberations. 'Isabel?'

'Sorry?'

'Where do you want me to drop you off?'

'At the Hibiscus Hotel near the Edward the Seventh Park. Do you need the address?'

'No, it's OK. It's next to that English tea shop, isn't it?'

'Yes, that's the one,' I said, surprised he knew it.

Seeing my expression, he added 'I did spend twelve years at school here. I know the city pretty well.'

'Of course. I really am very grateful for everything. I can't thank you enough.'

'Don't mention it.'

He pulled up outside the hotel, the engine still running. 'I'll be in touch as soon as I've heard from the garage.'

'OK. Thank you again.'

I watched him go, feeling absurdly grateful that he had rescued me and almost equally as stupid for needing to be rescued. 'So much for being self-sufficient,' I muttered as I headed through the reception.

* * *

The longer I stayed in my room, the more restless I felt. I had to do something constructive. I debated phoning Vanessa, but I was too angry to trust myself to speak to her even if she answered which, going on previous form, seemed unlikely. I phoned Lou, but she didn't pick up either. I imagined she could well be in the midst of trying to cheer up a group of tourists who had not been expecting a bleak, grey day.

It occurred to me then that Vanessa was not really missing; not in the sense that she had vanished from the face of the Earth. She had asked me not to tell the police about our meeting, but all bets were now off.

The walk to the police station filled me with familiar dread but also a sense of purpose. Before long, I was ushered in to see Inspector Mendes Silva. I had hoped I might see someone else who would prove to be easier to talk to, but I consoled myself with the thought that at least I wouldn't have to explain everything again.

'Good evening, Miss Foster.'

'Good evening, Inspector.'

'I was not expecting you to call in again so soon. What brings you here?'

I recounted my telephone conversation with Vanessa, her request to meet me and then her subsequent failure to turn up. Of the green car, the punctured tyres and lift back to the hotel, I said nothing.

'You agreed to meet someone who is listed as missing, and you didn't think it was necessary to contact the police.' We were back to the questions framed as statements, nudging me to respond, to give away information. But it was information I did not possess.

'She specifically asked me not to. I told her she had been reported missing and she should contact you to say she was safe, but she said she couldn't. I was afraid that if I did contact you it would frighten her off.'

'You thought we would send tens of cars up there with sirens blaring and lights flashing? Do you think we are fools?'

'No, no of course not.' I twisted the silver bangle around on my wrist. 'I realise now I should have contacted you, but I thought I was doing the right thing. But the good news is that means she's OK, doesn't it?'

'OK,' he repeated slowly.

'Yes,' I said, hope rising in me.

'But does it, Miss Foster? We only have your word that all of this happened and, even if it did happen exactly as you say, why didn't she meet you there?'

The flicker of hope quivered and died. 'I don't know.'

'And now we may never know either because you failed

to inform us. We are assuming for the moment that such a phone call even took place.'

'There must be a way for you to check that.' I remembered the message I had sent Vanessa and without thinking, I found my phone and showed it to him. 'Look, I sent her this message when I was waiting there.'

I'm here. Where are you? I told you this was your last chance.

'"Your last chance." That sounds rather like a threat, Miss Foster.'

'No. No, it wasn't like that. I simply meant that I wasn't going to play any more games if she didn't turn up. You know, after what happened at the café.'

'Quite so.' He tapped the palm of his hand with my phone. Time seemed to slow as I watched it move back and forth. 'Why do you think she chose that spot, assuming she did?'

'I really can't imagine. It's a creepy place.' Seeing his expression, I added, 'In my opinion.'

'It has a certain quality about it. It is very … particular and not for everybody, but the views are incomparable. I do wonder why she chose it. Are you quite sure she gave you no idea why?'

'She said it gave an amazing perspective.'

'Did she? And what do you think she meant by that?'

'I assume she meant that the view was good,' I said.

'Possibly. Then again, perhaps she meant something quite different.'

I recalled my own musings about that. I had also wondered if there was a subtext which I had missed and now

Mendes Silva seemed to be pursuing the same line. 'I honestly have no idea.'

No, Miss Foster, but it is something I would like to know. Along with a number of other things.'

I shrugged and looked down. 'I don't know what to say.'

He went to hand my phone back to me but, as I reached for it, he held on to it. 'Remember we have your details. Don't go too far.'

'What do you mean?'

'It means you must not leave Lisbon at this time.' With that, he finally allowed me to take my phone.

All my ideas about what I could say to persuade him to allow me to leave Portugal suddenly seemed ridiculous. Mendes Silva wasn't going to let me go anywhere. When I left the police station, I was utterly dejected. At every turn, by trying to do the right thing, I had done the worst possible thing. Now, I could not only not leave Portugal, I could not even leave Lisbon. And Inspector Mendes Silva clearly had me in his sights.

* * *

I retraced my footsteps back to the hotel, stopping on the way for something to eat which I had no appetite for. I pushed the food around the plate, attempted a few mouthfuls and finally gave up. In every sense, I felt as if I were going through the motions of what I should do. It reminded me of the months after Finn's death. I forced her from my mind and tried to reapply myself to the present.

Every day that I stayed in Lisbon seemed to make the

situation worse, and my natural instinct – to run – had been taken from me. That had been made very clear. I briefly entertained the idea of going back to Seville anyway; after all there were no border checks between Portugal and Spain. Then I realised that although I could leave, Mendes Silva had the numbers of my British passport and my Spanish Identification Card, which was linked to my French passport. If he wanted to find me, he would, and I would seem more suspicious and be in more trouble than if I stayed in Lisbon. I tried to reason that if I had to stay, I should at least try to do something productive. What that thing might be continued to elude me as I paid the bill, ignoring the disapproving look the waitress gave me for having barely touched the food, and returned to my room.

I stood in the shower, trying to wash the accumulated grime of the lookout at Monsanto and the police station off of me. I washed once, twice, three times, but still I felt dirty. Afterwards, slumped on the bed, I realised I had to try to switch off for a few hours at least. I got up and went to my bag to get the book I had packed. It had remained untouched since I had left Seville. Perhaps, I thought, I could lose myself in a different world for a while. I noticed that my bag was unzipped whereas I was sure I had zipped it up. It was something I always did when I left a hotel room; a silly habit of mine. I thought about all the distractions I had had and realised it could easily have slipped my mind. I pulled the sides of the bag back to rummage for my book and stopped dead in my tracks.

Placed on top of my clothes was the photo of Vanessa

and me in Seville, which I had seen in Lou's flat during my first visit there. I recoiled from it but, once I had caught my breath, I moved towards it and slowly picked it up. I turned it over, half expecting to see a note on the back, but there was nothing. I put it on the table and went through my bag. Nothing was missing, nothing had been displaced, but still it felt like a violation.

All thoughts of reading forgotten, I took the photo and perched on the edge of the bed. I searched her expression for something which I must have missed, some understanding of her true nature I had never previously noticed. The events of recent days had bestowed a knowing look to her smile, which I had never picked up on before, and a look of idiocy to mine, which was disconcerting.

As I stared at it, I became determined that one way or another I would find Vanessa, I would make her tell me what was going on, and I would clear my name.

Chapter 9

After breakfast the following day, I stopped off at reception. I was unsure how to ask the question without causing offence. Mariana was there, which made me feel better. She was the most approachable of the receptionists I had encountered during my stay.

'I know this is a strange question, but who has access to the rooms?'

Mariana looked taken aback. 'Normally only the cleaners. We do have spare keys of course, but we only use them in an emergency. Why do you ask?'

'I was just curious,' I said, realising how odd that must have sounded.

'Has something been taken from your room? If so, you must let us know. We would take something like that very seriously.'

'No, it's nothing like that. Really. Forget I mentioned it.'

'If you're sure,' Mariana said, looking anything but sure herself.

'Yes, yes, I am,' I said and hurried away from reception.

I set out to find another hotel with parking. I couldn't stand the thought of staying in the same room a day longer than I had to, knowing that Vanessa had somehow had access to it. I could have looked on the Internet, but I was consumed with that familiar feeling that I couldn't sit still, and searching for a new place to stay at least gave me something to do.

The search proved to be more complicated than I had hoped; finding an affordable hotel with a car park at short notice in July was not easy. I finally found a place in Areeiro; it was further away from the city centre than I would have liked, but at least Vanessa would not know where I was. With a promise to be in touch to confirm the details of the reservation, I made my way back to the Hibiscus to find out how much I would have to pay if I left at short notice.

As I got on the bus, my phone rang. 'Hello Nuno.'

'Hi Isabel. Your car will be ready tomorrow afternoon. When can I bring it over?'

'Whenever it's convenient for you.'

'How about six?'

'Six sounds fine.'

'OK, I'll see you then.'

I was relieved the car had been fixed, and it was one problem out of the way although it was an expense I could have done without. Thanking Nuno, I rang off.

When I returned to the hotel, Mariana was still at reception and stopped me. 'I had a call for you, Miss Foster.'

'Who was it from?'

'She didn't leave her name.' Mariana looked awkward

and shifted from one foot to the other.

'Well, what did she say?'

'It was strange. She said, "You might as well stay where you are."'

I felt my throat start to constrict. I had told absolutely nobody of my plan to change hotels. 'Was that it?' I managed.

'Yes.'

'How old would you say the caller was?'

'It's hard to say. Younger rather than older. About our age, maybe?'

'Thank you.'

'It's peculiar, isn't it? Does it mean anything to you?'

'Yes, yes, it does,' I said and retreated to my room before she could ask me any further questions.

Back in the room, the frustration built up in me further, and I paced up and down, trying to burn it off. I realised I had to do something. Anything. I phoned the hotel in Areeiro and told them my plans had changed. I paced some more and realised I couldn't bear to stay there, doing nothing, waiting for something else to happen to me. I phoned Vanessa and got no reply. The only person who I thought might be able to help me was Lou, but I wasn't going to phone her and risk being fobbed off. I decided I would go to her flat.

* * *

I climbed the final flight of stairs to Lou's flat, wondering how she put up with doing that every day. I knocked on her door, but if she was at home, she wasn't answering. I phoned her and heard nothing but silence from inside. Out of options, I slid down the wall and determined that I would wait it out. I had nowhere else to be. She would have to come home or leave at some point. I ran through everything that had happened again, searching for what I had missed, but I could find nothing. The more I thought about it, the more confused I became.

The hallway light flicked on, and I heard footsteps. I looked up, hoping to see Lou, but an elderly woman appeared at the top of the stairs. She said something to me and although I didn't understand a word, the idea was unmistakeable. She came closer and grabbed at my top, clearly indicating I should get up.

I complied, got to my feet and said sorry in English, French and Spanish, hoping one of them would calm her down. She huffed but appeared marginally less indignant. I pointed at the door and said 'Lou? Do you know Lou?'

She looked at me as though I had lost my mind, flapped her hands in exasperation, unlocked her front door and slammed it shut behind her, the sound filling the silence. I considered resuming my wait for Lou but noticing the spyhole in the woman's front door, I thought better of it. I was already on the police radar, and I had no desire to attract further unwelcome attention if she decided to call them. Mendes Silva, I was quite sure, would have something to say if he found out I'd been picked up waiting outside Lou's flat.

I walked back to the stairs and as I reached them, the automatic timer on the hallway lights clicked off. Plunged into complete darkness, I felt around in my bag for my phone so that I could put my torch on. What happened as I was searching for it I would have been unable to explain, even if Mendes Silva had been interrogating me and insisting on an answer.

I could not have said whether I somehow lost my footing in a moment of carelessness or whether the sensation of being pushed was real. I knew I must have passed out briefly because I regained consciousness at the foot of the flight of stairs with a young woman kneeling beside me whilst a man was pacing the hallway, talking to someone on the phone. The door to what I assumed was their flat was open, flooding the hallway with light.

'What happened?' I asked, hoping she could speak English.

'We heard a noise. We thought it was children being silly, but then we thought we should check, and we found you here. Rodrigo is phoning for an ambulance now.'

'No,' I said, my loathing of hospitals even stronger than my fear of the police. I tried to prop myself up and ignore the pain which seemed to radiate from numerous parts of my body at the same time. 'I'm sure that's not necessary.'

'You must see a doctor. You've hit your head.'

I touched my face and was faintly surprised to find that it was wet. I forced myself to focus on my fingers and saw blood. 'Perhaps you're right.'

Rodrigo and the woman waited with me until the ambulance came. I remembered being carried down the flights of stairs; a jerky, undignified exit with the tight turns on the stairs and the grunts of the men who were carrying me convincing me I would be dropped at some point.

At the hospital, I was swiftly processed. At some point, I gave up all hope of retaining any control over the situation and allowed them to examine my documents and my body as they wished. Relinquishing control was a disquieting sensation. Later that night, I was wheeled into a ward, hushed and dark, and the curtains were closed around me.

'I don't want to stay here. I want to go home,' I said to the nurse.

'Where is home?' She sounded sympathetic.

I looked at her and felt as empty as I ever had when I realised I had no idea where home was. I had only meant it in the sense that I didn't want to be in the hospital. 'I don't know.'

'You can't remember?' The sympathy became tinged with the concern of a medical professional.

'No, that's not what I mean. I know where I live, and I know where I am.'

She looked at me, clearly unsure what to say.

'It doesn't matter.'

She continued to gaze at me with a mixture of confusion and curiosity. 'We will check on you regularly during the night but try to sleep if you can.'

I managed to doze on and off although I was woken several times by lights being shone in my eyes and observations being noted on my chart. I had started to feel sleepy again, when I was disturbed once more.

'Isabel.' The whisper was urgent in tone.

I opened my eyes, but a light was shining in them, and I

couldn't see beyond it into the darkness where the voice came from.

'You just checked me,' I said drowsily, turning away from the light.

'Isabel.'

'What?'

'It's me. Vanessa.'

'Vanessa?' I turned back and squinted, trying to see past the light which abruptly shut off. 'Vanessa?' I repeated.

I sensed rather than saw her moving closer to me and felt her hair falling over my face. It tickled and irritated my bruised skin. I lifted my hand to move it away, but felt it being firmly replaced and pinned to the bed. The pressure on my injured arm hurt. She whispered in my ear. Even her breath against my bruises was painful. 'I'm watching everything you do.'

'I don't understand. What are you talking about?'

In the same way she had materialised, she disappeared. At some point, the painkillers must have overcome the fear her words had instilled in me because I drifted off to sleep and when I awoke, daylight had filled the ward. The ghosts of the night had been chased away, leaving me unsure whether I had had a vivid dream, or whether Vanessa had really visited me during the night.

* * *

'Good news, Miss Foster.'

I propped myself up on the pillows and waited for the doctor's conclusion.

'There are no signs of concussion, and you have nothing worse than some cuts and bruises so we are discharging you.'

'Thank you.'

'However, I understand you don't live here so you must rest in your hotel room for the next twenty-four hours and then continue to take it easy for the next week or so. If you experience any of these symptoms,' she said, passing a leaflet to me, 'you must seek medical attention immediately.'

'OK.'

'I cannot stress that enough.'

'I understand.'

'I would also like to send a copy of our report to your doctor in case you have any problems when you get home. It's unlikely, but I prefer to cover all possibilities.'

'I don't have one.'

'You don't have one?' She looked at me as though she could imagine nothing more extraordinary.

'No. I moved last year, and I didn't get round to registering at a doctor's surgery.'

'Very well. I will give you a copy and when you *do* get round to it, I suggest you give it to them.'

I nodded and the pounding it prompted in my head made me wish I hadn't.

After the formalities had been completed, I was allowed to leave. As a concession to what had happened, I took a taxi back to the hotel. I walked into reception and Ana, who was behind the desk, gasped, took a step back and then quickly recovered herself.

'Good morning, Miss Foster.'

'Good morning.' I saw hope in her eyes that an explanation would be forthcoming, but instead I headed for my room, leaving her to wonder.

It was only once I was back in my room that I caught sight of myself in a mirror for the first time and understood her reaction. My face was badly bruised all down one side, mainly bright red but already a sickly shade of purple in parts. I looked as though I had got into a fight and lost. Badly. Gingerly, I touched my skin; the slightest contact hurt. I wondered if I would ever look like myself again.

I lay down on the bed and stared at the ceiling, trying to remember how I had lost my footing. I also wondered if the visit from Vanessa could possibly have been real, but the events of the night before had taken on the quality of a dream. Or a nightmare, I corrected myself grimly. The more I tried to piece the events together, the more reality receded. It occurred to me that it was in some ways similar to the situation which had brought me to Lisbon. The more I sought the truth, the more elusive it became.

* * *

The call from reception to say that Nuno had arrived with my car interrupted an afternoon spent dozing. I had forgotten he was bringing the car over and had no time to make myself look even vaguely presentable. I went downstairs and was more relieved than I had expected to see a friendly face.

He took a step towards me rather than away, unlike Ana. 'Isabel, what happened? Are you OK?'

The concern in his voice touched me, but I wasn't about to let him see that. I felt vulnerable enough already. 'Yeah, fine.' Seeing how unconvinced he looked, I shrugged, aimed for humour and added, 'You should see the other guy.' To fill the ongoing silence, I decided it would be better to change the subject. 'Were there any problems getting the tyres replaced?'

'No, that wasn't a problem.'

I heard the emphasis on *that* and looked at him questioningly.

'Let's sit down.'

We moved out of earshot of Ana and sat down opposite each other on two of the sofas by the huge picture windows next to the revolving door.

Nuno leaned forward. 'Isabel, I don't know if I should mention this or not.'

'Well, you can't say that and then not say anything else so you'll have to tell me now.'

'No, I can't. You're right. The thing is Tiago, that's the guy who replaced your tyres, said it looked like they had been cut. It wasn't like you'd run over a nail or glass or something like that.'

I stared out of the windows, trying to form a question. 'How sure was he?'

'Pretty sure. He said there were clean cuts in both of them.'

'I see.'

'Maybe I shouldn't have said anything.'

'No, you did the right thing. I'm glad you told me.'

'You don't seem all that surprised,' Nuno observed.

'It's just one of those things, isn't it?'

'Is it?'

'Yes, of course. Vandals everywhere these days. What else would it be?'

'I don't know.'

'How much do I owe Tiago?'

Nuno pulled a receipt out of his pocket.

'I thought it was going to be a lot more,' I confessed as I opened my bag and found enough money to pay him.

'Mates rates.'

'Thank you again,' I said, wishing I had some reason to ask him to stay for a while if only to stop the walls closing in on me again.

'I'm sorry you had to pay at all.'

'Don't worry about that. I'm just very grateful.' I suddenly felt absurdly emotional at his kindness amidst everything else which was happening.

'Isabel, are you sure you're OK? Because if you're not, maybe I can help you.'

'Yes, I'm fine.' I forced myself to switch on my most impassive expression.

'Well, if you're certain.'

'I am,' I said, dragging a smile up from somewhere.

'I'll be going then,' he said, and we both got up. I watched him walk towards the door and then turn back. 'Would you like to get a drink?'

'Yes, I think I would.'

'I could meet you here tomorrow at seven.'

I had wanted to go there and then; anything to avoid yet more time alone with my thoughts in my room. Nuno seemed to have read my mind as he added, 'I would say tonight, but it looks like you should get some rest.'

Recalling how I had looked when I had seen my reflection, I was suddenly self-conscious. I put my hand to my face and winced as I realised how tender my skin was. 'Tomorrow would be good.'

'I'll see you then, Isabel. Try to get some sleep.'

I watched him go and then trudged back to my room, where I ordered room service and picked at food I had no appetite for until exhaustion finally overtook me.

Chapter 10

The following evening, Nuno and I walked through streets I had not taken despite their proximity to the Hibiscus. It occurred to me that my knowledge of Lisbon, given the number of days I had been there, was sadly limited while I was more familiar than I cared to be with my hotel room, Lou's apartment building and the police station.

I realised I was not being very good company, but Nuno didn't seem to mind. I was aware the silence was a comfortable one, so different from that day back in Seville when Javier and I had finally parted ways.

'Here we are,' Nuno said and guided me into a cosy bar on a quiet side street. 'What would you like?'

I remembered the advice on the leaflet to avoid alcohol and, as a concession, asked for a small glass of white wine and a large bottle of sparkling water.

The waiter appeared and disappeared. Drinks were produced. Still neither of us spoke. The earlier silence seemed to have become less comfortable, and I found myself apologising for being so quiet.

'You don't need to apologise, Isabel.'

'I bet you wished you hadn't asked me now,' I said, laughing awkwardly.

'Not at all. In fact, I'm pleased I did. You look as though you need someone to talk to.'

I took a gulp of the wine. It was too dry for my taste, but the chill was welcome. I topped the glass up with water. 'Perhaps.'

'I'm not a bad listener.'

'I don't know where to start. Don't say at the beginning.'

Nuno held his hands up in mock protest and smiled. 'No, I won't say that. How about you just tell me whatever comes to mind and then we take it from there?'

And so I found myself telling him the story of my friendship with Vanessa, which had taken us from Gdansk to Seville and then to Lisbon. I told him about Lou, the café, the police, what I had been doing at the lookout in Monsanto Park on the day we had met and about the photograph in my room, and the message at reception. I sat back and tried to judge his reaction, thinking that any sane person would by then have remembered an urgent appointment and be preparing to head for the door, but there was no trace of disbelief and no sense that he was about to get up and walk away.

'Why did you argue with Vanessa back in Seville?'

I realised I had glossed over that part. It was not an incident which would show either of us in a good light. 'There were two reasons, according to Vanessa. She said I had stolen her job and her boyfriend, well, potential boyfriend.'

'Go on,' Nuno said softly.

'I don't really want to get into it.'

'I can see that, but it might be relevant.'

'Last September we started work at the same school in Seville. One of the other teachers had to go home in January due to a family emergency, and I was asked to take her job. I agreed and didn't think anything more of it at the time. Then, just before the Easter holidays, Javier asked me out.'

'Javier was Vanessa's potential boyfriend?'

'Yes, but I didn't know that. Anyway, one night soon after he'd asked me out, Vanessa and I got into an argument. It started over something so stupid – the fact I hadn't done the washing up.'

I saw the look of confusion on Nuno's face.

'We shared a flat together,' I explained. 'It didn't stop there, though. She started yelling at me about stealing her job. I didn't understand. Nobody had applied for the job I was given because there hadn't been one on offer as such. The other teacher left so unexpectedly. I would never have accepted it if I had known Vanessa wanted it so much, but she never said a word when the other teacher left. They offered it to me because I was the teacher there who had the most experience with the courses she'd been teaching. I don't think they would have offered it to Vanessa anyway as she had only been teaching for two years. But, honestly, if I had known how much it meant to her ...' I broke off, unsure what else I could add.

'But it didn't end there?'

'No. Then she accused me of stealing Javier as well. I

remember her exact words. "It wasn't enough for you to steal my job, you had to steal Javier."'

'Can you steal a person?'

'I don't know about that, but it didn't make sense anyway. Vanessa and I had been out with a group of people a few times, and Javier was one of the group. They didn't have any sort of relationship that I knew about, and she had never mentioned having any interest in him.'

'It almost sounds like she wanted to have an argument with you.'

'I've thought that a few times too. I don't know. Sometimes I think I wasn't paying attention, and I didn't notice things I should have. You know, about the job and Javier. And then I think that perhaps she just wanted an excuse to have a bust up and leave Seville.'

'And Javier?'

'What about him?'

'Are you still together?'

'No. What with one thing and another, our first date didn't happen until May and then, our relationship, if you could even call it that, never really got off the ground. It dragged on longer than it should have done, but it was well and truly over by the time I left Seville to come here.' I thought I saw something relax in his face, but I didn't have time to think about it as he asked me another question.

'Do you think Vanessa slashed your tyres?'

'It's crossed my mind,' I admitted. 'At one time I wouldn't have thought her capable of doing something like that, but I've realised I'm not so sure about a lot of things lately.'

'You have to find her and sort this out once and for all,' he said.

'I know but how? I don't have a clue where to start, and I'm in a city I don't know where I don't speak the language.' I stopped, frustrated by my inability to deal with the situation.

Nuno sipped his drink. 'But I do.'

I looked at him, unsure where he was going.

'So why don't we decide where to make a start?'

I was the person who never needed anyone, but at that moment I sensed it was no longer true; at least not until I had managed to find Vanessa. My default was never to trust people completely, but it occurred to me I would have to take a leap of faith or remain stuck in a seemingly irresolvable situation. I studied the angles and planes of his face as he looked down at the table and felt something unknown to me give inside.

'It's a lot to ask of you; of anyone. And we hardly know each other.'

'Isabel,' he said and put his hand on top of mine. 'You're not asking, I'm offering. Let me help you.'

I looked at his hand on mine. As I tried to form a reply, we were interrupted by the waiter asking if we would like more drinks. Seconds later he had gone and so had the moment.

Nuno resumed in a more practical tone of voice and summarised the little we knew.

'Exactly,' I said as he finished.

'It seems to me the only person who might be able to help us is this Lou.'

'In that case, I should probably tell you something else.'

'What's that?'

'The accident I had happened at Lou's place.'

'I've been wondering what happened, but I didn't like to ask again. Are you saying Lou did that to you?'

'No, well, I don't think so.' I proceeded to tell Nuno about the events of that night as best as I could, including the fact I was not sure if I had been pushed or had simply lost my footing. I omitted to tell him about my possible visit from Vanessa as I was sure he would have thought I was crazy. 'Besides all that, she's not been very helpful so far,' I concluded.

'Maybe we need to ask her different questions then.'

'Yes, she's … strange. I don't know. Sometimes I think it's just her way and at other times, I wonder if she knows more than she's told me.' I thought about what Carolina had told me, and I was suddenly anxious about what I might be dragging Nuno into. It occurred to me that I had forgotten to tell him about Carolina's warning.

'Then that's where we'll start,' Nuno said.

'How are we going to succeed when the police have failed? Besides, I'm already in enough trouble with them without taking matters into my own hands.'

'That's why we need to do something.'

'Now?'

Nuno glanced at his watch. 'No, not now. Tomorrow morning. Have you seen anything of Lisbon since you've been here?'

'Not really. I seem to have spent most of my time here in places I'd rather not be.'

'Like the police station?'

'Yes. And the hospital.'

'In that case, this evening I want you to try to forget about everything and let me show you some of the city. What do you think? Do you feel up to it?'

I remembered I had to tell him about Carolina's warning. 'There's another thing too. I forgot to tell you about it before.'

'If it's anything to do with Vanessa and Lou, let's leave it until tomorrow. Take a break from all this for one night, Isabel.'

'A distraction would be welcome. I'm not sure I'll be very good company, though.'

'Don't worry about that. You have enough to think about already.'

Nuno proved to be a natural guide. He took me through winding back streets, revealing small squares and hidden corners of the city. He explained the history and meaning of the sights and for a while my worries faded into the background. As we arrived in Rossio Square, busy with people and traffic, real life intruded again.

'I thought you might like to listen to some fado,' Nuno suggested. 'There are other options, but fado is something unique. You need to know where to go, though.'

I had heard of fado but knew little about it. All I did know was that I was not yet ready to return to the hotel room. 'Yes, I would like that. Thank you.'

Nuno phoned someone, and I wandered across the waves of black and white cobbles to one of the mermaid fountains. I looked around the square, taking in the neoclassical façade of the national theatre at one end, the soaring central monument and then the shops and cafés, teeming with life. 'Where are you Vanessa?' I murmured to myself. I turned back to the fountain and looked up at the mermaids cast in bronze, their sightless gaze turned to the skies, impassive to the noise around them. They had no answers and neither did I.

'There's a table free so we can go to the fado club. Are you ready?' Nuno asked, as he joined me.

I took a final look up at the mermaids. 'Yes, I am.'

Nuno led me through the elegant neighbourhood of Chiado and into the Bairro Alto, through cobbled streets flooded with warm amber light. We arrived at an anonymous looking building with no signs outside and Nuno came to a stop.

'This is it,' he said.

'You'd never know it was here.' I said, looking at it sceptically.

'That's what makes it so special.'

We went down the narrow stairs into a softly lit cellar with vaulted ceilings. The walls were crammed with framed black and white photos of singers and guitarists. I gazed around at them, wondering what stories they would have told. On one side of the room, which I took to be the stage, a fringed black shawl was pinned to the wall.

Nuno guided me through the menu, and we ordered an assortment of cheeses, pickles and olives, which turned up with roughly cut chunks of fresh bread. It wasn't until I saw the food that I realised I hadn't eaten properly for a long time and that I was ravenous.

'Do you know anything about fado?' Nuno asked.

I shook my head, reaching for some bread.

'Do you know what saudade means?'

'No.'

'Saudade is almost impossible to translate, but it's like a longing that can't be satisfied; a feeling of loss and nostalgia for what you had but cannot have again, and the pain that causes. It's hard to explain and perhaps I'm not doing it well.'

He had my full attention by then. 'No, you've explained it very well.'

'Fado and saudade are entwined. Fate. Nostalgia. I heard fado described once as expressing what is left when everything has been lost.'

I looked at him but didn't trust myself to speak.

'They're going to start in a moment,' Nuno said, and I turned and saw the performers heading for the stage.

The two guitarists, one with a classical guitar and the other with a teardrop-shaped Portuguese guitar settled into their chairs and as the lights dimmed, leaving only candles to light the room, they started to play. I felt myself being transported far away to a place I didn't know yet which felt strangely familiar and then from the shadows, a woman dressed in black emerged. Her voice was powerful and haunting and although I was unable to understand a single word, I felt emotions I didn't know I still possessed and could not have articulated being wrenched from inside me. By the time they took their first break, all my thoughts of food had been forgotten.

'What do you think?'

'I don't understand the words, but I can feel the emotions.'

'People think fado is depressing. But it isn't. Well, I don't think so. It's sad but not depressing. It's a way of expressing sorrow and that's cathartic. Besides sadness is part of life, isn't it? It's pointless to deny that. Life is light and light casts shadows. One cannot exist without the other.'

I was saved from trying to form a reply by the return of the guitarists and the singer. Their second set of songs was, if anything, more intense than the first. I felt the sorrow but not the catharsis, and Nuno's words lingered in the air. I started to feel the need to escape, although I had no idea where I wanted to go. I could not continue to sit there, trying to hold myself together. There was too much emotion, too much intensity, in the air.

Nuno must have noticed something in my face or body language. In the next pause in the proceedings, he leaned across the table and whispered 'What's the matter?'

'Why did you bring me here?'

'I thought you would enjoy it, and I thought you needed to take some time out from everything.'

'I do, but what I really should be doing is looking for Vanessa and trying to find a way to clear my name. Not sitting here.' I felt tears threatening to form, something which had rarely happened to me since the day of Finn's funeral, and I backhanded them away. My protective layers were being stripped away, and I didn't know how to deal with that.

'You are allowed to take a break, you know. Enjoy this evening and then we'll start afresh tomorrow.'

'I'm sorry. I must sound so ungrateful, but I do appreciate you bringing me here. I'm just not the best company at the moment.' I summoned some composure and tried to recover the situation by posing a question. 'What were those two last songs about?'

'The first one was about being poor and marginalised. And the last one was about loss of life at sea. With our history that's very typical.'

I felt nauseous. I got up and stumbled up the stairs, desperate to get out of there. Nuno was some way behind me having, I assumed, stopped to pay and found me outside, my back pressed against the wall, cold and shaking despite the warmth of the night.

Chapter 11

My first feeling the next morning was one of unbearable embarrassment. To his credit, Nuno had seemed to sense the mortification which had set in shortly after he had found me and had not done what most people would have done; namely ask me what was wrong. At some point, I had mumbled something about having overdone it after my fall, which I doubted was convincing, but Nuno had appeared to accept my explanation without question and walked me back to my hotel. He had left me there having first made me promise to call him if I started to feel worse. We had also agreed he would be at the hotel the next day at around ten to talk about going to see Lou. I would have agreed to almost anything which would have enabled me to get away as soon as possible.

The thought of having to face him again was uncomfortable, and I was tempted to call him to postpone. Then I considered the need to find Vanessa and clear my name and thought better of it.

Nuno arrived just as I was finishing breakfast.

'Hi,' I said awkwardly, bracing myself for questions about what had happened the night before.

'Hi. How are you feeling?'

I was unsure if he was referring to my bruises or the night before so I chose to go with the former. 'Better, thanks. The bruises still hurt, but the pain isn't as bad.'

'That's good. Are you ready to see if we can find Lou?'

'Yes, I just hope she's at home,' I said, grateful he had not asked about my reaction the previous night.

'If she's not there, we'll try at the agency. We'll find her sooner or later.'

We took the bus as I had done on the previous occasions I had been to Lou's. As we got off, I looked mournfully at the hill. 'It's up there.'

'Come on then.'

We arrived at the top, and I took a moment to catch my breath. 'Where now?' asked Nuno.

I waved in the general direction of Lou's flat, still recovering from the pace Nuno had set and which I had tried to keep.

'Sorry. I forget that I'm used to these hills. I should have slowed down.'

I waved my hand again as I finished panting. 'It's fine. Follow me.'

By the time we reached the third floor, I felt hot, sweaty and fed up. I continued up the next flight, ahead of Nuno, and as I arrived at the top, I pulled up unexpectedly, causing him to bump into me.

'Isabel?'

I could say nothing because staring at me down the corridor was Inspector Mendes Silva, flanked by two other officers.

'Miss Foster?'

I managed a mute acknowledgement as I walked towards him.

'You appear to have had some sort of accident. What happened to you?'

'Nothing. I slipped on the bathroom floor. It looks worse than it is.' As I told the lie, I hoped the couple who had helped me the other night would not appear and recognise me. I assumed they had no reason to go up to the fourth floor, but the way things had been going, nothing would have surprised me.

'Nasty. What brings you here?' He glanced over at Nuno but did not address him.

'I wanted to speak to Lou.'

'Strangely enough so do we.'

I wanted to ask him why, but every time I engaged with him my situation became worse so I simply looked at him until I realised I could not outstare him.

In the silence, I heard Nuno speak, but he spoke in Portuguese so I could only pick out a few words, certainly not enough to follow what he was saying. Mendes Silva responded, and I wished I could follow the conversation.

'What's going on?' I asked Nuno when their exchange appeared to have come to an end. Neither of them spoke, and I watched as they eyed each other; Mendes Silva giving him that same appraising look he had given me so often, and

Nuno looking wary but unwilling to break eye contact.

'Why do you want to speak to Lou?' I asked.

Mendes Silva's gaze lingered a moment longer on Nuno, and then he reluctantly turned his attention back to me. 'That is our business, Miss Foster. A better question would be why do you want to speak to her?'

'I'm worried about Vanessa. You know that. I just thought Lou might remember something, or know something that would help me to find her.'

'You, Miss Foster?

'Me, you, us. Someone. Anyone. I don't care. I just want to know where she is.'

He appeared to ponder that point. 'I understand your concern, but you have done nothing to help us or yourself. When Vanessa went missing, you didn't contact us straight away. When she made contact with you, you neglected to tell us. You can see the problem. Vanessa is nowhere to be found. Lou is not here either. Yet you … you are … everywhere.'

I found I could contain myself no more. 'If I had done something to Vanessa, why would I have come to see you at all? I'd just have gone back to Seville as quickly as possible before you even knew I had been here.'

'It is an interesting point. Why did you stay here, Miss Foster? Really?'

'I told you. Initially, I stayed here because I wanted to find Vanessa. Then you told me I couldn't leave so I didn't have a lot of say in the matter.' I felt Nuno give my hand a warning squeeze and stopped myself from continuing.

'Perhaps or perhaps you had unfinished business.'

'What sort of unfinished business?'

'Perhaps Lou found out what you had done.'

'What do you mean? What I'd done? I haven't *done* anything.' I paused as his earlier comment registered fully with me. 'What do you mean Lou isn't here?'

'What I mean is that there are questions regarding Lou's whereabouts.'

'What?'

'You seem surprised,' Mendes Silva remarked.

'Of course I am. What sort of questions?'

'It's not entirely clear. Someone phoned her employer on her behalf to say she was sick. Yet she is not here. I always find the best place to recuperate is at home, wouldn't you agree?'

'Well, yes. I suppose so.' I seized on a possibility. 'Perhaps she's staying with the person who phoned in for her. Maybe she's taking care of her.'

'How do you know it was a woman who phoned?'

'I don't. I just assumed it was a female friend.'

'Why do I always get the impression you know more than you are telling us, Miss Foster?'

'I don't. I'm just as much in the dark as anyone else. Anyway, what's so sinister about being off work sick?'

'Nothing usually. However, Lou Johnson is a colleague of someone who has gone missing. By all accounts she is also a good friend of hers. Lou Johnson is not missing as such, but she is not at home, she is not answering her phone, and we don't know where she is. In the circumstances, I find that … concerning.'

'She's probably just recovering at her friend's house and not bothering to check her phone. She'll turn up.' I tried to sound more confident than I felt.

'Will she, though? We can only hope that is the case. In the meantime you have unfortunately dragged your friend into this.'

'What? No, no. He has absolutely nothing to do with this.'

Mendes Silva turned to one of his colleagues. 'Take his details.' He looked back at me, a hint of triumph in his eyes. 'I feel we may be getting closer to the truth, and the truth always comes out in the end. Don't you think, Miss Foster?'

* * *

Bruised by our encounter with Mendes Silva, Nuno and I decamped to a bar down the road from Lou's flat.

'I'm so sorry,' I said for at least the third time. 'It's one thing getting myself into trouble. It's quite another getting you into trouble too.'

'Stop apologising. You didn't force me to go to Lou's flat. If you remember, it was my idea.'

'Yes, but –'

'Listen to me, Isabel. It's not your fault. We might be in trouble now, but we've done nothing wrong so we'll just have to get out of trouble. Together.'

I massaged my temples, carefully avoiding the bruises. 'I know this sounds weird, but I came here to find Vanessa, and I've been looking for her ever since, but I feel … it feels more like she's pursuing me.'

'It doesn't sound weird. It's crossed my mind too.'

I pondered that for a while and then remembered my encounter with Carolina. 'In the absence of Lou, I can only think of one person who might be able to help us, and that's a long shot.'

'At this stage, that's all we've got. Who is it?'

'A woman from the agency Lou and Vanessa work for came to see me at the hotel. Carolina. She told me not to trust Vanessa … or Lou, come to that.'

Nuno sat up. 'When did that happen?'

I thought back; weary of my brain feeling so woolly. 'It was before we met. I was going to tell you last night and then you said we should forget about everything for the evening. I should have remembered to tell you before we went to Lou's today. I can't seem to think clearly at the moment.'

'That's understandable after everything you've been through. What else did she say?'

'Not much. She seemed frightened of Vanessa. She didn't even want me to say her name. She said Vanessa had found out things about her and threatened her. She also said she couldn't help me to find her, and I shouldn't even try.'

'Why?'

'She suggested it would be dangerous.'

'Vanessa seems to be good at manipulating and intimidating people.'

'Yes, that and getting under their skin.' I realised how well she had succeeded with me; someone who thought herself impervious to people in general. 'Perhaps Carolina was right, Nuno. Perhaps I should just give up the search and hope everything resolves itself somehow.'

'But you can't, can you?'

'No, I can't. I hate the fact we seem to be under suspicion for something we haven't done and despite everything, I'm still worried Vanessa has got herself into some sort of serious trouble. I need to know what's going on.'

'So we'll go and see Carolina and find out if we can get anything else out of her.'

'She might have left by now.' Seeing Nuno's confused expression, I added, 'She said she was going to change jobs. And anyway, she'll clam up if she sees me.'

As we sat in the bar, continuing to brood over our predicament, I abandoned all attempts at following the advice on the hospital leaflet and ordered a vodka and tonic. I hadn't eaten properly in days, and I felt my inhibitions loosening faster than I had anticipated.

A second drink appeared, and I swirled the liquid around, stabbing at the slice of lemon with my straw. I had become trapped in a prison with no walls and no longer felt certain of anything. It occurred to me how convenient it was that Nuno had appeared on the scene to rescue me at the Panorâmico de Monsanto.

'Why were you there?' I asked.

'Where?'

'At the Panorâmico de Monsanto. The weather was terrible, and it was deserted that day. Apart from the person who slashed my tyres.'

'You think I did that?'

'No, I don't. I didn't mean that. It's just that I didn't see anyone else there.' As I said the words, I remembered the green SUV cruising past. I thought of all the kindness and patience Nuno had shown me. He had done more for me than most friends would do for each other, let alone a total stranger. I would have done anything to take the words back, but they had been said, and there was nothing I could do to retract them. 'I'm just saying it's … odd.'

'Isabel, I know how much you've been through since you got here, but please stop and think for a moment. All I've done is try to help you. All I want to do is help you.'

'So why were you there?' It was no longer an accusation but a desperate need to believe that somebody around me could be trusted without reservation.

Nuno must have picked up on my change of tone as his changed as well. 'I go there to remember and to clear my head. I find it helps. Everything looks so small and unimportant from up there.'

I pushed my drink to one side, suddenly feeling completely sober. 'What do you go there to remember?'

'Not what. Who.' He paused. 'Teresa.'

I felt a strange stab of an emotion I could not identify. 'Teresa?'

'My sister. She committed suicide three years ago.'

I wasn't sure if I could have reproached myself more at that moment. Any remaining traces of suspicion fell away. 'I'm so sorry,' I said, wishing I could have found better words.

'The thing people don't realise about suicide is the guilt …' His voice trailed away, and I wasn't sure if he was even aware I was still there. But I was, and I knew a thing or two about guilt.

'The grief dulls a little, the anger burns itself out eventually, but it's the guilt that's the killer; it just seems to keep growing.' I said the words without even thinking.

Nuno looked up at me and in that moment I felt a bond with him which he could not know we shared.

As we left the bar and set off for the agency, I found myself apologising again.

Nuno stopped me. 'Isabel, you don't need to keep saying sorry.'

'I do. It was awful of me to say what I did when you've been … you …'

'What is it?' Nuno asked gently.

'You've been the only person who has helped me. You've shown me nothing but kindness.'

'After what you just said to me in the bar, I have a feeling you need a bit of kindness.'

I half nodded, half shrugged, and he smiled at me. 'It's forgotten.' He raised my chin, encouraging me to look him in the eye. 'It really is forgotten. Come on.'

* * *

There seemed to be no sign of Carolina at the agency from our vantage point in the street. We had taken up a position behind by a large advertising hoarding from where we could observe the comings and goings at the agency, thanks to its large windows. We saw tourists milling around but of Carolina, there was no sign.

'She's probably not there anymore, Nuno. We might as well go.'

'Let's give it another five minutes.'

I sighed, but there were no other avenues to explore so I didn't pursue it. The minutes dragged by, and the crowds started to thin out a little.

'Have another look. Can you see her?' Nuno asked.

I peered cautiously round the hoarding. 'Yes, that's her. At the counter by the window.'

'Wait here,' Nuno said, and he had gone before I could ask him what he was going to say to her.

I watched him as he went into the agency, approached the counter and said something to Carolina. It struck me again just how attractive he was. Carolina apparently thought so too, judging by the huge smile that had spread across her face and the way she twirled her hair through her fingers as she spoke to him. She appeared to have ripped a page from a manual on how to flirt. Nuno, meanwhile, seemed to be totally oblivious and had an earnest look on his face as he explained something to her. In any other circumstances, it might have been comical.

I had a sudden vision of Finn beside me, commenting on our attempts to watch what was going on whilst trying to remain hidden by the hoarding and then dissolving into giggles. I remembered how infectious her laugh had been, and a shard of pain worked its way through me. I forced myself back to the present and wondered what they were saying and if it would bring us any closer to finding either Vanessa or Lou.

Nuno emerged into the sunshine and gestured at me to walk away. I started moving, keeping the hoarding between me and the agency and met Nuno around the corner.

'What did she say?'

'I've set up a meeting for a drink.'

'How did you get her agree to do that?'

Nuno looked sheepish. 'I said I was interested in arranging a private guide for my friends, and I would pay good money if she could arrange it for me. I didn't mention you.'

'I'll be a pleasant surprise in more ways than one.'

'What do you mean?'

'I was watching her. She was flirting with you like mad. She thinks she's going to be making a lucrative deal and getting another chance to spend some time with you. I'm the last person she'll be expecting or wanting to see.'

Nuno shifted around awkwardly. 'I had to improvise. It wasn't my intention for it to work out like that.'

'Well, there's nothing we can do about it now. What time have you arranged to meet her?'

'In half an hour at that bar opposite the agency.'

We agreed Nuno should meet her alone, and then I should join them. As he left, I wondered what would come of our meeting. I couldn't imagine her taking too kindly to seeing me. I counted the minutes until I judged I could join them. I walked over to the bar and stopped in the doorway. Nuno looked up, and Carolina, who was sitting opposite him with her back to the door, turned to follow his gaze.

'What are you doing here?' Carolina asked.

'I'm sorry, Carolina,' Nuno said. 'I haven't handled this very well, but Isabel needs to speak to you.'

'You brought me here to see her?'

I heard the way her voice landed on *her* and felt my heart sink. We would learn nothing, I was sure of that.

'Yes. I was just about to explain.'

She got up, but I stopped her and sat down in the seat next to hers, blocking her exit. 'Carolina, I'm sorry if we've upset you, but I really need to talk to you. It is important or I wouldn't ask.'

She looked from me to Nuno. His presence seemed to reassure her, and she sat down again. 'I don't have long.'

'Do you know where Lou is?'

'She's off sick so I suppose she's at home.'

'Well, she isn't and for reasons I won't go into now, the police seem to think we know more about where she is than they do.'

'And what can I do about that?' Carolina asked defensively.

'They also seem to think I was involved in Vanessa's disappearance.'

'What? Why?' She looked genuinely startled, her previous attitude momentarily forgotten.

'I don't know. We hope you might be able to tell us something else about Vanessa or Lou that will help us to clear our names.'

'I told you everything when I came to see you at the hotel. I wish I hadn't bothered now.'

'I can imagine,' I said, hoping to placate her and, in truth, I could imagine. 'But please, just think. Is there anything you know that could possibly help us?'

Carolina stared at the table, chewing her lip. Whether that was a sign of resistance or consideration, I couldn't tell.

'Please Carolina,' Nuno said.

She sighed and seemed to come to some sort of decision. 'Before Vanessa came to work at the agency, Lou was in a bad way. I don't know what was wrong with her, but she obviously had problems of some kind. Then Vanessa arrived and within a few weeks, she and Lou were best friends, and Lou was much happier.

'At first, I was pleased. Lou being in a better mood made the atmosphere at work more pleasant, and Vanessa seemed like a fun person to have around. Until my problems with her started.' She shot me a look. 'I don't intend to tell you all the details, and they're not relevant anyway. What I will say is that Vanessa is good at making you feel great about yourself when it suits her. She gets you to open up, and then she turns round and uses what she knows against you. She did that to me, and I reckon she did that to Lou too.'

'Why?'

'Because that's what she does.'

'And there's nothing else?' Nuno asked.

Carolina looked past Nuno towards the bar. Her desire to get away was palpable. The silence stretched out, but I could wait, and I felt sure Nuno could too.

'There is one thing.'

'Yes?' Nuno said quietly.

'One day I arrived at work, and I was in the back office. That's where we leave our coats and things,' she added unnecessarily.

This time Nuno remained silent, and I followed his lead.

'You must never repeat this,' Carolina said.

'I promise,' I said and Nuno murmured his agreement.

Carolina started chewing on her lip again. 'I was making coffee. I like to have a drink before I start work.'

I could sense every extra detail she disclosed was pushing her closer to the point where she would tell us something we needed to know so I resisted the urge to rush her.

'Anyway, I'd left the back door slightly open. There's a little courtyard out there. The smokers use it sometimes.'

Nuno and I both looked at her expectantly.

Carolina swallowed hard. 'I heard them talking. Lou and Vanessa, I mean. They were talking quietly at first. I recognised their voices, but I couldn't hear exactly what they were saying. I wasn't paying attention anyway really. Then Lou raised her voice a bit and said "You never told me I'd have to do anything for it."'

Nuno and I exchanged glances.

'That caught my attention. I mean it was an odd thing to say, and she sounded stressed. Vanessa said she'd make sure it would be bad for her if she didn't go through with it. She said she was already committed.' Carolina took a deep breath. 'I was really curious by then. I didn't want them to see me, but I went to the door and looked through the crack by the hinges. Vanessa handed Lou an envelope and said that should help her to get over her issues.'

'Did you see what was in it?' Nuno asked.

'What?' Carolina looked startled as if she had forgotten we were there.

'Did you see what was in the envelope?'

'Yes, I did. Lou opened the envelope and took some money out. Well, lots of money actually. I didn't want to risk them seeing me so I got out of there as quickly and quietly as possible and went to my desk. When I next saw them, they were all smiles. You would never have known anything had happened, but …'

'But?' I asked.

'It was the look on Vanessa's face when they were outside. I can't even describe it, but it was like if Lou had dared to cross her …' She shook her head.

A silence settled around us, which Nuno finally broke. 'Thank you Carolina. Is there anything else you know which could help us?'

She looked around the room as though hoping to draw strength from somewhere. 'They met out there a few times,' she ventured. 'I couldn't always hear them or see what was happening, but there was one other occasion when I could.'

She stopped again and I thought she would not continue, but then I heard her take another deep breath. 'They were out there, and I heard Lou. She said she didn't like it and besides it wasn't practical. I don't know what *it* was. Vanessa said she didn't have to like it; she only had to do it. There was something about her tone. It was like the look on her face the other time.' She shook her head. 'I was frightened, and it wasn't even directed at me. Anyway, Vanessa gave Lou a small bag and said she – Lou, that is – knew what to do.'

I could bear it no longer. 'Did Lou open the bag while she was out there?' I asked as softly as I could.

Vanessa met my eyes for the first time. 'Yes. She took out a phone. One of those old-fashioned ones. And some papers. I couldn't see those properly. I don't know what they were.'

I sat back in my chair. Money; a phone; paperwork; Lou's protests and Vanessa's insistence. I had no idea what any of it meant. And yet … there was something stirring in my brain as I tried to slot all of the pieces together. It was like an infuriating itch I couldn't scratch. I became aware that Carolina was speaking again.

'… so I stepped back and that's when I knocked a cup off the table. They both looked round when they heard the noise, and I ran out of the room. By the time they found me, I was at my desk. They couldn't really ask me if I'd been in the other room without sounding as if they'd been doing something suspicious. But later Vanessa came to see me. She made it clear that "people who poke their nose into other people's business and then blab" as she put it, have to accept that there will be consequences.'

'That's when she threatened you with … something?'

Carolina nodded and swallowed hard. 'I had done something wrong, something stupid. I admit that, and I'm not proud of it. That's why I won't talk about it. And now I'm going to make a fresh start away from everything. Away from Vanessa.'

'We really appreciate the fact you've told us all this,' Nuno said.

'You mustn't tell anyone ever,' Carolina said as if suddenly aware just how much she had said.

'We won't,' I said, hoping events wouldn't force me to break my promise.

Carolina glanced at me, uncertainty and anxiety written across her face and got up.

I moved out of her way. 'I thought you might have left the agency by now.'

'This is my last week. You were lucky to find me there.'

We watched as Carolina walked out of the café and crossed the road. 'Do you think she's told us everything?' I asked.

'Everything that's relevant, yes. I doubt whatever hold Vanessa had over her has anything to do with this. It's obvious she's still afraid of her, though.'

'I wonder why Vanessa was giving Lou money,' I said, as wild, unformed theories started to race through my mind.

'It was clearly to force her to do something she wasn't happy about, but that could be almost anything.'

'And the phone. What was that about?'

'I have no idea, but it means Lou knows more than she's letting on.'

'So the key is to find Lou. How, though?'

'I'm not sure yet. But we'll find a way.' He smiled at me, and I found I liked the way that made me feel.

Chapter 12

Nuno had to excuse himself from our hunt for Lou for the rest of the day to go to a birthday party at his cousin's house. Left to my own devices, I walked down to the old town, waited in a long queue and took the Santa Justa Lift to the viewing platform. The last time I had been there, Vanessa had diverted me and sent me running off to the café in Chiado. As I surveyed the scene with the city spread out before me, I realised again how glorious Lisbon was and wished I was seeing it under different circumstances.

Mariana was at reception when I returned to the hotel. 'Good afternoon, Miss Foster. Don't forget check-out time is eleven.'

I looked blankly at her.

'You're due to leave the day after tomorrow so I thought I'd remind you now in case I don't see you tomorrow,' Mariana added.

I realised I had completely lost track of the days. 'Is there any chance I could extend my stay again?'

'I'll have to check the reservations. Just a moment.'

I waited as she tapped on the keyboard. 'Yes, we can accommodate you. How long would you like to stay?'

My frugal lifestyle meant I had never gone through all of my inheritance, and I was able to afford the occasional unexpected expense. Nonetheless, I didn't intend to end up emptying my entire bank account to keep Mendes Silva happy, and I had to get the car back to Seville by the end of the rental period. 'I'm not entirely sure. I'd better say another week, but I might leave earlier if my circumstances change.'

Mariana typed something in and looked at the screen. 'Yes, that's fine. If you could let us know by eleven the day before, we might be able to give you a refund for any nights you don't stay. I'll have to check with my manager first, though.'

'Thank you. That's very kind.'

In the lift up to my room, I wondered what would happen if neither Vanessa nor Lou had reappeared by the time I was due back in Seville. I supposed I would have to try to hope for the best, which went against my pessimistic nature. I needed someone to cheer me up. 'I wish you were here, Finn,' I sighed as the lift doors opened.

* * *

The following afternoon, as Nuno had promised, he arrived at my hotel room to discuss what we should do next. We had just settled ourselves at the small table in my room to consider what we knew and what we could do when there was a knock on the door. As I jumped, I realised how conditioned I had become to expect bad news.

'Who is it?' I called.

'Police.'

If I had been alone and I hadn't been in a room on the sixth floor, I might have considered trying to escape, but there was no way out.

Nuno and I looked at each other. He shook his head looking fatalistic and gestured for me to open the door.

'Just a moment,' I said, trying to sound composed.

I felt my legs start to shake and the rest of my body go rigid. I forced myself to get up and set my face to what I hoped was neutral as I opened the door.

Mendes Silva was standing there with one of his officers. 'Miss Foster. May we come in?'

'Of course,' I said. I couldn't stop trembling, and I was starting to feel faint. Images of Nuno and I being arrested, going on trial and being thrown into prison flashed in front of me. The thought of being locked up somewhere and of the same fate being inflicted on Nuno was too much to bear.

I resumed my seat at the table, not trusting myself to stand much longer as the room swam before my eyes. Mendes Silva and the other officer looked around for seats and seeing none, Mendes Silva started to speak.

I heard nothing he said, too caught up in what I had anticipated would happen next.

'Miss Foster?'

'Sorry?' I replied, looking up at him.

'Your friend Miss Taylor has reappeared. She walked into a police station in Tondela earlier today.'

Relief coursed through me, leaving me unable to respond.

'Miss Foster? Did you hear me?'

'Yes, yes, I did. Is she OK?'

'Apparently. She offered no explanation as to why she hadn't been to work, but that is not our concern. That is between her and her employer. She said she had been unaware that her disappearance had been reported and that people were looking for her until she read a report in this morning's newspaper.'

'But that's not true. I told her the police had opened an investigation. I told you about that as well the second time I came to the police station.'

'Quite. Frankly, even leaving your statement to one side, what she said stretches credibility, but credibility is not as stretched as far as our resources so I am inclined to close the matter.'

'What about wasting police time?'

'We don't have a strong enough case to make it worth pursuing.'

'And not registering her new address?'

'She is within the time limit to rectify that. You seem keen to see her get into trouble,' Mendes Silva remarked drily.

'No, it's just that everyone has been so worried and she's caused so much … stress. And then that's it. It's over.'

'She has not committed a crime.'

As the reality of the situation started to sink in, I asked him the question I should have started out with. 'So Nuno and I are not under suspicion anymore?'

Mendes Silva sighed. 'The case of Miss Taylor's disappearance will be closed. At the moment, Lou Johnson is simply off work sick, and there is no case to pursue. However, it is a loose end in a way.'

I didn't like the way he had said loose end. 'Why?'

'First Miss Taylor disappears and then when she turns up, she gives no reason for her disappearance. She is not required to but still … then another employee, a colleague from the same agency, becomes impossible to contact. I would like to establish her whereabouts. Yes, someone called in sick for her, but she is not at home, and she is not answering her phone. I feel there is something here that is not quite right … some connection which has been missed. We may need to speak to you again Miss Foster so although you are not under suspicion as such, you must still check with us before you can leave the country.'

'I see,' I said.

'Mr. Ferreira da Costa, the same applies to you.'

Nuno nodded but said nothing.

'Goodbye for now, Miss Foster.'

'Goodbye.'

As I closed the door behind them, I turned to Nuno. 'What do you make of that?'

'I honestly don't know what to think.'

'How much trouble do you think we're still in?'

'A lot less than we were a few hours ago, that much is for sure. And I don't see how he can connect us to whatever might have happened to Lou so I think he'll have to drop that too. The only question is what happens first.'

'What do you mean?'

'Whether Lou makes an appearance or whether he decides to drop it.'

I started to pace the room. I hated being in a situation where I was dependent on the actions of others and could do nothing to influence the outcome. I needed to do something, however ineffectual it might be. I also had a few choice words I wanted to say to Vanessa. I got up, grabbed my bag and headed for the door.

'Where are you going?' Nuno asked.

'Tondela.'

Nuno followed me and caught my hand. 'Why?'

'That was the place where they said Vanessa went into the police station, wasn't it?'

'Yes, but Isabel she could be anywhere by now. Tondela must be at least a three-hour drive from here.'

'I think she wants me to follow her.'

Nuno looked at me, doubt evident in his expression. 'Has it occurred to you that you're wrong, and you're chasing someone who doesn't want to be found?'

'You said yourself that you thought she'd orchestrated our falling out. She's planned all of this so I don't believe for a minute that her reappearance is the end of it.'

'You're stubborn. You know that, don't you?' But there was the hint of a smile on his face.

'You don't have to come with me,' I responded.

Nuno and I were still debating the merits of going to Tondela by the time we got to my car. In the gloom of the underground car park, I turned to Nuno. 'I'm more grateful to you than I can say for everything you've done, but I don't expect you to come all the way to Tondela with me. I can take it from here.'

'I haven't done anything.'

'You have. And I'm not just talking about getting the tyres fixed. You listened to me, you believed me and even when I got you into trouble, you didn't blame me. But now you're more or less in the clear. As you said, it's just a matter of time. I don't expect you to pursue this any further …' I trailed off, not sure why I was trying to talk him out of going with me when I really wanted his company.

'So I can go back to my life, and you can get on with yours?'

I found myself realising that wasn't what I wanted, but the instinct for self-preservation kicked in and overrode other feelings I didn't want to acknowledge. Every time I let someone get close, it led to disaster. For them and for me. 'I suppose so.'

I got my car keys out and opened the door. I had to end the conversation before my resolve to go it alone disintegrated. 'Trust me, you'll be better off.'

I got in and, as I did, Nuno moved around the car and slipped into the passenger seat.

'Trust me, I won't,' he said.

'I'm going to Tondela. You do know that, don't you?'

'Then let's go.'

The drive to Tondela took us just over three hours, and I sensed the weariness we were both experiencing by the time we arrived. We had spoken little on the way. I had been preoccupied with my own thoughts, and I assumed that Nuno had been as well or had decided to allow me the luxury of uncomplicated silence.

'Can you check the directions to the police station?' I asked, after I had passed the same street corner three times.

Nuno consulted his phone. 'I think you need to turn left at the next junction.'

I followed his directions and within a few minutes we had drawn up outside. I parked, and we looked at each other.

'Do you want to wait here?' I asked.

'I think you might need a Portuguese speaker.'

I wanted to believe I could handle it alone, but I realised he was right. We walked to the door of the police station, and I was suddenly relieved that he was with me. Having to rely on someone had never sat well with me and the sensation left me off-balance.

Lost in a myriad of thoughts, I let Nuno take care of all the formalities until we were seated in front of a police officer. I awoke from my reverie to hear her saying, in English, 'You are here about Vanessa Taylor?'

I heard Nuno reply in English to confirm that was indeed why we were there, and I forced myself to engage with the conversation.

'What do you want to know?'

'I'm a friend of hers, and I've been very worried about her. I was hoping she might still be here.' I realised then what a forlorn hope it had been, and Nuno had been right to say we were on a fool's errand. The police officer's next words confirmed my thoughts.

'I'm sorry. She left here some hours ago. We had no reason to detain her, and I suppose she had no reason to stay.'

'How did she seem?' I ventured.

'I don't understand.'

'I mean was she well? Did she seem distressed in any way?'

The officer paused. 'No. She was very calm and apologetic. She said she hadn't realised what a fuss she had caused.'

'And that was it?'

'Yes.'

'Did she say anything about where she was going?' I asked.

'No. In my opinion, Miss Foster, you will just have to wait and hope that your friend makes contact with you.'

She got up, and it was clear the conversation was over. Pleasantries were exchanged, and we found ourselves outside.

'Perhaps she's staying in Tondela for the night.' I said.

'Perhaps. Or perhaps she's in Lisbon or Porto or back in Spain. She could be almost anywhere by now.'

The unfairness of the fact that Vanessa was free to do whatever she pleased and go wherever she chose whilst Nuno and I were still required to obtain permission from the police if we wanted to leave Portugal, stung me.

'You're right, but we've come all this way so I'm going to check the hotels. You don't have to come with me,' I added hastily, feeling even Nuno's patience had to have its limits.

'Isabel, I don't mind if you want to do that. I'll go with

you if you'd like me to. I just think you're wasting your time and energy.'

'I've come all this way. I might as well try.'

Consulting our phones, we discovered Tondela was happily, from our point of view, relatively short of hotels. A tour around those closest to the centre proved as fruitless as Nuno had predicted. With one closed for renovation and the others fully booked but unwilling to disclose any information about their guests, we stood outside the last one, looking at each other, tired and dispirited.

'Do you want to get something to eat?' Nuno asked. 'I don't know about you, but I'm really hungry.'

I realised I hadn't eaten since breakfast. 'OK,' I said, rummaging for my keys. 'Can you look for a place to go?'

Following Nuno's directions, we drove back through the centre of Tondela, an attractive, well-kept town, which was not as short of restaurants as it was of hotels. Nuno selected one with good reviews and before long we were being seated at a table.

'Where do you want to go from here?' Nuno asked.

'I don't know. I think you were right. Vanessa doesn't want to be found, and I'm probably going to have to accept that I'll never really understand what all this has been about. I'll just have to wait it out and hope Lou turns up soon, and then I'll be able to leave Lisbon.'

'How do you feel about that?'

I looked at him, unclear whether he was referring to never clearing up the mystery or leaving Lisbon. Or both. 'I don't know. I'm so exhausted right now, I can't think clearly.'

'Do you want me to drive back?'

'No, you're not insured to drive my car. The last thing either of us needs is another brush with the law.'

'You're too tired to drive, Isabel. When was the last time you slept properly? I mean really well?'

'It feels like a long time,' I admitted. 'How about finding a hotel for the night? Unless you need to get back tonight?'

'No. I'm in no hurry.'

We finished dinner and headed back to the car. I drove around, hoping to find a place which had not made its presence known on the Internet and might therefore be more likely to have some free rooms. Nuno, meanwhile, was busy looking up hotels further away. He made a couple of calls and shook his head at the end of each one.

On the edge of a hamlet to the south of Tondela, I saw signs for a hotel somewhere off the main road.

'Have you tried that one?' I asked.

'No, the name's not familiar. I'll give them a call.'

I pulled over and waited.

'No reply.'

'Let's try anyway,' I said and turned onto the unpaved road indicated by the sign.

Minutes later we had parked and were standing in reception, ringing the bell. The foyer was richly decorated in reds and golds with intricately carved, dark wood bookcases lining the walls.

A man in rumpled trousers and an ill-fitting cardigan eventually appeared rubbing his eyes and said something in Portuguese, which I didn't catch.

Nuno and the man had a brief conversation, and then he turned to me. 'They only have one room.'

I turned to leave, but Nuno stopped me. 'It's a twin room, and you need to sleep, Isabel.'

I looked out of the window by reception and saw that it had started to rain heavily. All thoughts of sleeping in the car or attempting the drive back to Lisbon were finally abandoned. 'OK,' I agreed.

We were given the key and directions to the room and then the man shuffled off again.

I unlocked the door and found it was decorated in the same style as the reception; the same dark wood furniture and red and gold colour scheme. I headed for the bathroom, grateful to find toothpaste, toothbrushes and soap.

When I came back out, Nuno was sitting on the end of one of the beds, looking uncomfortable.

'This is awkward, I know.' I said, thinking that if the obvious was stated it would somehow make the situation less difficult.

'I can sleep in the car if you would prefer that.'

I looked at the rain streaming down the windows. 'While I'm warm and comfortable in here? No, you can't do that.'

'I think I'll have a shower then.'

I walked over to the window. I heard the bathroom door close, and the sound of the water running; an accompaniment to the rain outside. I watched it fall, hypnotised by the rhythmic splashes hitting the panes. Somewhere out there was Vanessa. What was she doing? What was she thinking? Was she planning the next step in some elaborate game or had it finally come to an end? Was it time to give up the hunt and wait it out in the hope I would be allowed to go back to Seville soon? So many questions and no answers.

By comparison with everything which had happened in Lisbon, Seville, even with its complications, seemed a preferable option. Except I was not yet free to leave. My invisible chains were chafing. I caught sight of my reflection in the glass; a stranger with shadows and valleys etched deep in her face. The last two weeks had cost me a lot, and I was overcome by exhaustion.

I phoned the Hibiscus to tell them I would be back the next day, imagining them innocently reporting that a hotel guest had gone missing. The thought of another run in with Mendes Silva was something I was keen to avoid at all costs. That done, I turned off the overhead lights and leaving only Nuno's bedside light on, took off my sandals and slipped under the heavy brocade cover, leaving the bed fully made up.

The sunlight hitting my face woke me up. I turned over to find myself alone. Nuno's bed was almost undisturbed although there were small indentations in the cover which suggested he had slept on the bed if not in it. I wondered if he had perhaps decided at some point during the night that it was all too much trouble and quietly left. I wouldn't have blamed him.

I got out of bed and saw that my car was still outside and then felt guilty for allowing myself even the fleeting doubt that Nuno might have taken it. On the way to the bathroom,

I noticed his phone was still on the bedside table. Puzzled but not yet alert enough to make sense of everything, I showered and got dressed. I was starting to feel almost human and when I opened the bathroom door, Nuno was sitting at the small table with two cups of coffee and a paper bag, streaked with grease stains.

I felt obscurely pleased to see him. 'Good morning.'

'Hello. I thought you might appreciate some breakfast.'

'Thank you.' I sat down opposite him. 'Is this from the hotel or did you have to go out for it?'

'From the hotel, luckily. There's not much in the way of shops around here.'

'I'm really not sure what's near here. I was so tired last night.'

'You slept well,' Nuno observed.

'For once. You didn't?'

'Mostly, but I was awake for a while.'

'Snoring, was I?' I said, trying to laugh and feeling embarrassed.

'No.'

'Oh.' I could feel the tension in the air, crackling like static.

Nuno stirred his coffee. I thought he would never stop, but finally he put the spoon down and looked up at me. 'Who's Finn?'

* * *

I had been so consumed with thoughts of Vanessa and what, if anything, I should do next that Finn had slipped into the background. I stared at Nuno, wondering how he knew about Finn. He wasn't supposed to know about her; nobody was.

I tried to think of various ways to respond but came out with only one word. 'Why?' I heard my voice catch on the question.

'You were talking in your sleep. I woke up and I thought you were talking to me at first, but then I saw you were still asleep.'

'And what did I say?'

'I couldn't understand most of it, but I caught the name "Finn" a couple of times and "find".'

Playing for time and in need of coffee anyway, I carefully opened a sachet of sugar, stirred it into my coffee and took a few sips.

'I was obviously dreaming about Vanessa if I said "find". You know what dreams are like; all muddled up.'

Nuno nodded, took the croissants out of the paper bag and balanced them on the plastic lids of the coffee cups. The simple act pulled at me. He had stuck by my side at moments when most people would have walked away. He had never blamed me or got angry and he was sitting there organising breakfast as best he could. He had never asked me for anything until that moment and I was stalling him, refusing to give anything away or let him in. I hesitated. He hadn't judged me up to that point, but if I told him about Finn he wouldn't be able to stop himself from thinking badly of me, and I couldn't bear that. But I couldn't bear not being honest with him either. My carefully constructed walls had not just been breached; they were crumbling around me.

'I do know someone called Finn,' I began slowly. 'Or at least I did.'

Nuno met my gaze but said nothing. He broke eye contact and retrieved some paper napkins from the bag, spread them out and placed the croissants on them.

'Finn was my best friend.'

'I thought he must have been someone special.'

'He? No.' I looked at him, confusion turning to comprehension. 'No, Finn is – was – short for Fiona. She hated Fiona and insisted on Finn.'

'Was?'

'She died. It was a long time ago.' I sighed. 'A very long time ago.'

'But she's still in your thoughts.'

'Of course. I think all of this business with Vanessa has brought a lot of stuff to the surface.'

'I'm sorry. I shouldn't have pushed you to talk about her.'

I shook my head. 'No, it's OK, and the thing is I do want to tell you, but I just can't find the words.'

Nuno took my hand. 'Then don't. Not now. There'll be a right time and the right words.'

I let my hand rest in his for a moment and then pulled away, terrified by the intimacy of the moment. 'We should think about getting going soon.'

Once we had checked out and I had negotiated the dirt track and we were back on the main road, Nuno spoke for the first time since we had left the hotel. 'Have you made a final decision about Vanessa?'

'I've asked myself that so many times, and I'm not sure I'm any closer to an answer. Perhaps Mendes Silva was right. The first time I met him, he said searching for Vanessa was like chasing a shadow. There's no perhaps about it, is there? He was right. You were right. I thought she did want me to find her, but I was wrong. I thought I knew her. I thought we were friends, but now I think I never knew her at all and the friendship never really existed. I thought a lot of things that have turned out to be wrong.'

'That must be hard to come to terms with.'

'Yes, and so is the fact that I still don't know what any of this is about, but I think I'm done with running around in circles and chasing after her.'

Out of the corner of my eye, I saw Nuno nod. 'That makes sense. I can't see how you can find her, and what would be the point?'

I thought about that and concluded there was no point at all.

* * *

We had been on the road for what felt like a long time, but when I looked at my watch barely an hour had passed. I pulled at my shoulders and moved my head from side to side. I normally enjoyed driving, but recent events had left me out of sorts.

'Do you want to take a break?' Nuno asked.

'I wouldn't mind, but don't you need to get back? Won't

your family be worried about you?'

'No. I phoned my aunt last night to say I wasn't sure when I'd get back. You were asleep by the time I called her.'

'In that case, can you have a look to see where we could stop?'

'How about Leiria?' Nuno suggested, looking at his phone. 'It's pretty close.'

'OK.' After another ten minutes or so, the signs for the Leiria exit started to appear. Straight on for Lisbon or right for Leiria. The thought of being back in my hotel room, the thought of being alone, made the decision to break the journey easy. With Nuno navigating, we found a place to park and got out.

'Have you been here before?' I asked.

'No, never. I've heard it's worth a visit, though.'

We set off for the town centre, taking a circuitous route through the gardens near the river. It was a gorgeous morning; the sun high in a clear sky and just the lightest of breezes. The area was busy with people of all ages enjoying the surroundings and the weather. It was a blissful moment of normality.

'Would you like to go for a walk by the river?' Nuno asked.

'I think I'd rather see the main square and the old town if that's OK.'

'Sure.'

We turned in the direction of the old town and, as we were about to leave the gardens, a man selling roses approached us. 'A flower for your lovely lady.'

'Oh no, I mean we're not …' I started to say, feeling embarrassed by the misunderstanding, but while I was still protesting Nuno had bought a rose and presented it to me.

'You needn't have,' I said.

'No, but I wanted to.'

I looked at him, wishing I knew what to say. I felt myself trying to reinforce the familiar walls I had constructed, but they didn't seem to be as strong as they had been in the past. Aware I was still staring at him, I managed a shy thank you, and we continued on our way to the square. Arriving there, we got a view of the castle rising above the town.

'Are you up for a climb? Nuno asked.

'Why not?'

The route took us on a winding road through the old town and then onto a road which switched back and forth before finally arriving at the gateway leading into the castle grounds. We wandered along the ramparts and through the ruined church and eventually found ourselves in the loggia we had seen from the main square. From there we had a view over the city and the thickly forested slopes of the surrounding countryside.

'No offence to Lisbon, but I prefer this lookout point to that one in Monsanto Park,' I said.

'A castle wins over an abandoned restaurant,' Nuno agreed.

And, I thought, I had no concerns about that green SUV appearing. I wondered again who had been driving it and why I had been followed, but everything which had happened seemed hazy and far away on that morning in

Leiria with Nuno. We walked back into town and had lunch at one of the cafés close to the main square.

'It's a lovely place. I'm glad we made a stop here.'

'You haven't had much of a chance to enjoy Portugal yet, have you?'

'Not really,' I admitted.

'A trip you'll remember, I imagine. I know I will.'

I met his eyes and saw layers of meaning in what he had said. I hated the fact I was unable to find a way to respond.

He paused, and I think he must have sensed I couldn't find the words I wanted because he changed track. 'What will you do to fill your time when we get back to Lisbon?'

'I had thought about taking a road trip round Portugal for a few days, but I'm not sure now. I still want to see more of Lisbon. And then I'll have to contact Mendes Silva to find out about leaving Portugal. I can't stay here indefinitely. Apart from anything else, I've got to get the car back to Seville soon. After that, I need to decide what to do about the next school year.'

'What is there to decide?'

'Whether to stay in Seville or move on. Rent is pretty expensive, and my living situation isn't exactly ideal.' I didn't feel the need to mention that every place I went to had a maximum shelf life of two years whatever it was like.

'Where would you go?'

'I don't know. I'm a bit of a nomad. See where the wind blows me.' I tried a smile, but it didn't even convince me.

* * *

We were back where we had started in the dim light of the hotel's underground car park. I told myself it was time for us to go our separate ways. I didn't want to say goodbye, but I knew we had to; it would be better for Nuno. And, I told myself, it would be better for me too although I couldn't quite convince myself that was true.

Nuno's hand moved to the car door, and I hoped he would make his departure fast. Instead he hesitated and turned to me. 'I'd like to see you again.'

'I'll be here. I have to wait for the police to say I can leave.' I realised I hadn't actually agreed to see him again, much as I wanted to.

'I'll call you tomorrow then?'

'OK.'

'And make me a promise, Isabel?'

'What's that?'

'If Lou turns up in the meantime, please don't disappear without saying goodbye.'

I nodded, and watched as he got out of the car and disappeared into the shadows. I picked up the rose on the dashboard and wondered what it meant or if it meant anything at all. I didn't like the fact that I cared so much, but still I took it back to the room, stirred sugar into a glass of water and carefully placed the rose in it.

Chapter 13

I was momentarily confused when I woke up the following day. My thoughts were still back in the hotel room where Nuno and I had stayed the night before and the strange mix of intimacy and distance between us both there and during our visit to Leiria. I noticed the rose in its glass and thought how carefree I had felt for those few hours in Leiria. It was strange to be alone and back in my room in Lisbon.

Some sleep seemed to have resolved what I would do, though. I abandoned the idea of a road trip in favour of staying in Lisbon and exploring the city over the next few days. The tantalising slices of it which I had seen had made me want to take the opportunity to enjoy it as a normal visitor. I would say goodbye to Nuno, but I would try to keep it short and sweet. I didn't want to leave him with the impression that I had used him and then discarded him; nothing could have been further from the truth, but I couldn't tell him why I needed to get away from him. I didn't even dare articulate why to myself.

Feeling decisive if not exactly cheerful, I made my

habitual coffee and sat cross-legged on the bed with my phone and the maps and guides I had collected from the hotel reception desk and the Algarve Welcome Point. I determined that it was time to put Vanessa behind me once and for all. As Nuno had said, she could have been anywhere by now, and she clearly didn't want to see me. If only Lou would turn up, I'd be in the clear. As would Nuno. And I would be as relieved for him as I would be for myself.

Leaving the Hibiscus, I walked down the Avenida da Liberdade one more time and took the little funicular from close to Restauradores Square up to the lookout terrace of São Pedro de Alcântara. Families, friends and couples were taking in the view and behind them was a kiosk café, full of people enjoying the sun.

Walking to the railings, I gazed out over the rooftops of Lisbon. On the hill opposite, the Castle of São Jorge with its crenellated walls and towers rose high above the Alfama, the oldest district of Lisbon, packed with winding narrow streets I had yet to explore. An assortment of terracotta roofs and white and pastel coloured buildings, dotted with patches of green, covered the space in between the hills and tumbled down to the waterfront. It was impossibly beautiful and, for a moment, I felt relatively content. I decided that the next day I would visit the castle and the Alfama. And after that? I told myself that surely by then Lou would have resurfaced and Mendes Silva would tell me that everything had been resolved and I was free to leave.

As I stood there gazing out over Lisbon allowing the sun to warm me through, I heard my phone buzzing. My first reaction was a combination of hope and alarm at the thought it might be the police, followed by the hope that it might be Nuno. I was surprised and dismayed by the disappointment I felt when I saw that it wasn't him.

'Hello Lou.' I said warily.

'Hello Isabel.'

'What's going on? Where are you?'

'We need to talk. I'll meet you at that tea shop near your hotel. I'll be there in twenty minutes.'

She hung up, leaving me to try to recall if I had ever told her where I was staying. I was fairly sure that was information I hadn't shared with her.

* * *

'You're late,' Lou said as I joined her at her table. Her hands were wrapped around a steaming cup of tea as though she was frozen to the core. Her previous composure had cracked, and there were deep purple smudges under her eyes.

'I wasn't nearby when you phoned. As I would have told you if you'd given me time to reply. How did you know which hotel I was staying in anyway?'

Lou gave me a look, which could have been anything from frustration to fear. 'It's very difficult to know where to begin. You must understand I had no idea at first.'

'Had no idea about what?'

'What she wanted me to do.'

By she, you mean Vanessa?'

'Of course,' Lou responded irritably.

'Do you plan to tell me?'

'Yes. Give me a chance.'

'Go on then.'

Lou shifted around in her seat. 'When she first came to me, I thought she was crazy. But Vanessa has a way about her. She is very good at working out what people need and giving it to them. For a price.'

I recalled how, the first time I had met her, Lou had described Vanessa as "capable". It hadn't sounded complimentary.

'So?' I prompted her.

'I needed money. I went to the bank and they wouldn't give me a loan so in desperation I did something I should never have done. I borrowed some money from a loan shark. The trouble with that is you can never pay it back. One stupid decision and I've paid for it ever since in more ways than one.'

She sipped her tea, and I felt the closest I would come to any sympathy for her.

Lou put the cup down and continued. 'I was getting deeper and deeper in debt. Stupidly, I confided in Vanessa or she got it out of me. I'm not entirely sure now which way round it was. But, anyway, she knew I needed money, and she offered to give it to me. Not to lend it to me; to give it to me. It was the answer to all my problems. Or so I thought at the time.'

'You must have been close if you talked about that.' As I said the words, I had an image of Carolina sitting opposite me in the hushed breakfast room at the hotel, whispering to me. *'She has a way of getting things out of people and then using that information to get what she wants.'* I also remembered what Carolina had told me about Lou and Vanessa becoming the best of friends, and Lou's mood suddenly improving. I heard Lou start to speak again and pulled my attention back to her.

'That's the thing. I only met her in April. But I was at my lowest ebb, and she was so kind and helpful. We just clicked, and I was grateful to her. I needed a shoulder to cry on.'

I found it hard to imagine Lou needing to cry on anyone's shoulder but let it pass. 'And then?'

'As I said, she offered me the money I needed to make the weekly payments. For the first couple of weeks there were no strings attached but then, when she gave me the next instalment, it turned out it was for a price. I had to do something for her. I wasn't very happy about it, but then I thought it seemed harmless enough.'

The silence hung between us. I told myself not to say anything and risk the delicate balance.

'She wanted me to go to the Algarve Welcome Point and follow you from there. She showed me photos of you. I felt like I knew your face as well as I know my own by the time she'd finished bombarding me with them. She said she knew more or less when you'd be there, what type of car you'd be driving, even the registration number, and that I should follow you.'

I recalled how Vanessa had casually asked me what type of car I'd hired, apparently concerned I'd chosen something suitable for the streets of Lisbon. She'd asked for the registration number so she could try to get me a permit, and

I had thought nothing of giving it to her. I'd even sent her a message to let her know when I was leaving Seville and another to tell her which town on the Algarve I would be staying in overnight. I'd inadvertently played into her hands and helped her to help Lou. As others had observed, but I had clearly missed, Vanessa was good at getting whatever she needed from others. Even so the Algarve Welcome Point was a busy place and there would have been no guarantee Lou would have seen me there.

'You could easily have missed me at the Welcome Point,' I observed.

'That's what I said to her, but she said I had to try. She said she had other things for me to do as well when I got back to Lisbon so she'd give me the next instalment as long as I agreed to go there and try to find you. She made it clear there would be no chance of any more payments unless I went. She also said that once I'd done everything, she'd pay off all my debts once and for all.'

'What type of car were you driving?'

'A green SUV.' She could hardly look at me.

'The one parked in your garage the first day I met you at your flat.'

'Yes.'

'The one you said you knew nothing about.'

'Yes.'

'I recall you told me to get a grip when I challenged you about that. You tried to make me feel like I was being completely irrational.'

'I couldn't exactly tell you the truth, could I?' Lou looked guilty and exasperated in equal measure.

'I saw you in Faro too, but I didn't see you follow me there from the Welcome Point.'

'I had some problems at the toll booth. I was there for a long time trying to sort it out, but Vanessa had told me Faro was where you were probably heading. I drove around Faro for ages before I saw you. It was pure luck I found you there at all.'

'And you were parked outside the hotel in Olhão?'

'Yes. When I was in Faro, Vanessa sent me a message to say you were going to spend the night in Olhão.'

I remembered sending Vanessa a message about going to Olhão when I was in the car park in Faro. She must have contacted Lou immediately to pass that information on.

Lou continued. 'The problem was she didn't know where in Olhão you were going to stay. Anyway, I started to follow you there, but there was a lot of traffic, and I lost you. Then once I got to Olhão, I stopped at the first hotel with parking and saw you'd done the same thing. I left before you the following morning. I didn't know if you'd picked up on being followed, and I didn't want to risk a confrontation at the hotel as I had no idea what I'd say or how you'd react. Vanessa said you could be … volatile.'

'Did she? I bet she said a lot of things.'

Lou carried on, ignoring my comment. 'I was pretty sure about the route you'd take to get to Lisbon from Olhão so I waited for you at that petrol station. If I hadn't seen you …' Lou shrugged. 'I followed you as far as Castro Verde.'

'Didn't Vanessa want you to follow me all the way to Lisbon?'

'She didn't explicitly say I had to follow you all the way and in fact she told me to stay away from my flat for a couple of days so I decided to have lunch with a friend in Castro Verde and stay there.'

'What I don't understand is why she wanted you to go all the way there and follow me at all. I told her I was going to Lisbon. She had no need to check up on me.'

'I didn't understand it either. I didn't understand much at all, but I quickly learned that questioning her about anything wasn't a good idea. Vanessa seems to be driven by some strange internal logic which never made any sense to me.' Lou paused, sipped her tea, and I saw the frown lines between her eyebrows deepen. 'I got the impression she wanted me to follow you to spook you so that you were already on edge when you arrived in Lisbon. If that worked, I suppose it suited her purposes and if it didn't, it wasn't the end of the world. The rest of her plans seemed designed to do the same. You know, rattle you. Psychological games. Weird as anything. But that's Vanessa.' Lou looked away.

A waitress appeared and Lou fell silent as I ordered a cup of tea. 'Were you at that viewpoint in Monsanto Park?' I asked once the waitress was a safe distance away.

'I drove past it a few times, yes. Vanessa arranged for me to pick up the car again so I could do that.'

'Did you take Vanessa there?'

'No.'

'Did you get out of the car at any point?'

'No.' Lou looked genuinely puzzled by the question. 'Why?'

'My tyres were punctured while I was there.' I spoke as evenly as possible, trying to gauge her reaction.

Lou clutched the cup closer to her as though the warmth provided her with some comfort. 'I don't know anything about that. I swear.'

'Let's say I believe you. What else did she get you to do?'

'She told me what to say when you showed up at my flat although you seeing the car in the garage certainly wasn't part of the plan. She arranged for that man to pick up the keys so early because she said you'd never make it to my flat at that time of day. It did confirm what she'd said to me about your behaviour, though. I suppose it made me trust her a bit more when you proved to be the way she had said you were.'

'Volatile?'

'Exactly.'

'Who was that man who picked the car up?'

'I don't know. Someone Vanessa organised. I just had to give him the keys. I was convinced he was going to turn up while you were at the flat.'

'That's why you were so keen to see me leave.'

'That and what I'd heard about your behaviour.'

I decided not to pursue that. 'What else did she get you to do?'

Lou examined her tea. 'She told me to suggest that you went to the police to offer your help with the enquiry into her disappearance. When you didn't go straight away, she told me to phone you again and push you to go. Make you feel as if it was your duty.'

'Wait a moment. She contacted you *after* she had gone missing?'

'Yes.'

'Why didn't the police know she'd called you?'

'You don't need ID to get a phone here.'

I thought about that for a moment and decided not to get sidetracked. 'And you didn't think, just perhaps, that it would have been a good idea to tell someone that she'd been in touch? You know, with a police investigation going on?' I could feel my indignation rising along with my voice although as I spoke, I was aware that I had also kept that information from the police when Vanessa had told me to meet her in Monsanto Park.

'Keep it down, will you? By then I knew I was into something worse than just doing a few strange things. You don't understand what it's like. You get into something and then you can't get out of it. And I still had to pay those people off. I was caught between Vanessa and her demands and the other lot and their demands. It wasn't much fun for me either.'

I found it hard to find much sympathy for Lou. She had helped to make the last two weeks of my life as stressful as possible. As I thought about what Lou had told me, I also began to realise just how thoroughly Vanessa must have planned everything although precisely what the purpose of all that planning amounted to still eluded me.

From my bag, I heard my phone ringing.

'Aren't you going to get that?' Lou asked.

We eyed each other across the table. I didn't want

anything to destroy the confessional mood Lou seemed to have found herself in, but I thought it might be the police calling so reluctantly I pulled the phone out of my bag. Nuno's name came up on the screen. I wanted to answer it, but it was not the moment. I let it go to voicemail. The waitress arrived with my tea, and I feared the continual interruptions might damage Lou's sudden desire to confide in me.

'Anything else?' I ventured, putting my phone on silent mode.

'She got me to leave that photo in your room.'

'That's how you knew where I was staying.' I paused. 'How did you get into my room?'

'I'm a licensed tour guide. I put the photo in an envelope, flashed the badge at reception and explained I had some lost property to return to Isabel Foster who had been on one of our tours. I said the hotel was on my way home. The receptionist said I could leave it with her, but Vanessa had been quite explicit – it had to be left in your room. I let her take it so I could see which pigeonhole she put it in. That's how I got your room number. Then I had to wait for her to take a break. I thought I was going to be there all day. As soon as she disappeared, I grabbed it and took it to your room. It wasn't difficult to get in, particularly when I offered the cleaner fifty euros to open the door.'

'Well you had money to burn by then, didn't you?' I observed, unsuccessfully keeping sarcasm out of my voice.

'I suppose I deserve that.' Lou said, releasing the cup and picking at her nails.

I tried to resume more calmly. 'All so simple.' I paused and looked out at the people passing by in the sunshine, apparently without a care in the world.

'Did you phone the hotel with a message for me?'

'No. What message?'

'It doesn't matter. Was it you who pushed me down the stairs?'

'What? Push you down the stairs? What stairs? No. I've never done anything violent. I wouldn't.' Lou sounded so indignant it was almost laughable in the face of everything she had been willing to do, but I found myself believing her.

'If you say so, but what I don't understand is why you are telling me all this now.'

'I called in sick.'

The change of track left me confused, but I decided to go along with her line of reasoning. 'The police told me someone called in sick *for* you. That's not quite the same.'

'You've spoken to them about me?' Lou looked shocked.

I ignored her obvious desire to know how that had come about and continued. 'They seemed to think I might know something about your whereabouts as well as Vanessa's disappearance.'

Lou massaged her forehead. 'I needed to get away from anywhere Vanessa could contact me for a few days. It was like she could reach into every corner of my life and my mind. I was exhausted by it. A friend Vanessa didn't know about, the one in Castro Verde, let me stay with her and phoned in sick for me. She said I'd lost my voice. It was a good excuse – you can't do a very effective tour if you can't speak, can you? Then I turned my phone off.'

'Both phones?' I asked before stopping to consider the consequences of revealing what I knew. I had made a promise to Carolina, and I owed it to her to keep it if I could.

'What? How do you know I have more than one phone?'

I scrambled for an answer which would protect Carolina. 'I assume you have two phones. One for work and one for home?'

'Oh, I see. Yes, both. It was the first time I'd had any peace since the whole thing with Vanessa had started.'

'And now?'

'Well, I realised I couldn't hide forever. There was work to think about, and I still owed the rest of that money. I turned my phone back on so I could call work to say when I'd be going back. I didn't get round to that because there were lots of missed calls from Vanessa. I started to feel that sense of panic again. I told myself to ignore them, but then she called while I was sitting there with the phone in my hand. It was almost like she knew I'd turned it on or something … and then she told me I didn't need to worry about anything anymore.'

'What did she mean by that?'

'She said it was over, and I could go back to my normal life. As long as I didn't say anything about what had happened between us, then that was the end of the matter. She said the final instalment plus a 'bonus', as she put it, would be in my bank account. She'd always given me cash before which was more convenient, but I wasn't about to complain. She's the last person I want to see. Anyway, the money was in my bank this morning, and I've finally paid my debts off.'

'So why are you telling me all this? Why not just keep quiet and get on with your life? You've happily done everything else she told you to do.'

Lou registered my tone of voice but ploughed on. 'Because I don't know if I believe her. What if she decides there's something else she wants me to do? What if it's something worse next time?'

'You could always say no.' I responded. 'You don't owe anyone any money now, I assume.'

'No. I've learned my lesson on that score, but it's not that simple.'

'Why isn't it?'

'At one point, I tried to push back even when I needed the money. It was just all too … creepy for me.'

'And?'

'She threatened me.' Lou said quietly.

'With what? Telling everyone you'd been desperate enough to borrow money from a loan shark? So what? People would gossip for a while, but they'd move on. Telling everyone what you'd done for her? That would only implicate her too. Surely nothing she could say amounts to enough for you to be beholden to her forever.'

'You really don't understand, do you?'

'Obviously not.'

'She threatened me physically.'

'Physically?' I searched my mind for any memories I had of Vanessa doing anything which suggested she could be violent. I could think of nothing but then, I reminded myself, I had missed a lot about her.

'Do you think she was serious?'

'Yes. I have no doubts about that. So, yes, I can go back to my normal life. I have to. But as I told you, I'm afraid of her. If something were to happen to me …'

'You'd like someone to make sure the police are pointed in the right direction?' I realised at that moment Lou really was all about herself.

'I can't hide forever, can I?' Lou repeated, searching my face. 'I just need some "insurance".'

'And that's what I am?' I continued to stare at her.

Lou broke eye contact first and nodded. 'I hope Vanessa has crawled back under whichever rock she emerged from. If I never see her again it'll be too soon. But I can't be sure.'

I was about to tell Lou that Vanessa had resurfaced in Tondela when I saw a way out of the predicament which Nuno and I were in. I wasn't proud of keeping the information about Vanessa from her, but I couldn't afford to stay in Lisbon indefinitely at the mercy of Mendes Silva's whims, and I saw even less reason why Nuno should have to suffer. Lou had already said she needed to come out of hiding. All I was going to do was give her a little push. I didn't want to risk Lou scuttling for cover again by mentioning Vanessa's reappearance.

'I'll make a deal with you,' I said.

'What's that?'

'If you phone the agency and the police right now, I promise the police will be pointed in Vanessa's direction. If it ever becomes necessary. If you don't, you're on your own. No "insurance".' I shrugged, trying to sound much more indifferent about Lou's decision than I felt.

'I have to phone the agency anyway but the police? What do you want me to say to them?'

'Phone the agency first. And put it on speaker phone. After all, Vanessa said you could go back to your normal life. Going along with that is probably the best thing you can do right now.'

I listened as Lou explained how sick she had been and apologised profusely. She could be quite charming when it suited her. She went on to stress she had fully recovered and was ready to get back to work. The man at the other end, who I took to be her boss, sounded relieved.

'I'll see you at nine-thirty tomorrow then to run through the programme,' he said.

I shook my head.

'Just a moment,' Lou said and, moving the phone away, hissed at me, 'What?'

'I pointed at my watch, held up four fingers and mouthed 'This afternoon'.

Lou looked exasperated. 'Could I come in this afternoon? At about four?'

'Yes, I suppose so. Actually that would be better for me.'

'Right, I'll see you later then,' Lou said and hung up. She placed the phone on the table. 'Happy?'

'So far. Now the police.'

'And what do you expect me to say to them?'

'Ask for an Inspector Mendes Silva and if he's not there,

find someone who can give him a message.'

'And then?'

'Say that I phoned you, and I mentioned that the police are concerned for your safety. Say you had no idea about that, you're fine and you're going back into work now. Tell them if they need to check on you, you'll be at the agency at four.'

'You seem very keen to get me back to work as soon as possible.'

'You've been off for a few days. You might as well get back into the swing of things as quickly as possible. After all, you wouldn't want to lose your job and end up with money problems again, would you?'

Lou shot me a look, one which I knew I deserved.

'And you can clear things up with the police too so they can close their file on you.'

'Conveniently for you. It still leaves you under suspicion for Vanessa's disappearance, though.'

'One thing at a time.' I said, avoiding a direct answer and pointing at the phone. 'On loudspeaker. In English.' I had no idea if Lou could speak Portuguese, but I wasn't going to take any chances that she might say something I wouldn't understand.

Lou phoned the police station and during the pause while she waited to be connected, I realised Vanessa's reappearance might come up, but I would have already got Lou to do what was necessary. I would just have to deal with her reaction.

I heard someone answer in English. Not Mendes Silva. I

would have recognised his smooth, insinuating tones immediately. I relaxed a little; speaking to another officer minimised the chances of Vanessa being mentioned. Lou followed the script I had given her to the word.

'Thank you for informing us,' I heard the officer say.

'You will be sure Inspector Mendes Silva gets my message, won't you?'

'Yes, of course.'

'Satisfied now?' Lou asked as she ended the call.

'I will be soon.' I glanced at my watch. 'Come on.'

'Where are we going?'

'To the agency. I'm not taking any chances that you might change your mind. I'm sick and tired of being suspected of things I haven't done.'

'You heard me say that I was going in. I don't need an escort to get me there,' Lou said, sounding tetchy.

'Well you're going to get one anyway.'

We walked to the agency in stony silence, and I saw a man wave through the window at her.

'Goodbye, Lou.'

'Wait a moment. There was one other thing Vanessa asked me to do during our last conversation.'

'What was that?' I asked.

'She wanted me to pass a message on to you.'

'Go on.'

Lou swallowed hard. 'To quote Vanessa, she said, "If you do what I say, it's over for you, Lou, but it's not over for Isabel. Far from it. Make sure she knows that."'

Chapter 14

All thoughts of more sightseeing and enjoying my remaining days in Lisbon had been abandoned. I retreated to my room to reassess the situation.

My first instinct, as it always had been, was to run. Far and fast. And now I could. But then other considerations started to creep in. I had promised Nuno I would meet him before I left, and I felt I owed him that much at least after everything he had done for me. I realised I wanted to see him although that in itself worried me. Then it also dawned on me that if I left Lisbon immediately, I would never know why Vanessa had behaved as she had and what she had meant by the message she had given Lou. I wasn't sure if I wanted to know or not, but I could at least say my goodbyes to Nuno while I was mulling it over.

My phone rang, and I saw Mendes Silva's name come up.

'Hello?'

'Hello, Miss Foster. We have established Lou Johnson's whereabouts and confirmed she is safe and well although I understand you are aware of that. I gather you spoke to her and asked her to contact us.'

'Yes.'

'How did that come about?'

'I kept phoning her and eventually she answered. She'd lost her voice apparently. That's why she couldn't go to work.'

'It was fortunate for you that you were able to contact her.'

'I suppose so.' I hated speaking to him. I always felt he was looking for an angle which would incriminate me.

'You will no doubt be pleased to know you are no longer required to stay in Portugal. Both you and Mr. Ferreira da Costa are free to go about your business without any restrictions. We will of course be contacting him as well to let him know. No doubt, though, you will be in touch with him shortly to tell him the good news.'

I refused to engage with him. 'Thank you.'

'Goodbye, Miss Foster.'

I phoned Nuno, wanting to be the one to tell him the news. I was more pleased to hear his voice than I cared to admit and touched by the fact he sounded happy to hear from me as well.

'I'll admit I'm relieved,' Nuno said.

'I know. I feel so much better too.' And although that was true as far as Mendes Silva was concerned, Vanessa's message was still playing on my mind. I paused, unsure what to say next.

'I tried to call you earlier. I was wondering if you were free this evening.'

'Yes.'

'Would you like to go out? We can finally spend some time together without all those worries about Vanessa and Lou hanging over us.'

An image of Lou relaying Vanessa's words came to me, but I didn't want to inflict another round of my worries on Nuno. 'We might not have anything to talk about.' I said it as a joke and hated how awkward I sounded.

'I doubt it. How about I pick you up at seven?'

'Sounds good,' I said as lightly as I could, thinking about the fact that the evening would bring another farewell; one that I knew would be harder than most.

As I was about to go for a shower, the phone rang. I didn't recognise the number but answered it anyway.

'Hello?'

'Isabel.'

'Vanessa? What do you want?'

'I don't have time to explain now.'

'I think you should make ti–'

'Woolacombe Sands.'

'Vanessa's words cleared my head of any other thoughts. 'What did you say?'

'You heard. I'll be at Praia do Guincho at eight-thirty tonight. Don't be late.' The phone went dead. Woolacombe Sands; a connection to a past I was always trying to outrun. And in the time I had been in Portugal I had picked up a few words of Portuguese. Praia was Portuguese for beach.

* * *

I called Nuno. 'I'm sorry. I can't meet you tonight after all.'

'Has something happened?'

I hesitated. 'Yes.'

I suppose that Nuno must have picked up on the anxiety in my voice because I heard him say, 'What's the matter, Isabel?'

I wanted to lie, partly to avoid dragging him back into whatever Vanessa was planning and partly because the words Woolacombe Sands were seared in my mind, and I didn't want him or our friendship to be sullied by association with that. Despite that, I could think of no plausible alternative to the truth. 'I have to see Vanessa.'

'Vanessa? I thought all that was over.'

'So did I, but she just called me, and she wants to see me this evening.'

'It's going to be another game, Isabel. Another pointless pursuit. You know that, don't you?'

The echo of Vanessa saying the words *Woolacombe Sands* rang in my head, and I wasn't so sure. 'I think this is different.'

'Why? What hold does she have over you?'

'I'm really sorry; I can't explain now, Nuno. But I have to go and see her tonight. I'll catch up with you tomorrow, I promise.'

'Where does she want to meet you?'

'Some beach. It's called Praia do Guincho.'

'I know it.'

'Where is it?'

'It's out past Cascais. It would take about half an hour to drive there.'

'OK, thanks.'

'I take it you're going? I can't change your mind?'

'No, you can't. I have to go.'

Nuno sighed. 'It's your decision but think about it, Isabel. Lou's flat, that café in Chiado, Monsanto, Tondela, Praia do Guincho. There's a pattern here. She sends you running off all over the place and then disappears, leaving you wondering what the hell is going on.'

'There's no point in getting angry.'

'I'm not angry with you. I'm angry with her, and I'm worried about you.'

'I'm worried too,' I admitted. 'But I'm going anyway.'

'Then let me go with you. Vanessa gives me a bad feeling.'

The thought that Nuno might hear whatever Vanessa might have to say about Woolacombe Sands was too much to bear. 'No, I need to go alone. I'll be in touch tomorrow. Bye.' I ended the call before Nuno could protest further and weaken my resolve.

I headed down to the car park, pulled out of the hotel and cautiously negotiated the Marquês de Pombal roundabout again. No horns blared at me that time and then I was back on the IC15. I remembered the last time I had driven that route to go to Monsanto Park. This time, though, I didn't have to turn off anywhere. Crossing the whole width of the park now as the shadows lengthened, knowing I was heading for the coast, for a beach where Vanessa would finally meet me, was as unnerving as it suddenly seemed inevitable.

I realised there were potential dangers in going through with the meeting. Both Lou and Carolina were clearly afraid of her, but the need to know why she had planned all those things overrode the sensible options of not going or going with Nuno. That was the hold she had over me now – the need to know. Besides, I had a feeling I would never get any peace until there had been a final showdown and the situation had been resolved once and for all. In an hour or so, I would finally find out what she wanted from me. It was one of those fork-in-the-road moments, and I could only hope I had chosen the right road.

The IC15 finally petered out and turned into a road with one lane on either side, running through small towns. Beyond my car, the world seemed so normal; people out for a walk, chatting with their friends, walking their dogs, carrying bags of shopping. I craved some of that normality. The surroundings became ever more rural, and I drove on for miles, not seeing a soul. I thought I had taken a wrong turn somewhere but as I crested a hill and arrived at the next junction, I finally saw the sand dunes and, in the distance, the sea. I was getting close.

I took the road which would lead me down to the coast. The sand ran up to the side of the road as though the beach could no longer be contained. I turned off and parked in the car park of a small hotel as far from both the hotel and the beach as possible.

Walking around the hotel and over to the entrance to the beach, the smell and sound of the sea hit me as the Atlantic air whirled around and the waves broke on the shore. I could feel panic rising like bile in my throat and burning. I remembered long ago the sea rushing into my throat and burning too. I had never set foot on a beach since that day with Finn. I wasn't sure I could do it for all that I needed to know what it was Vanessa wanted to tell me. I glanced back to where I had parked, but the car was out of sight now. Go back or go forward; it was impossible to know which was right.

Buffeted by the wind, I took a few more tentative steps. I was still on tarmac even though it was sprinkled with sand. In another few steps the paved road beneath my feet would finally disappear, surrendering to nature. I closed my eyes and tried to find some courage. I told myself that I would not have to go into the water and the sand couldn't hurt me. I removed my sandals, took another step and felt the sand give beneath my feet, enveloping them in damp coldness as my feet sank deeper.

Despite my fear and the biting chill of the wind, I forced myself to keep going. The dunes reminded me of those at Woolacombe and for a moment, I was clambering up them again with Finn on a calm, clear morning, bickering good naturedly about whose turn it was to carry the picnic basket. I came to a stop at the top of the dunes, from where I could see the whole sweep of the beach and the Sintra hills beyond, framing the bay. I turned, almost expecting to hear Finn saying 'Well, we made it.' But of course she was not there. The wind was picking up even more, and the beach was almost deserted, but I knew that somewhere down there was Vanessa.

My phone rang. With the howling of the wind, I felt it vibrate rather than heard it. 'Yes?' I shouted into it.

'I can see you up there. Come down here.'

'Where are you?' I yelled, scanning the beach again.

'Don't worry about that. I'll find you.'

I continued through the dunes, slipping and sliding in the soft sand and then emerged out onto the beach on level ground again. I looked around me, not caring to go anywhere close to the water. And then I saw her. For a moment, I felt obscurely pleased. Then I thought of everything she had put me through, and I felt something closer to pure anger. She was standing at the exact point where the waves were breaking, leaving the sand wet and compact in its wake. She beckoned to me, but I shook my head.

'Come here,' I heard her say faintly although she must have been shouting to make herself heard over the waves and wind.

'Why don't you come here?' I called back.

She cupped her hand behind her ear and shrugged her shoulders before motioning for me to move closer once more.

The wind howled around the beach, depriving me of hearing. I scrunched my eyes up to protect them from the sand. One by one my senses were being stripped away. A sense which was still intact was the one I wished would desert me – that of feeling; the sand stung my skin like a million tiny needles being pushed into it.

Determined to put an end to her games once and for all,

I forced myself to approach her. I pulled up a short distance from where she stood. Close enough to be able to speak without shouting but not too close to the water. I watched it swirl around her feet and then pull away, and I shuddered.

'Good to see you again. It's been a while.'

'Why are we here, Vanessa?'

'You seem rather ill at ease, Isabel. Any particular reason?'

'You know I don't like the water. I told you …'

'Oh yes. The swimming pool; getting pulled under as a child. Quite a plausible story. Except that's not the real reason you don't like it, is it?'

'Get to the point, Vanessa.' As I spoke, another gust of wind drove more sand into my skin and my hair into my eyes. Instinctively, I closed them and when I opened them again, Vanessa had gone. I looked around, wondering if I had only imagined she was there. Vanessa appeared from behind me; she had been circling round me, leaving me feeling like her prey.

'Let me take you back. Ten years ago. Woolacombe Sands, Devon. Ring any bells?'

I had known from the moment she had uttered those words on the phone that something such as this had to be coming, but I found myself as unprepared as if I had had no idea.

'Nothing to say?' Vanessa asked, stopping to pick up a pebble, examine it and toss it out to sea. 'That's not surprising really. After all, how do you explain killing someone?'

'Kill? No. No, I didn't kill anyone.'

'Two of you went into the water, but only you came out alive.'

I was on the verge of tears. Since that night in the hotel on the way back from Finn's funeral, I could count on one hand the number of times I had cried, and I didn't want Vanessa to see how deeply her words had affected me. I heard the mournful call of the gulls as they wheeled overhead. A lone kite surfer tracked through the sky, his vivid red kite reminding me of the young boy flying his kite all those years ago. There was the same vast tract of sand backed by dunes; the same Atlantic waves. Woolacombe Sands. Praia do Guincho. Past and present were colliding in a hazy mist, leaving me dizzy and disorientated. Vanessa had chosen her spot well, whatever her reasons might have been.

'Only you came out alive. Isn't that right?' Vanessa walked up to me and grabbed me by the arm.

'Yes,' I whispered.

'Say it.'

'Say what?'

'Admit what you did to her.'

'I didn't do anything. I suggested that we went for a swim, that's true. But I never dreamed ...' I shook my head.

'So you killed her through sheer stupidity and recklessness. If you hadn't suggested going for a swim, she would still be alive.'

'Don't you think I know that?' I heard myself yelling despite her proximity. 'Don't you think I've thought about it every day since and wished I could turn back time? Who the hell are you to tell me that?'

'Who the hell am I? You mean you haven't worked it out yet? I thought you were a bit brighter than that.'

'Well clearly I'm not so why don't you tell me?'

'Ask yourself who would care enough to plan everything you've been through in the last few weeks? Who would want to make you suffer?'

I looked around, searching for an answer but came up with nothing.

Vanessa walked into the water. It was now around her ankles rather than washing over her toes. 'Still no idea?'

I shook my head and watched as Vanessa waded deeper into the water. It was now around her knees and her dress was soaked through and clinging to her legs. 'Come on, Isabel. Come a bit closer. I can't hear you from over there.'

'I didn't say anything,' I replied but edged a little closer. I had to know the truth even if it was only her version of the truth.

The water was at Vanessa's waist. 'I'm not a very good swimmer,' she shouted.

I thought back to my teens and early twenties. I had been a strong swimmer, which coupled with my youth, had been a dangerous combination. The perceived invincibility of young people had a lot to answer for, and the follies it could lead you to could never be forgotten or forgiven.

'If you come out, I'll tell you everything,' I said although there was not much to know. Finn and I had gone to the beach, I had suggested a swim, and we had got into difficulties. I had survived; Finn hadn't. But if I could only get Vanessa out of the water, I could deal with what to say next. 'Please come out.'

'No, I don't think so.'

'Well at least don't go any further in. It's not safe to swim here. It's too rough and too cold.'

Vanessa's laughter reached me before the wind whipped it away. She started to wade towards me, and I was filled with relief. She stopped short of getting out of the water, but it was a start. 'Come in.' It was an order rather than an invitation.

I watched the sea swirl around her knees. 'You know I can't.'

'What's more important, Isabel? Knowing how I know about Woolacombe or not coming in?'

She had me, and she knew it. My legs felt so heavy I thought I would not be able to move them, but I found myself standing ankle deep in the water, the chill biting into me. The water washing around my legs made me feel queasy. 'Satisfied?'

'For now.'

'You planned all of this to punish me, didn't you? Why Vanessa?'

'Perhaps you should start by not calling me Vanessa.'

'What are you talking about?'

'Perhaps you should call me by my original name.'

'You're not making any sense.'

'But I am.' She waded closer to me and grabbed my wrist. 'Why don't you call me Caitlin?'

A multitude of emotions and memories filled not only my mind but my body. Caitlin, Finn's moody Gothic sister. The shadowy figure of a fourteen year old bent over a coffin.

Caitlin would be twenty-four now, a few years younger than Vanessa had told me she was, but clearly she thought nothing of lying. Even allowing for the changes wrought by time, she looked nothing like her. Her hair was long and fair, not spiky or cut in jagged layers or dyed purple or jet black. Vanessa's eyes were pale blue, but all I remembered of Caitlin's eyes were two smudges of black in a pale face. There was nothing about her appearance or bearing which was suggestive of Caitlin. The ages didn't tie up either yet somehow I knew that for once she was not lying to me.

'Caitlin,' I said slowly as if trying out a word in a foreign language for the first time, unsure how it would sound.

'Yes.'

'How did you find me?'

'When I first tried, I just met dead ends. I went to the address Finn had for you, but you'd gone, and you hadn't left a forwarding one. Not surprising; I wouldn't have either. After a while I gave up, and I tried to get on with my own life. But, you see, I never really had my own life.'

'What do you mean?'

'All I heard growing up was how amazing Finn was. What a tragedy losing her was. Like I didn't know that. But in all that, I got lost. You took Finn. And you took my teenage years too.'

'I –'

'I haven't finished. I became Finn's poor substitute. I went to the same university, did the same degree. I thought if I could become her, my mother would stop resenting me. I tried my hand at a few jobs back in England, but I still wasn't good enough so then I went on to do what Finn had wanted to do but didn't get a chance to. I went abroad to teach English.'

'You expect me to believe you just happened to turn up at the school I was working at in Poland?'

'No, of course not. I taught in Finland for a year. Helsinki. I only went there because that was where Finn had wanted to go.'

I had a flashback to the conversations Finn and I had had about where we would like to teach and remembered her telling me she wanted to go to Helsinki. I recalled her rolling onto her back on the grass, staring up at the sky and saying 'Finn in Finland. I like the sound of that. And think of all those gorgeous men.' She laughed; that infectious laugh I missed so much. Teaching English had been more my dream but teaching in Finland had been Finn's. The reason I had never even contemplated going there was because Finn had not had the chance to go.

Caitlin was speaking again. 'In the spring before I started at the school in Gdansk there was that big English conference in Riga. "Teaching English in the Baltic Region" it was called. Do you remember it?'

I remembered it all too clearly. I had been dragged along, having failed to come up with a suitably pressing reason for not being able to attend. I had always hated events like that and even an expenses-paid trip to Riga hadn't made the prospect of three days of lectures and socialising seem more enticing. I had managed to wriggle out of similar events before, but the director of the school had made it clear that one wasn't optional. Subsequently, I had spent the time between talks trying to avoid the interminable opportunities to mingle, which everyone else seemed to enjoy so much.

'I saw you there. I recognised you immediately.' She looked appraisingly at me. 'You hadn't changed that much you know.'

'Unlike you.'

Caitlin tilted her head in acknowledgement of the point. And then?' I asked.

'And then all the feelings I had been trying to suppress about you came back; the anger, the resentment. Everyone was wearing those stupid name tags so it was easy to find out which school you worked at. I tracked down the Director of Studies and was pretty much hired on the spot. I can be quite persuasive.'

'But the director of the school must have known your name wasn't really Vanessa Taylor.'

'I changed my name by deed poll a while back. I thought a fresh start might help. Everything is in the name of Vanessa Taylor. To all intents and purposes Caitlin Williams is long dead and gone.' She laughed bitterly. 'Just like her sister.'

'But where did you get an Irish passport? Finn had a British one.'

'Haven't you heard? If you have an Irish grandparent, you can become an Irish citizen and get a passport. It's become quite a thing.'

'What happened to Suzanna?'

'She fared better than me. At some point my mother realised she couldn't go on as she had been. She went to therapy, she got better. Well, better than she had been, and she didn't make as many mistakes with Suzie as she had with me.'

'And your father?'

'He walked out. Parents often split up after the death of one of their children. You can add that to your list of successes.'

'So all this has been for revenge?'

'Of course. I made a point of befriending you. The strange thing is I think I would have liked you in another life. As it was I hated you.'

'You hated me all along?'

'Yes.' Caitlin said it as though it was the most natural thing in the world.

'Then why did you agree to go to Seville with me? Why didn't you have it out with me in Gdansk or at that conference come to that? Why go through all this?'

'Because I needed to time to plan, and I needed to gain your trust. I could see that was going to take time. You were quite a tough nut to crack.' She sounded as though she grudgingly admired the fact.

'And the row we had before you left Seville?'

Caitlin waved her hand as if batting it away. 'About the job? It was a pretext.'

'You never wanted it?'

'I couldn't have cared less about the stupid job. And why would they have given it to the most junior teacher there anyway?'

'And Javier?'

'I could see he liked you before you could. I flirted with him, but that was all. I really wasn't interested in him. I was just playing.'

'Is that when you got the photo of the two of you? When you were "playing"?'

'Yes. I got him to take it and forward it to me because I thought it might be useful. I just wasn't sure how at the time.'

'I know about all the things you got Lou to do,' I said, neglecting to think about the position I might be putting Lou in by telling her that.

'She's been blabbing, has she?'

'It was you who phoned the hotel and left that message for me about not bothering to move to another hotel, wasn't it?'

'Yes.'

'How did you know I'd be looking for a new hotel after Lou left that photo of us in my room? Were you following me?'

'No, that would have been far too risky. A missing person has to be seen to be missing, so to speak.'

Her mocking tone infuriated me. 'So, how did you know?' I repeated.

'Because I know who you are, Isabel. I know what you are. When it all gets too much, you run. I knew the photo would send you dashing off looking for a new place to stay, a way to escape.'

Her words hurt because I knew they were true, but I was determined to keep going. 'When did you plan all this?' I said, waving an arm around me.

'It was quite time consuming. I started kicking ideas around in Poland, but I just couldn't get the plan straight. When I came here at Christmas it all started to come together.'

'You came here? I thought you went back to England to see your family. You told me how great it had been to see your brother again. Except you don't have a brother, do you? You told me so many lies.'

Caitlin laughed. 'I certainly did, and you believed every single one. I had to be careful of course not to let you see my passport. You'd have seen I'd lied about my age, and that could have been tricky.'

Ignoring that, I moved on. 'What was all that about at that café in Chiado? Why did you want me to go there?'

'I wanted to see you to gauge how you were.'

'And sending me off to Monsanto Park?'

Caitlin shrugged. 'It was all part of making your life miserable.'

'Was it you who slashed my tyres there?'

'Guilty as charged,' she said, as if confessing to nothing worse than having returned a library book a day late.

'And I suppose it was you who pushed me down the stairs at Lou's?'

'It was. I thought I'd be stuck there all night if I didn't get you out of the way. I was worried I'd killed you for a moment. I ended up having to go to the hospital to check up on you. That was very inconvenient.'

'So that wasn't a dream? You really were there?' I was

speaking to myself more than Caitlin and felt the tension inside me ease a fraction. If Caitlin hadn't wanted to kill me then and had gone as far as going to the hospital to check on me, she couldn't be planning anything too drastic now. She had just wanted to put me through a bad time and finally confront me in a place where she knew I would be out of my comfort zone. Once she had unburdened herself, we would both move on, albeit in very different directions, never to meet again.

She started to speak again, ignoring my questions. 'Killing you would certainly have messed up my plan.'

'What do you mean?'

'I mean we had – we still have – unfinished business.'

My frustration boiled over. 'It's more like you have unfinished business with the police. I don't know how many offences you've committed, but it must be a fair few.'

'Really? Name one.'

'Criminal damage, pushing me –'

'I mean one that someone could prove I've committed.'

I thought about everything she had done. I couldn't prove she had slashed my tyres or pushed me down the stairs. The only other possibility I could think of was a charge of wasting police time, trivial in comparison, and Mendes Silva had made it clear the police would not be pursuing that.

'I'm not a legal expert,' I responded, irritated that nothing Vanessa did seemed to have any repercussions for her; only for those around her.

'Well it doesn't matter now anyway.'

A fatalistic tone, which disturbed me, had entered her

voice. 'Why doesn't it matter?' I asked.

'Because I've done what I set out to do. I wanted to make your life as miserable as mine has been. As miserable as you made it. I wanted you to know what it's like to suffer, and I've made you think about Finn's death and –'

'How dare you say that? I think about her every day. About what happened. I miss her every day. I feel guilty every day. I suffer every day. I didn't need you to come along to be reminded of her.'

'And,' Caitlin continued as if I hadn't spoken. 'I wanted you to know that you didn't just destroy Finn's chance to have a life. You destroyed my life too. And my parents' lives.'

'So now what?'

'Planning all this was the only time I felt better. I had a goal, and it kept me going. But now I realise there's only one way to end it.'

'What do you mean?'

'I've had enough now. Enough of everything.' She started wading out into deeper water. I heard a sharp intake of breath as it reached her chest, and then she turned back to look at me. 'I meant what I said,' she called out. 'I'm not a good swimmer.'

'Come back to shore. We can talk. We'll sort this out.' My previous frustration and anger had vanished, and all I felt at that moment was an overriding desire not to see any more tragedy play out.

'No, I don't think so.'

'If you want me to beg, I will.'

She gave me a look akin to disgust and then turned away

and moved deeper into the water, leaving only her head visible. A wave washed over her and she disappeared from sight. I saw her head reappear a moment later and felt relief flow through me. I yelled her name at the top of my voice, but it was no match for the wind and waves, and I knew it wouldn't carry far enough for her to hear me.

The colour was draining from the sky, and it was growing colder. The force of the wind and surf were punishing the beach, and in a moment it would be too late. I dropped my bag and sandals on the sand, knowing what I was going to have to make myself do. I was shivering before the water had even reached my knees. I waded deeper and felt the weight of the water sink into my shorts and T-shirt. I gasped as the waves hit my chest and then my face. I didn't believe I could do it, but I knew I couldn't turn back either.

I was lifted off my feet by the next wave and forced to start swimming. I reached Caitlin and grabbed her from behind just as another wave cascaded over us. Having taken hold of her from behind, I should have had the advantage. Theory again. She was strong and determined to fight me. And her other advantage was that she seemed to want to drown. She flung her arm out of the water and caught me a glancing blow across my face. I fought to stay conscious and afloat and started to tow her towards the shore. She was not going to be rescued without a battle though, and I felt her grab at my hand and bite it, causing searing pain which shot up my arm. I wished at that moment that I could have knocked her out as she would have been easier to manoeuvre that way.

We seemed to have been in the water for an eternity. Still I persisted, convinced that we could not be far from safety by that point. I was as determined to save her as she was determined not to be saved. She threw her arm back and hit me again. A much better shot the second time, and I blacked out.

I was back on the beach. Someone was kneeling over me. At first, I thought I was in Woolacombe, but there it had been daylight and now it was dark and there was only one person there instead of all the concerned onlookers who had crowded around me in Devon. 'Where is she?' I asked. I saw stars overhead, stretching into infinity, and then I remembered no more.

Chapter 15

The first thing I recalled clearly after that was the jerky movements of being taken out of an ambulance on a stretcher and then being wheeled into a hospital. From my perspective, all I could see was a white ceiling, blinding white strip lights and odd snippets of people's bodies: a forearm here, someone's elbow there, a glimpse of part of someone's face. I could hear people talking, but I couldn't understand what they were saying and, in any case, I sensed they were talking about me, not to me. I wanted to talk, to ask questions, but unlike my last trip to the hospital in Lisbon, the willingness to relinquish control and let other people take charge of my fate proved to be irresistible, and I gave into it without a fight. Time passed, which could have been minutes or hours, and then I fell asleep.

When I woke up, I stared up at the ceiling for a while as I tried to piece everything together. I wondered where I was and if at some point someone would come to find me and tell me what was going on. My head was pounding, and I saw that my hand was lightly bandaged. Then I heard a voice nearby.

'Hi.'

I slowly turned my head and saw Nuno sitting in a plastic chair, wrapped in a foil blanket. I felt surprise, relief, confusion and a multitude of other emotions, yet I could not express any of them.

'Hi.' I looked around the featureless, windowless room which gave no clue as to our location or the time. 'Where are we?'

'Cascais hospital.'

'What time is it?'

Nuno checked his watch. 'Getting on for eleven-thirty.'

'Morning or night?'

'Night.'

'Why are you here?'

'There was no way I was going to leave you here on your own.'

It wasn't what I had meant, but the fog was starting to lift, and I remembered being on the beach.

'Where's Vanessa?' I used the name out of habit, and it crossed my mind that I should have called her Caitlin, but then Nuno wouldn't have known who I was talking about.

'She's here too.'

I looked at Nuno in alarm. 'She's not … I mean, she's still alive, isn't she?'

'Yes. She's getting the best care possible. They think she'll be fine, but she won't be leaving just yet. She's in intensive care, but they have given her a ninety-six percent chance of a full recovery.'

'I have to see her.' I tried to get up but my body protested more than Nuno, and I sank bank into the pillows.

I gazed up at the ceiling again. 'It's my fault she's here.'

'No, it's not. You saved her life, Isabel.'

I looked back at Nuno. 'What do you mean?'

'Don't you remember going into the water to save her?'

Further fragments of memory started to return and coalesce: watching Caitlin go ever deeper into the water as I called out to her, urging her to return to the shore. I remembered the dawning horror; the realisation I would somehow have to go in to try to save her; the water washing around and over us; the biting cold; the terrifying force of the Atlantic; Caitlin fighting to make me to let go of her.

'Yes. I didn't think I could … How do you know what happened? How is it that you're here?'

'I drove out to the beach. You told me not to, and I wasn't going to, but then I had such a bad feeling about the whole thing, I couldn't stop myself. When I arrived I saw you pleading with her to get out of the water, and I saw Vanessa refusing and going further in. I mean, I couldn't hear either of you; I was too far away, but it was clear from your body language that was more or less what was going on.

'I didn't want to interfere, but then she went further out and disappeared under the water, and you went in after her. That was when I started running down to the beach to get to where you were. When I reached you, you were trying to get her back to shore, but she kept fighting you, and you passed out. I helped you with the last part, but you had already done the hard work.'

'I wondered why you had that blanket around you. You're not hurt, are you?'

'Not at all. Just cold.'

'You don't have to stay, you know. In fact, I think you'd be better off staying well away from me. I seem to be very good at getting you into trouble.'

Nuno smiled. 'Thanks, but I think I'll stick around. There is one thing, though,' he said.

'What's that?'

'When you're feeling stronger, will you tell me everything?'

'Yes,' I replied and, with that, I felt my eyes closing.

* * *

When I awoke again, Nuno was still there. I found his presence comforting, and I felt safe despite my hatred of hospitals.

'Nuno, I need to tell you something.' I risked sitting up again and found the movement easier than I had done before.

Nuno pulled his chair closer to the bed, the foil blanket rustling and unfurling as he moved. He pulled it back around him. 'What is it?'

'It's a long story, and I'll explain it all later, but there are some things you need to know now.'

'OK. Go on.'

'Vanessa's real name is Caitlin, and she's Finn's sister.'

'Finn?' It took him a moment to recall our one and only conversation about her. 'Finn?' he repeated once he had registered the significance of the name.

'Yes.'

'And you didn't know who Vanessa, I mean Caitlin, really was?'

'No. I had absolutely no idea. Not until earlier on the beach. Between when I saw her as a teenager and meeting her as Vanessa a couple of years ago, eight years had passed. To say she'd changed her appearance in that time would be an understatement.'

'But why has she been going by a different name? And why did she do all those things?'

I fell quiet. Telling Nuno the whole story would expose me for who I was and what I had done. 'I will tell you the whole story,' I said prevaricating, 'but at the moment the crucial thing is she shouldn't be here alone.'

'You're here.'

'Believe me, I'm the last person she wants to see. We have to try and get in touch with her family.' I remembered what her parents were like; neither seemed a good choice. Suzanna, her sister, would probably have been a more approachable option, but at fourteen, she was also an impossible one. Jennifer or Robert it would have to be.

I propped myself up more and looked around the room. 'Where's my phone?'

Nuno got up and retrieved a bag from a table in the far corner. 'You dropped your bag on the beach before you went in after her. I guess it's in here.'

He passed the bag to me, and I found my phone and scrolled down to Finn's name. I had never been able to bring myself to delete the entries; it would somehow have been like turning my back on her. Delete and move on. I had two entries: Finn mobile and Finn home, her parents' number. Whether either Jennifer or Robert still lived there, I had no idea, but I had nothing else to go on.

My finger hovered over the number. I wondered what the people at the other end would think when they heard the phone ring. A phone call that late at night would seldom be the herald of good news, but the thought of not contacting them as soon as possible was unthinkable.

I tried to block out the things Jennifer had said to me the last time we had met and find the courage to make the call. I tapped the number and heard the phone ringing. Feeling physically sick, half of me hoped a complete stranger who had never heard of the Williams family would answer.

'Hello?' Jennifer's voice echoed down the line, as clipped and distinctive as ever.

'Hello. Is that Jennifer Williams?' I asked to give myself a moment to collect myself. I already knew the answer.

'Yes. Who's calling?'

Concerned she would put the phone down if I told her, I ignored the question and kept talking. 'I'm calling from Cascais Hospital in Portugal, but I don't want you to panic. Caitlin is here. She's been involved in an accident and although we expect her to make a full recovery, we feel she should have someone from her family here with her.'

While I had been speaking, I had heard something which could have been a gasp or a sob at the other end of the line. 'What type of accident?'

It was the other question I had been dreading; she had already lost one daughter to the sea. I reminded myself she didn't know who she was talking to and was unlikely to start screaming at me down the phone. 'She got into difficulty in the sea. Fortunately, someone was able to help her. They, that is, we, admitted her and she's now in intensive care, but the recovery rate is ninety-six percent for someone in her condition, and she's young and fit so there is every reason to be optimistic.'

I heard a man's voice in the background and Jennifer's reply. 'It's a hospital in Portugal, Robert. Caitlin's there.' I could hear no more of what she said to him. I had noticed the fact she had called the man Robert yet Caitlin had told me they had divorced and she held me responsible for that as well. I wondered if that had been another lie.

'That was my husband. We'll be on the next flight over.'

Her husband. Her husband, Robert. A stab of anger went through me at being blamed for a divorce which had not happened.

'I think that would be advisable. Please try not to worry in the meantime, though. She is in very good hands.'

'Thank you. What's your name, by the way?'

I desperately searched for a Portuguese surname. I wasn't about to use Nuno's. I thought of Mendes Silva. 'Doctor Silva.' I said.

'Thank you, Doctor Silva. We'll be there as soon as possible, but would you please let us know if there is any change in her condition in the meantime?' Without waiting for confirmation, she gave me her mobile number, which I repeated back to her while I wrote it on a scrap of paper I had grabbed from my bag.

She saved me the trouble of saying whether it would be possible to contact her or not by hanging up.

'I need to speak to one of the nurses or doctors,' I said to Nuno. 'Could you find someone and translate for me if necessary?'

Nuno nodded and left the room. He returned with a nurse and, through Nuno, I explained that Caitlin's parents were flying over from the UK. I gave them the torn piece of paper with Jennifer's phone number on it.

I glanced from the nurse to Nuno and back again. 'Could I see Caitlin?'

A further conversation took place, and then Nuno translated for me again. 'The nurse said she's sedated so you won't be able to talk to her.'

'I just need a moment with her. Please?'

I heard Nuno speak, and then the nurse nodded. I slowly got out of bed and felt the world spin. The nurse motioned at me to stay still and disappeared, returning a moment later with a wheelchair. Reluctantly, I accepted it, and she wheeled me to the intensive care unit, Nuno following by my side. As we arrived, the nurse stopped and said something to Nuno.

'She said ICU can be frightening for visitors, but Caitlin is stable. And only one of us can go in.'

I looked up at Nuno and hesitated, but he squeezed my hand. 'Go in, Isabel. I'll wait here.'

The nurse took me into the unit and wheeled me up to Caitlin's bed. She made a gesture, which I took to mean I wasn't allowed to touch Caitlin, and held up one finger and tapped her wrist. She was not wearing a watch, but I understood the gesture was a reminder that the clock was ticking on my visit. She backed away, but I sensed she was watching me from a distance.

Now I was there I didn't know what to do or say. I felt helpless, adrift in a world of whirring and clicking machinery which was completely alien to me. Caitlin finally looked peaceful, which was the only scant consolation I could draw from the situation.

Slowly, I got to my feet. I leaned over, getting as close as I could to Caitlin without touching her. 'I'm so sorry,' I whispered and with that the nurse approached me, eased me back into the wheelchair and took me out of the unit. Nuno prepared to wheel me back to the room, but I got out of the wheelchair. 'I'm going to walk.'

'You don't have to.'

'Yes, I do.'

'At least take my arm then.'

In the room, Nuno tried to get me to go back to bed.

'No, I don't want to stay here any longer, Nuno.'

'I think you should so they can keep an eye on you.'

'Please.' I looked at him, desperate for him to agree. 'I hate being here. I'd feel much better in a hotel.'

Nuno sighed and disappeared again. He reappeared with a doctor, who asked Nuno something. A discussion followed, and I wished I could understand even half of what they were saying.

'The doctor is going to check you over and then if he's happy, we can leave,' Nuno said and left the room again.

I let the doctor run various checks on me, and he asked me a few questions, which I was able to answer truthfully. I wasn't sure whether I would have lied if it had been necessary, but I suspected I might have done just to get out of there. Finally, he seemed satisfied and muttered 'OK' before leaving the room.

Nuno came back in and before long we were given the hospital's blessing to leave, by which time it was around two in the morning. Nuno had not asked me any further questions and for that I was grateful. I wasn't sure if I would have been able to show as much restraint if the roles had been reversed. We stood outside, the warm air wrapping itself around us. 'What now?' I asked.

'I thought we could get a taxi back to the beach, and check in at the hotel there if we can. We shouldn't drive tonight, but we'll be close to our cars in the morning.'

The wait for a taxi, the journey back to the beach and checking in at the hotel took another hour, and we agreed that explanations could wait.

'Ring me immediately if you start to feel unwell,' Nuno said.

'I will, I promise.' I watched him walk down the corridor to his room. I wanted to follow him, to spend the night in the same room as him, just to have the reassurance of knowing he was close by. 'Bad idea,' I told myself; I would have to get used to Nuno not being around soon enough. I unlocked the door to my own room instead and sank down on the bed. Wearily, I pulled my clothes off and left them where they fell on the floor.

Chapter 16

I woke to the sound of waves crashing on the beach. If I had been confused by the various places in which I had woken up during the trip, it was nothing as to how I felt that morning. I would never have chosen a room near the sea. As I got up and looked out of the window, I realised my head had stopped pounding.

Having showered, I pulled on my clothes from the day before, which were crusty with salt and sand and generally much the worse for wear. I felt dirty and unkempt, but then I thought about Caitlin in intensive care and Jennifer and Robert flying over to Portugal, and I felt guilty for allowing myself such thoughts.

I found Nuno in the breakfast room, staring out to sea, apparently hypnotised by the waves. For some reason, I felt nervous about approaching him, unsure how he would react after the events of the previous night. 'Morning,' I said, cautiously.

He turned and smiled at me, and I felt my nerves start to dissolve. 'Good morning. Did you sleep well?'

'Yes, better than I would have expected. I suppose everything just caught up with me. How about you?'

'Likewise. Do you want some coffee?'

I willingly accepted the offer and after we had selected breakfast, I waited for Nuno to press me for a full explanation, but he didn't.

'I suppose you want to know everything?' I ventured.

'When you're ready,' he said, placidly. 'I'll admit I have been wondering about a lot of things.'

'I can imagine.'

I allowed the coffee to get to work and the room to start to clear. I knew after I had told Nuno everything, my fledgling friendship with him would be over, and that hurt more than I cared to admit. I decided to play for a little more time although I knew I was only postponing the inevitable.

'Can we go to the hospital first? Then I promise you I will tell you everything.'

Nuno simply nodded and offered me some more coffee as I wondered at his patience.

* * *

Emotionally and physically drained as we both were and easy as it would have been just to sit there together, practicalities intruded on us. Nuno drove us into Cascais to buy some clothes which were cheap but clean. After a stop back at the hotel to change, we set off in Nuno's car for the hospital.

'I think I should speak to Jennifer and Robert if they are there.'

'I thought you only wanted an update on Caitlin. You

could be waiting for ages for them to turn up.'

'Yes, that's true, but there are things I think I need to say to them.' I hesitated, afraid to say too much and give away what had happened to Finn, and the part I had played in it.

Nuno looked at me, but I looked away and out of the window at the passing scenery and silently thanked him when he didn't press me for more details.

After various enquiries during which I was grateful Nuno was there to help with translations, we finally established that Caitlin was stable and that her parents were expected shortly.

Once I knew that, what I really wanted to do was find some reason for Nuno not to be there when Jennifer and Robert arrived. The thought that he would get to hear their mangled version of what had happened to Finn before I had had the chance to tell him the full story, made me sick to my stomach.

I racked my brain to think of some plausible reason why he should leave. Without much hope, I made the only suggestion which came to me. 'Why don't you go back to the hotel? It's not much fun sitting around here.'

'I don't mind waiting.'

'Well, at least go outside and get some fresh air.'

'I really don't mind staying here. I'd tell you if I did,' Nuno said, smiling and squeezing my hand.

I forced a smile in return, wishing I could think of a more creative reason for him to leave.

We sat in the waiting room and an eternity seemed to pass. I memorised every detail of the floor tiles, the posters on the wall, the other people waiting for news and the expressions of the staff as they moved back and forth.

Time elongated and I felt as though the wait would never end, but when I looked at my watch, it was not even ten o'clock. Nuno bought us cups of coffee from the vending machine at the end of the hallway, each one less appealing than the last. He spoke to me a few times, but he must have realised I was not up to making conversation and allowed me the privilege of silence.

With every passing minute, I was losing my nerve. I had just decided to leave, as keeping Nuno and Caitlin's parents apart was more important than what I needed to say to them, when I heard a voice I recognised all too well. The voice of my old accuser, and the voice I had heard on the phone the night before. Jennifer was demanding to be allowed to see Caitlin immediately, and someone was assuring her that would not be a problem.

They rounded the corner just as I stood up, and we all froze in our tracks. Jennifer and Robert were instantly recognisable, but the intervening years had changed them. Jennifer still had the demeanour of a woman who expected to get what she wanted when she wanted it, and she had retained the figure of a model, but her hair was shorter and the shadows under her eyes and the lines carved into her face spoke of great strain and sorrow. I remembered Robert as a physically imposing man of well over six feet, but his posture was now stooped as though the burden he had been carrying for so long had simply proved too heavy to bear anymore.

The teenage girl beside them had to be Suzanna, no

longer the diffident young child. She was only fourteen, but she radiated a maturity beyond her years and looked weary. She had Finn's dark hair but Caitlin's eyes although they were a warmer shade of blue.

Jennifer spoke first. 'Isabel?' She sounded as though she could scarcely believe what she was saying.

'Jennifer.'

'Why on earth are you here?'

'I, that is …'

'Wait, was it you who phoned me last night?'

'Yes, it was.'

'There is no Doctor Silva, I take it?'

'No. I thought if I told you who I was, you'd put the phone down on me.'

She ignored that. 'Why are you here?'

As I was casting around for the right words, I heard Nuno speak. Isabel was with Va … Caitlin on the beach yesterday. She saved Caitlin's life.'

'But Caitlin has hated the beach ever since …' My heart and stomach were performing somersaults, waiting for the next words, the ones which would end my friendship with Nuno. But her voice trailed away, and I saw Suzanna put her arm around her. I was transported back to the church, but now Suzanna had taken on the role of the protector rather than the protected. Before any of us could speak further, a doctor appeared and ushered Caitlin's family to one side.

Nuno and I watched them from a distance. 'We might as well go,' I said, desperate to get Nuno out of the hospital before Jennifer could say anything else.

'Are you sure? I thought you wanted to speak to them.'

'I've changed my mind.'

'OK. If you're sure.'

We turned to leave, and I heard Suzanna call my name.

'Isabel, wait.' She caught up with us and looked uncertainly from me to Nuno and back again.

'I'll be in the café,' Nuno said. He squeezed my hand and then left us alone.

Looking at Suzanna, I felt the power of speech desert me. I hoped she had something to say because I could find nothing.

'The doctor said only my parents can go in for now. Could we go somewhere and talk?'

'OK, but not here. I hate hospitals, and I need some fresh air.'

'Depressing places, aren't they?' Suzanna agreed.

We found a bench outside and settled ourselves on it. The view of a car park offered nothing to lift the spirits.

'Everything's a bit unclear at the moment. All we know is what that man who was with you said. That you were on that beach with Caitlin, and you saved her life. I didn't even know you were in touch with her, let alone that you were here in Portugal together. I thought she was living in Poland. Mind you, we hadn't seen or heard from her since last summer. She came to visit us, and it didn't go well.'

'Why? What happened?'

'I don't know really. I came home one day to her and mum screaming at each other. Caitlin was yelling about never being good enough, and mum was shouting back that she'd taken what she'd said the wrong way.' Suzanna puffed her cheeks out and sighed, and I got the feeling she had witnessed other similar scenes play out over the years.

I wondered whether I should tell Suzanna an edited version of the truth, but then I realised Caitlin was going to need help if she was ever going to have a chance to get better. That was, after all, the reason I had decided to brave a meeting with Robert and Jennifer. I took a deep breath and opted for an unsparing version of the truth, covering everything from the friendship with me which Caitlin had engineered in Gdansk, to the move to Seville and everything which had happened since I had arrived in Portugal.

Suzanna said nothing until I had finished. 'It's my fault.'

'What is?' I asked, astonished by the comment. Whatever I had expected her to say, blaming herself had not been it.

'I knew Caitlin was ... damaged. I should have intervened years ago.'

'I'm not being rude but you're only fourteen now. What could you possibly have done as a child?'

Suzanna gave me a lopsided, sad smile. 'Ours is not a normal family. I'd hazard a guess that my fourteen years have not been like the average fourteen year old's. At school, everyone in my class seems very immature to me. I'm not sure whether I envy them or not.'

I let that sink in and remembered my own complicated childhood which had left me feeling older than my years. Then I asked her about something I had not understood, and I had forgotten to ask Lou. 'Caitlin needed money to do what she did. I still don't know how much she paid Lou, but

I'd imagine it was a lot. Lou said she had big money problems. Where would Caitlin get that sort of money?'

'My dad knew how my mum treated Caitlin, but he has always given way to her. My mum, that is. About everything. From something as trivial as the colour of the walls to … anyway, I think he felt guilty so he tried to compensate in the only language he really understands.'

'Money?'

'Yes. Caitlin had a very healthy bank balance by the time she was eighteen, and it just kept growing. I know he's set up some sort of trust fund for me.' She kicked at the paving stones. 'Some compensation for a messed up childhood, eh?'

'I suppose it shows he cares even if not in the way you'd like.'

'Maybe.'

We sat in silence for a while. I had no idea where to take the conversation and, it appeared, neither did Suzanna although she showed no inclination to leave. She seemed to be fizzing with a pent up need to say something, but I could not imagine what more we had to discuss.

'I always hoped I'd meet you one day,' she said, finally breaking the silence.

'Why?'

'Because you knew Finn. My parents won't talk about her. Well, only sometimes, and then it's in these weird, reverential tones. Caitlin has never talked about her at all. I want to know what my sister was really like. Will you tell me?'

I sighed and looked at the sky and then at Suzanna's

earnest, enquiring face. It was not a conversation I wanted to have, yet I felt Suzanna was owed that much at least; I had no right to refuse her. 'OK, I'll try. Finn and I met on our first day at university. I was nervous; she was exuberant, larger than life. She found the fun in everything. She found humour in the moments when others struggled. She could cheer me up with just a word or a look. She brought a lot of light into everyone's lives, mine included.'

'So she was as perfect as they say?' I saw something which looked akin to disappointment cross Suzanna's face.

'Nobody's perfect, but we learn when we are still children not to speak ill of the dead, don't we? And particularly when someone dies so young … besides your parents and Caitlin are the last people who are going to think badly of her.'

'What were her faults?'

'Why do you want to know?'

'Because all of our lives have been touched by her death. Maybe Caitlin's most of all. I need to know who Finn was – all of it. You have to understand she's this almost saintly, untouchable figure. I feel I have so much to live up to, so much to … to compensate for. Particularly with Caitlin being the way she is. It would actually be a relief to know she wasn't perfect.'

I considered that. 'Finn could be pretty outspoken. She wasn't shy about making her opinions known. She was never cruel and she never meant any harm, but her honesty didn't always sit well with everyone. Diplomacy wasn't a word she was familiar with.'

'Anything else?'

'She was a bit lazy sometimes, but then again, she could get away with it. She was bright. I was more of a plodder; the one who had to study hard and make notes. Finn didn't work nearly as hard as me, but she did just as well as me academically.'

'So you were envious of her?'

'No. Well, only when I was exhausted after spending a night studying, and she was lively and ready to go. Mostly, though, I admired her for it. I admired a lot of things about her. Her positivity, her optimism. As I said before.'

'What happened at the beach, Isabel?'

'With Caitlin or with Finn?' I asked, knowing the answer but playing for time.

'With Finn,' Suzanna said softly.

I took a deep breath and tried to give words to the events of the day which had haunted every subsequent one. 'We decided to go to Devon for a long weekend. The forecast was for spectacular weather, and you know how it is in England. When you get sunshine, you have to make the most of it so it seemed too good an opportunity to pass up.

'We arrived on the Friday afternoon. It was a normal weekend for two students in their twenties – bars, sunbathing …

'We had originally planned to go back around midday on the Tuesday, but the forecast was so good that we changed our minds. If we hadn't …' I twisted the bangle around on my wrist and was temporarily blinded by the sunlight as it reflected off it.

'We booked an extra night at the hotel, and then we

headed down to the beach for the afternoon. It was me who suggested going for a swim.' I paused, struggling with the next part. 'Finn didn't want to go into the water. She wasn't a great fan of swimming. In fact, she thought exercise of any kind was slightly suspect.' In spite of everything, I found myself smiling at my memories of Finn. 'She was happy with a book, but I thought it would be fun to go swimming together.'

I stopped, hoping Suzanna would let me off at that point, but she was staring at me as though mesmerised.

'So it was me who convinced her to go in,' I said.

I wanted Suzanna to say something, but she continued to stare at me.

'Don't you see?' I said. 'That's why it was my fault. I convinced her to go in. And then the weather changed. It was as fast as someone clicking their fingers. I was desperate to find her and get her out, but she had disappeared, and I could feel myself being pulled under. I couldn't even save myself, much less Finn. And that's why it's totally and utterly my fault.

'I was the one who persuaded her to go in, I was the one who promised her she would be safe, and then I let her down. When she needed me, I wasn't there for her.' I emerged from my memories to find my fingernails digging into my arm hard enough to break the skin and draw blood.

Suzanna followed my gaze to the bright red beads appearing on my arm. 'I think we've all suffered enough, don't you?'

I looked at her again, only fourteen, yet so much more

mature than any of the teenagers I taught. I couldn't begin to imagine what her life had been like. I didn't know how much of Caitlin's testimony to believe, following the revelations that she had lied to me about so much, so I decided to ask Suzanna. 'You were very young when it happened. Did you … did you suffer very much?'

'Not as much as Caitlin. She told me that our mother always compared her unfavourably to Finn. She told me that once mum had said to her she wished Caitlin had died instead of Finn.'

I could barely imagine the horror of hearing a parent say that. Even my own distant parents had never said anything remotely as cruel as that. For the first time, I could truly understand the hatred Caitlin must have felt for me. In the place within where absolute honesty resides, I couldn't say whether I would have felt differently if I had been in her place. I could not imagine, however, what level of torment must have driven her to devise and execute her plan for me.

We let Suzanna's words hang in the air and slowly dissolve, and then she continued. 'By the time I was old enough to really understand what was going on – and what had happened – mum was seeing a therapist. So I got off lightly compared to Caitlin. Not that it was exactly a happy home to grow up in and mum is still … fragile at times.'

'You must hate me as much as your mum and dad do.'

'We don't hate you, Isabel.'

'But you must do …'

'Mum and dad might have hated you at one time; I couldn't say how they were in the early days, but if they did, it was the shock. They have grown to realise you didn't set out to hurt Finn. Caitlin, well, Caitlin, was always angry – with my parents, with me, with the world, with everyone and everything. You're just one on a long list. I don't know where we go from here with getting her the help she needs.'

It struck me again how much she sounded like the adult in the situation, the one tasked with finding a solution. 'I truly hope you do manage to help her.' I hesitated. I thought of the night before and wondered if Caitlin had heard my apology. 'If the opportunity ever presents itself, will you tell her I'm not angry with her? She'll have enough healing to do without thinking I bear her a grudge. And tell her I'm sorry.'

'You don't have to apologise, but yes, I promise you that when the moment is right I will tell her that. If you give me your phone number, I'll let you know when she's out of intensive care.'

'I'd appreciate that.' I gave Suzanna my number and added, 'I think I'll be changing it soon. You know … in case …'

'In case Caitlin decides to contact you again?'

'Yes.'

'Somehow I don't think she will, but I'd probably do the same thing.'

'I won't see any of you again. You know that, don't you?'

'I know, and I can't say I blame you. There's nothing you can do to fix things anyway. We're a bit of a mess really.'

We got up, and she held her hand out to shake mine. It was an oddly formal gesture which somehow suited the moment; a final parting of the ways. The moment when she would leave to try to help to repair her family and I … I didn't know at that point.

I watched her return to the shadows cast by the entrance and then took my own path to the café.

* * *

Nuno and I drove back to the hotel and settled ourselves in the same room where we had had breakfast. I knew the moment had come when I would no longer be able to find a reason or an excuse to put off the explanation he deserved. As I launched into the story, he didn't interrupt or ask for clarification. He allowed me to pour everything out in my own way and my own time. I spared no details. I told him about my childhood; about Finn; about how she had died; about how I had run ever since and about Caitlin's desire for revenge. Nuno's judgement would come, but it would come with me having held nothing back. He would go his way and I would go mine, but there would be no lies between us.

'Finn was the better person yet somehow I was the one who survived,' I finished. I bit down hard on my lip, steadied my voice and added, 'so that brings me up to where we are today.' I couldn't look him in the eye. I didn't want to see the disapproval or disappointment. I looked out of the window and found myself staring at the spot where Caitlin had decided to exact her final revenge on me.

'I can't believe Caitlin blamed you for what happened to Finn. It was just a terrible accident. And then to plan all this …'

I dared to glance in Nuno's direction and saw nothing but kindness and concern. 'I can. I blame myself every day.

My whole life since that day has been about trying to run away from the guilt I feel.'

'You can't though, can you?'

'No, not unless I ever manage to run away from myself.'

'So why don't you stop running if you know there's no point?'

I bit my lip again. 'Because I don't know any other way to live now. I ruin other people's lives. Look at what I did to you. And … I'm not even sure who I am anymore. If I allow myself to stop, I'll have to face myself, and I don't think I'll like what I see.' I had never been that honest before, even with myself, and the impact of what I had said stopped me in my tracks. I looked at Nuno, unable to say anything else although I desperately wanted to fill the silence.

'I like what I see,' Nuno said.

'But you don't really know me.'

'After all you've been through and what you've just told me? I may not know everything about you, but I think I know you well enough to say you're an amazing person.'

I heard an embarrassed laugh coming from me, but I no longer felt as if I were in my body. I was remote and observing a conversation between two strangers from a distance.

'You didn't have any support from your parents and then with what happened to Finn … and being blamed for her death. You were only twenty-one at the time with nobody to turn to. I'm not surprised you ran away. But what I see now is someone who overcame her worst possible fear to save the life of someone who had set out to destroy her. I think that's pretty incredible.'

The woman sitting opposite the man dropped her head and blushed. The man leaned over the table and took her hands in his. 'You are a very special woman, Isabel,' he said, and I found myself back within my body, looking across the table at him.

What would have happened next, I was never to know as a member of the hotel's staff approached us.

'Mr. Ferreira da Costa? Miss Foster?'

We both looked up, and I recognised the receptionist who had checked us in during the early hours. She looked tired and apologetic in equal measure.

'We do need you to vacate your rooms, please.'

With nothing to pack, we were standing outside in the car park within twenty minutes.

'What next?' Nuno asked.

I looked around as if the answers would magically appear in front of me. 'I haven't had time to make any plans. I'll have to go back to Seville soon – for starters, at least.'

I saw something flicker across his face, but it was fleeting and indecipherable.

'What is it?' I asked.

Nuno hesitated. 'I hoped you might stay here for a while.'

'Caitlin has the people she needs here. There's nothing I can do for her.'

'I wasn't thinking about her.'

I had spent so many years alone, protecting myself from the damage caring about other people could inflict that I didn't follow him at first. I stared at him stupidly.

'I meant that I thought we might spend some time together,' he added, my awkwardness transferring itself to him.

'We've found Caitlin,' I said. I was clumsy, out of practice.

'Yes, so now we could enjoy spending time together without worrying about Caitlin or Lou or the police. Get to know each other better.'

'I don't think I'm the easiest person to get to know.'

'I'm not interested in easy.'

I looked at Nuno and thought that any other woman would know what to say. 'I guess we should make a move.'

As we both had our own cars, the drive back to Lisbon was a moment of peace, a moment for reflection. It was not long enough as there was too much to process, but it was welcome nonetheless.

Nuno's car followed mine into the hotel car park. 'Can I see you tomorrow?'

I hesitated. I wanted to say yes, but something had been building inside of me. 'There's something I need to do first.'

'Would you like some company?'

'Don't take this the wrong way, but it's something I need to do alone.'

Chapter 17

I set off soon after dawn the following morning and drove west out of Lisbon along the coast. Looking at various websites the night before, I had found somewhere close to what I was looking for. Tamariz Beach in Estoril was described as a soft, sheltered crescent of sand with calm waters.

After I had parked the car, I put my phone in a plastic bag and shoved it out of sight under the seat. I locked the car and walked through the gardens of the casino and down to the promenade which ran behind the beach. At one end, a seventeenth century fortress kept watch. I found a strange comfort in historic buildings which had managed to remain intact, impervious to the march of time: they had seen the centuries come and go and yet still they had endured. The shops and restaurants which lined the promenade meant the spot wasn't as peaceful as I would have liked, but I had arrived early enough to have a measure of solitude.

Finding the quietest part of the beach, I stripped to the swimsuit I had bought the afternoon before, dropped my clothes and towel and walked down to near the water's edge. The sun had climbed higher during the drive, and I stood there for a while, enjoying the warmth on my skin and remembering how much I had once loved the sea. Its vastness, its unknowability, even its unpredictability had all once fascinated me, but I had become repelled by them.

The water rushed in and touched my toes, making me jump. Now I was there I wondered if I could do it. I took a few steps into the water. Ankle height; shin height; knee height; waist height; feeling the water wash around me and pull at my body. I forced myself not to turn back, to remember the breathing exercises I had been taught, and then I was floating, swimming; sensations which had once been as natural as breathing. There had been a time when I had been tipped for some success as a swimmer but that, like so much else, had been lost along the way.

I started to welcome the resistance of the water against my body, and then I turned over and allowed myself to float, gazing up at a cornflower blue sky.

My twenty-one year old self turned to Finn. 'Come in.' I was beckoning her from the shoreline.

Finn laughed and shook her head.

I walked back up the beach towards her. 'Come on.'

'What would I want to do a daft thing like that for?' Finn asked, peering at me over the top of her sunglasses.

'Because swimming is fun.'

'For you athletic types maybe. I, on the other hand, have a good book and a cold drink.' She curled up on her beach towel, and I thought how she was almost feline in her love of comfort and pleasure.

'Humour me?' I said, holding out my hand to pull her up.

Finn sighed and put her book down, carefully marking her place. 'You do know I wouldn't do this for anyone else, don't you?'

I smiled as angelically as I could and pulled her to her feet. 'It'll be fine. You're safe with me.'

I continued to stare up at the Portuguese sky, slowly turning to cobalt. 'I'm so sorry, Finn,' I whispered and felt tears rolling down towards my hairline before being absorbed by the sea.

* * *

When I finally made it back to the car, I retrieved my phone from its makeshift hiding place. Switching it on, I left it on the seat while I sorted out my swimsuit and wet towel. I heard it ring and saw Suzanna's number on the screen. A moment of anxiety hit me as I imagined answering it to find Caitlin at the other end.

'Yes?' I asked cautiously.

'Isabel, is that you?'

I recognised Suzanna's voice and relaxed a little. 'Hi. Yes. What's happened?'

'Caitlin is out of intensive care. We're going to take her home as soon as we get the green light from the doctors.'

Once again, her tone and phrasing struck me as mature beyond her years. 'Thank you for letting me know, Suzanna. I appreciate it. I imagine you have far more important things on your mind right now than updating me.'

'I promised that I would contact you. I … I don't know how she is. Emotionally, I mean. I haven't really had a chance to speak to her yet. Not properly. At the moment, I just want to get her back home.'

'Just try to take it one step at a time.'

'Yes.'

'I think that's all any of us can do.'

'Will you make me a promise, Isabel?'

'What's that?'

'Please don't spend the rest of your life blaming yourself. I know Finn loved you like a sister, and I'm sure you felt the same way about her. I know you would never have hurt her.'

I was confused. Suzanna had been a young child when Finn and I had been friends. She wouldn't have known what Finn thought of me. I said as much to Suzanna, expecting nothing more by way of explanation than a few kind but empty words.

'My parents left Finn's room as it had been for years. I went in there from time to time to look through her things. That sounds awful, but I was trying to learn more about her. I found a present she had wrapped up and hidden away at the back of a cupboard.' Suzanna cleared her throat. 'My only defence is that I was still quite young. I opened it.'

The line went so quiet I thought she had gone. 'Are you still there?' I asked.

'Yes. It was a present for you. For your graduation. There was a card with it and in it she said you were her much loved extra sister and she was so excited about the two of you going off to discover the world together. I meant to mention it to you the other day, but with everything else that was going on, I completely forgot about it.'

It was my turn to go quiet. I didn't trust my voice to remain steady.

'Isabel?'

'I'm here.' My voice cracked on the words.

'I'm sorry. I thought that would bring you some comfort, but all I've done is upset you.'

'No, you haven't.'

Suzanna spoke again, more hesitantly. 'I was wondering if you'd like me to send it to you. It was always meant for you.'

'I don't think your parents would approve.'

'They don't know about it. I hid it away in my room. I didn't know why at the time, but I do now.'

'In that case, I would love to have it.'

'Send me your address, and I'll get it off to you.'

'OK. There's only one thing. I don't know how long I'll be staying on there.'

'I'll send it to you by courier as soon as we get back home,' she promised.

'Thank you. Not just for the present. For forgiving me, I mean.'

'No forgiveness required. Take care of yourself, Isabel.'

'And you Suzanna.'

I sent Suzanna my address and was about to turn the key in the ignition, when a message from Nuno appeared.

When you've finished what you had to do, will you call me?

I phoned him, and he answered almost immediately. 'Hi. Are you OK?'

I thought about the swim and my conversation with Suzanna. 'Yes. Yes, I think I am.'

'Did you do what you needed to do?'

'Yes.'

'That's good.'

The silence stretched out and became strained, which I realised was entirely due to my reluctance to give anything away. 'I'm in Estoril,' I added, feeling that saying something was better than nothing.

'Would you like some company?'

'Here?'

'They often have fireworks displays there in the evening in summer. If you like the idea, I could come and join you. We could have dinner and if the fireworks are on, so much the better.'

'Yes. I would like that. I'd like it very much.'

'I'll take the train. Meet you at the station at eight?'

I spent the afternoon in Estoril and much to my own surprise found myself not just trying on but buying a dress. Nuno had only ever seen me in my well-worn T-shirts and shorts or jeans. I couldn't do much about the bruises which marked my face and hand, but I found some mascara at the bottom of my bag and as I applied it and looked at myself in the mirror, I felt there was some improvement.

As I waited at the station for Nuno, I started to feel nervous again although I had no idea why. All of my secrets were out in the open; there was nothing to feel anxious about. But I had bought a dress and gone to more lengths than normal to tidy up my appearance for reasons I didn't care to examine.

Nuno got off the train, and I saw immediately that he had noticed the transformation. 'You look beautiful.'

'I felt like a change,' I said, trying to brush off the compliment and my embarrassment. 'It seems like I've been living in T-shirts and shorts forever.'

'I wouldn't complain about that either,' he said.

We walked along the promenade and found a restaurant overlooking the beach.

'What made you come to Estoril?' Nuno asked.

I fell silent, wanting to tell him but feeling it would somehow diminish the significance the moment had held for me. I hoped he might add something, but there wasn't a lot he could say when I kept shutting him out. I took a deep breath. 'I went swimming this morning. That's what I needed to do alone. I needed to know if I could do it, and I needed to say sorry to Finn where I lost her. In the sea, I mean. Not here. That probably sounds stupid. It does to me when I put it into words.'

'It doesn't sound stupid at all. And I can understand why you needed to do that alone. Did it help?'

'It did, yes. Suzanna phoned me too. Caitlin is out of intensive care. They're hoping to take her home soon.'

'So this really is the end of the whole thing?'

'It looks that way, yes.'

We made small talk about the food and the view, and then Nuno brought up the subject we had skirted around.

'When are you leaving, Isabel?'

'The day after tomorrow. I have to get the car back.'

'Do you think you will stay in Seville?'

'I've thought about it, and I don't think I can. It's such a gorgeous city, but I moved there with Caitlin, and we lived and worked there together. Everywhere is going to remind me of her, and I'd always be expecting her to track me down if I stayed. I don't want to be looking over my shoulder all the time. I'll have to resign and give notice on my room. Then I'll need to think about where to go so there are a lot of things I need to take care of.' It was all true, but I was rambling, and I knew it was because I was running scared of my feelings for Nuno and what he might say, given the chance.

'It sounds like you're set on leaving Seville them. Have you thought about where you'll go?'

'I haven't got that far yet.'

'Évora is a pretty good place to live.'

'Évora? Your home town?'

'Yes.'

I looked at him, waiting for an "I got you going there" moment followed by a big smile, but he continued to return my gaze.

'I've never been to Évora,' I said.

'You really should go. It's a lovely place.'

'I'll think about it,' I said, when I wanted to say so much more than that.

'Is that a promise?' Nuno asked.

'To think about it? Yes.'

We finished dinner and moved outside to the promenade to watch the fireworks with the gathering crowds. The breeze picked up and as I shivered, I felt Nuno tentatively wrap his arms around me. I could tell he was unsure and was seeking reassurance that I was comfortable. I gently took his hands and held them where they were, not wanting him to pull away.

We stayed like that for a while until I turned around in his arms. He withdrew his arms from around me and cradled my face in his hands, tenderly kissing the bruises and scrapes I had acquired over the weeks. I closed my eyes and focused on the feather-soft sensations. When he stopped, I opened my eyes. The fireworks had ended at some point and the crowds had started to disperse, but they were events I was only vaguely aware of by that point. We looked at each other and with the soft murmur of the waves breaking on the beach in the background, we finally kissed and the world dissolved.

* * *

I woke up the following morning, once more wondering where I was. Forcing my brain to engage, I sat up and realised I was in a hotel room in Estoril. We had not made it back to Lisbon the previous night. There was something else that was different as well. Nuno was there beside me, also half-awake. I felt his fingers trace down the length of my spine and as I turned to face him, he smiled, drew me close and put his arms around me. There were difficult conversations and decisions ahead, but they were not for that moment. I had lived in the past for too long, and I was not yet ready for the future. For a little while at least, I wanted to find out what it was like to live in the present.

We had lunch in Estoril and took a walk along the beach. I was in no hurry to go back. I felt that as long as we were in Estoril, we were in our own little bubble, which would be burst if we strayed too far.

When we could put it off no longer, we drove back, still avoiding any discussions about the future. Having parked, we walked up to the top of the Edward the Seventh Park. It was where I had taken in my first views of Lisbon on a morning which although only three weeks ago seemed so much longer.

'You know I want you to come back, don't you?' Nuno asked, taking my hand. 'I meant what I said about Évora.'

'I know, but I have all those things to sort out in Seville before I can do anything else. And besides …' I broke off, unsure how to explain what was on my mind.

'Besides what?'

'Despite what you said before, we still don't know each other that well. I would need to get my own place there, and I'd need to find a job.'

'You wouldn't want to move in with me?'

'I wouldn't want to risk spoiling things by putting too much pressure on us; for us to feel we have to make things work out.'

'I understand that.'

'You do?'

'Yes. I'd just be happy if you were in Évora.'

'Perhaps I should go back to Seville that way. Take a look. I've heard it's worth a visit.' I smiled at him.

'I wish I could go with you, but it's my aunt and uncle's anniversary the day after tomorrow, and they're having a big dinner. I have to be there. Are you sure you couldn't stay for a few more days? You could come to the dinner and meet some of my family. Then we could go to Évora together.'

'It might come as a surprise if you turn up with someone they've never heard of.'

'I was rather hoping to tell my family about you before then,' Nuno said.

'Can we wait? Just for a little longer?'

'OK. But I don't want to keep you a secret.'

'Well, I could only stay one day longer at the very most. If I don't get that car back on time, I dread to think how much they'll charge me. And if I leave tomorrow, I'll just have enough time to squeeze in a visit to Évora.' I couldn't find the words to tell him how hard it was going to be for me to say goodbye. Of all the many goodbyes, I knew that was one which was going to cut deep.

Nuno and I postponed our parting that night for as long as we could. We walked up to the lookout point of Graça, with the castle to our left and views which stretched across both the city and the Tagus.

'I never did get to the castle.'

'Next time,' Nuno said and put an arm around my shoulders.

The sun was setting, and the city was bathed in warm light. We sat under the pine trees, the air heavy with their scent, and watched as the sky flamed ochre and red until finally darkness fell. We lingered over a late dinner, and we talked until the restaurant finally closed its doors for the night.

Much as we tried to ignore it, the moment when we would have to say goodbye was drawing ever closer. Ana, stationed at the reception desk in the Hibiscus, was never going to allow anyone who was not a registered guest to make it past reception at that time of night.

Out in the street, I turned to look at the brightly lit reception again, visible through the vast glass windows. 'I hate this, but I really should go.'

'I know, and I hate it too.' Nuno wrapped his arms around me. 'Before you go, I want you to know I'm not going to put any pressure on you about moving. I know there's a lot to think about, and I'll respect whatever you decide. But I don't want this to be the end for us. I hope it's just the start.'

Part 4

Seville, Spain

Chapter 18

The next morning I left early, keen to get underway before I had time to brood about leaving; ripping the plaster off again. My route to Évora took me back over the April 25th Bridge, a feat I achieved with just a few butterflies in my stomach. The heat built as I drove into the scorched countryside of the Alentejo region. An hour and a half after leaving Lisbon, I arrived in Évora, found a place to stay for the night and then set out to explore.

Évora didn't have the more widely known attractions of Seville, but it still had its share of beautiful spots and a rich history. More than that though, it had an understated, sleepy charm. Having given up on the map, I wandered the cobbled streets lined with white-washed houses with mustard yellow accents, stumbling across the city's sights from time to time. Along the way, I found a place to print off my CV and handed it in at a few schools. I also picked up some information about flats for rent.

The following morning, I sat out on the terrace of the hotel, surrounded by huge terracotta pots brimming with flowers, listening to bird song. I tried to take Nuno out of the equation and think about how I would feel about living in Évora if I was alone and found myself thinking it was a place in which I would be comfortable.

By late morning, I realised I would have to make a move back to Seville. I had no desire to return to the messy remains of my life there, but I could put it off no longer so I got into the car once more for the final leg of my journey.

With the car safely returned to the agency, I walked back to the flat, my feeling of despondency growing as I walked through the door. The room was as gloomy as ever. I sank onto the bed and caught up on my messages with Nuno. I had already told him how much I had liked Évora, but I had avoided giving him a definitive decision about moving there. I needed to know how I felt once I was on my own again without the distractions of being with Nuno or visiting a new place.

The next day, I walked to the María Luisa Park. Everything was much the same as it had been before I had left: the deep blue skies; the heat; even the sound of Entre Dos Aguas drifting across the park. It was almost as though the last three weeks and the trip to Lisbon had never happened, yet I had been fundamentally changed.

I headed for one of my favourite spots in the park, the monument to the romantic poet Gustavo Bécquer, and took a seat on a bench. The monument was fashioned around a swamp cypress, which sheltered the statues placed around its trunk. There was the marble statue of the poet himself and, to his left, three young women, also captured in marble, each depicting a state of love – I remembered I had read they represented hopeful love, possessed love and lost love. I got up and examined their expressions. Above them hovered a mischievous Cupid, cast in bronze. Walking round the tree, I looked at the other reclining bronze figure with broken wings, representing wounded love and then, completing the circle, I came back to the statue of Gustavo Bécquer again.

I returned to the bench and contemplated a monument to love in all its complexity; its light and shade; its joy and grief. I imagined sitting there with Finn, commenting along those lines. 'Ah Isabel,' I heard her saying 'you have the tortured soul of a poet.'

I wondered if I could risk the hurt which I was sure would inevitably follow if I dared to allow myself to love Nuno and let him love me in return. I sensed Finn closer to me than she had been in years and felt rather than heard her say 'Take a chance.' I looked round almost certain that if I had been quick enough, I would have seen her, but I was alone.

I found my phone and looked again at the messages I had exchanged with Nuno the previous night. He had been true to his word and had not put any pressure on me, but his messages had made it clear how much he hoped I would seriously consider a move to Évora or even somewhere close by. My own messages had continued to be more reticent. I had lost the ability – or perhaps more accurately I had never learned – to express certain feelings. I was too practised at keeping everything bolted down deep inside to change overnight.

I looked around me, wondering what to do for the best. As I had predicted, every corner of the city had a memory of Caitlin attached to it. Equally, the endless moves to new countries had lost their previous, compelling attraction. But perhaps I could move one more time because I would be moving to something, to someone, rather than running away again.

The arrival of tourists posing for photos in front of the monument woke me from my reverie. I forced myself to go back to the room, where I looked at my half-unpacked bag; a symbol of my uncertainty.

It dawned on me just how empty it felt. There had to be more to life than that sad, stark room with its sagging blind and temperamental fan or somewhere equally bleak in another lonely corner of the world. I had nobody to blame but myself; I had shaped my life into that bare existence, filled with transient people and superficial friendships. I wondered if I had the ability to take it now and reshape it into something more worthwhile. I wondered if I had the courage at least to try. I thought about Nuno and felt that shift inside of me again, which simultaneously excited and terrified me. I would see every hour of the night come and go as I wrestled with my decision.

* * *

The following day I tendered my resignation, and I told my housemates I would be leaving. They were surprised enough to stop arguing for a while. As I sat in my room, thinking about the recklessness of making myself homeless and jobless, my phone rang. It was a Portuguese number I didn't recognise.

'Hello.'

'Hello. Is that Isabel Foster?'

'Speaking.'

'This is the Ashdown School of English in Évora. We've received your CV. We'd be interested in interviewing you, but I see that you live in Seville. Where are you at the moment?'

'I'm in Seville, but I'm actually moving to Évora in a couple of days.'

'That's perfect. Would 10.30 next Thursday be a convenient time for an interview?'

'Yes. Yes, it would,' I heard myself saying.

'Good. We'll see you then.'

Later that day, a courier arrived with a parcel from England. I found a note inside from Suzanna along with a small package and a card.

Dear Isabel,

As promised, here is the card and present from Finn. I have tried to seal the envelope and wrap the present again in the original paper, but it all looks a bit of a mess. I suppose that doesn't really matter, though. What does matter is that they are finally going to be with you as Finn had intended.

Caitlin is going to be evaluated next week, and we will see what happens after that. One step at a time, right?

Best wishes,

Suzanna

I picked up the card and found my hands were unsteady. I carefully opened it, and an exuberant twenty-one-year-old Finn was speaking to me.

To my dearest wonderful friend Isabel,

I am so happy we met and that I get to call you my friend. I have always been too embarrassed to say it, but you really are like a sister to me. I love Caitlin and Suzanna very much, but it's wonderful to have a sister of my own age as well. My bonus sister!

I'm so excited about our plans to go travelling together and teach abroad. Think of all the adventures we'll have. Those Finns won't know what's hit 'em!

Lots and lots of love,

Finn, xxx

I felt the tears rolling down my face. They made cold tracks against the heat of my skin. I let them fall and let myself feel the pain. As they slowed and the dried tears made my skin itch, I rubbed at my face. I picked up the present in its scrunched up paper, imagining a younger Suzanna inquisitively ripping it open and then the Suzanna I knew carefully trying to smooth it out and wrap it up again properly.

Opening the box, I found a silver pendant nestled on a cushion of midnight blue velvet. It was the accompanying piece to the silver bangle I had bought Finn; the one I so rarely took off. I gently removed it from the box and held it in the palm of my hand, allowing years of memories, emotions and regrets to wash over me. Walking to the mirror so that I could see the clasp, I put it on, and then I returned to the bed. I packed Suzanna's note, Finn's card, the box and wrapping paper into a small bag and tucked them inside my rucksack.

I sent Suzanna a message, unwilling to risk phoning her at the wrong moment. I tried to keep it as cryptic as possible.

Received. Thank you so much.

Suzanna appeared online. *Thanks for letting me know. Glad it's reached you safely.*

Goodbye Suzanna.

Bye Isabel.

Our final exchange was over. I had seen a lot of Finn in Suzanna and was sorry I would not have the chance to know her as she got older. Yet another goodbye.

* * *

It was my last night in Seville. After a walk around the old town, I took a seat at a small bar in the tangle of streets in the old town and watched the world go by. The feelings I had were all too familiar. Throughout my years of wandering around the world and however much I had believed it was time to move on, I had always experienced a wave of sentimentality on my last day somewhere, a desire to remember all of the details of the place so I could summon them at a moment's notice. That evening was no exception.

As midnight approached, I walked back to the flat. The only certainty was that I would not be in Seville the following night. I read for a while and at some point drifted off to sleep. A young boy was running along a vast, sandy beach, chasing a bright red kite. He was shouting, but the words were indistinct. I saw the kite veer out over the sea and we both stopped, waiting for it to crash into the water. My heart was in my mouth, but another gust of wind pushed it back over the beach.

As the wind died down, it fluttered to the ground. I ran to grab hold of it before it could take flight again. The boy raced up to me as I bent down to give it back to him. 'Here you are,' I said. 'Hold on tightly to it this time. Don't let go.' The boy nodded his head vigorously, his eyes shining with delight at being reunited with his kite.

'James?'

I turned to see his mother at the top of the dunes. I waved at her and then pointed at the kite. She smiled and then called out to her son again.

'James, come on.'

The boy turned to me. Thank you,' he said shyly.

'You're welcome.'

I saw him scramble back up the dunes to his waiting mother, clutching his kite with both hands. They disappeared from view, leaving me alone on the beach once more.

I heard Finn's voice. 'It's time for you to go too, Isabel.'

'Not yet. I'm not ready. I want to stay here a bit longer.'

'No, it's time. You have to go.'

I woke with a start, her voice recalled with absolute clarity for the first time in years. It was still dark outside, and I switched on the bedside light. The bracelet, necklace and my watch sat next to my phone. I checked the time; it was almost five in the morning. I wanted to go back to sleep, to return to the beach, to recapture the moment which had brought me comfort, but I knew it had gone. I could not go back.

Before most of Seville had woken up, I left my keys on the kitchen table and slipped out of the flat for the last time. I walked through the pre-dawn streets towards the bus station. I had plenty of time before the bus was due to leave, but the walk was my chance to stop and remember and say more goodbyes to places and memories. Nuno had offered to pick me up in Seville, but I needed a few more hours of solitude to contemplate a new type of future. We had agreed instead that he would pick me up in Badajoz where the bus would leave me, and we would drive from there across the border to Évora.

Finn had gone. There was no way I would ever be able to change my past, but I had been forgiven by her sister, and I had proved to myself that I could overcome my fears and be stronger than I thought. I didn't need to go through the rest of my life as a ghost drifting through a dream, searching for meaning but finding none because I was too afraid to form any human connections. I vowed that from then on, I would continue to keep Finn's spirit alive inside me but without being consumed by it.

There was still guilt within me over how badly Caitlin had been affected by Finn's death, but I found comfort in the fact she had been reunited with her family. I knew Suzanna would somehow do whatever was required to get her the help she needed, and I had to accept that I could play no part in that.

I stood outside the Plaza de Armas bus station in Seville in the cool, grey light of an overcast morning; a day which made it easier to leave. I went in and looked up at the board; so many destinations. There was a bus leaving for Madrid, and from there I could get to the airport. The desire to run again was second nature, and I had to check it.

To fill some time, I went to the bar in the bus station and ordered a drink I didn't want as it was more comfortable in there than in the waiting room. My phone rang. I looked at the screen and smiled. Nuno.

'Is your bus on time?'

'Yes.'

'So you'll be in Badajoz by about eleven-thirty?'

'I should be,' I said, keeping my voice light.

'I can't wait to see you.'

'Likewise.'

'See you later.'

'Bye.' I ended the call but continued to gaze at the screen, thinking about everything and nothing.

I went back into the waiting room, looked up at the board again and thought about Madrid and the airport. I could take a flight to somewhere, anywhere. Or I could go to Badajoz and meet Nuno.

I remembered what Caitlin had said to me on the beach. *I know who you are, Isabel. I know what you are. When it all gets too much, you run.* The problem with running was that eventually you realised you were running from yourself, and there was nowhere left to go. You had to face yourself.

With sudden clarity, I realised I didn't want to go to Madrid. I didn't want to fly off somewhere. I didn't want to run and be alone anymore. It was just old habits raising a final protest before they were laid to rest forever. The reality of continuing my transient life, friendless and alone, and worse, the thought of not seeing Nuno again – I knew I didn't want any part of it. I wanted him in my life. I was ready to take a chance on living rather than existing. When you had lived in too many places, it was hard for anywhere to truly feel like home, but I thought I was ready to give it a try.

Nuno was the only person beyond Finn's family who knew what had happened, and he hadn't judged me. Better than that, I hadn't relied on him to save me. Although I knew he had given me courage and support along the way, I had saved myself and, in the strangest of ways, Caitlin had also saved me. Something beyond the worst my imagination could ever have conjured up had happened and yet somehow I had survived. Whatever the future held, that was something for which to be thankful.

I hoisted my rucksack onto my back and headed downstairs to the concourse to catch the bus. In less than three hours I would be in Badajoz and by the afternoon, I would be in Évora. It was finally time to stop running and discover what it would be like to build a life.

About the Author

Alex Milan was born in England but has spent over twenty years living and working in other countries. Her first two novels, The Last Carriage and The Ghosts of Summer, were published in April 2020 and April 2021 respectively. You can find out more about Alex at alexjmilan.com.